METAPHASE

Metaphase

Dna Strand 2

Jordana Wells

METAPHASE
DNA Strand 2
Jordana Wells

Edited by Karen Robinson
Proofread by Jennifer Oberth
Formatted and Typeset by Jo Michaels
- all of INDIE Books Gone Wild
Cover Design by Robin Ludwig Design Inc.

CONTENTS

CONTENTS

PROLOGUE

The penetration was slow, exquisite. Had I ever been so acutely aware of another person before? Had I ever felt so alive? I caught a momentary whiff of Chase's protection, the latex smell foreign among the organic scents of sweat and musk.

His eyes bright and hot with focus, he touched me. His fingers were delicate but sure as he spread me wide. At the flash of silver in his hand, I looked away.

"Stay with me," he said huskily.

"I'm here," I murmured, fingers twisting in the white sheet.

A gasp escaped me as he unerringly found the knot of nerves beneath the surface, and his eyes crinkled with a victorious smile at the proof he knew my body better than I did.

My fingers clenched, sweat popping from my skin.

"Pain?" he asked.

"A little."

He retreated, studying my face to determine if that was an exaggeration or an understatement.

"Breathe," he encouraged, checking my restraints. "Try to relax."

I forced my back to lose its arch, willed my fists to unclench.

His hand flexed, creating a sharp, bright pain that made me gasp.

"Damn," he muttered. "I'd hoped Blue was glitching, but all that new tissue is already dying."

His tech, Deni, peered at the monitor, discreetly tilting it away from my sight. "We don't have enough nanobots on hand to clean out this much necrotic tissue. Are you going to clear it manually?"

"No, it's too close to the nerves for me to attempt it while she's conscious. Break out the reserves. We need to get this under control."

Sweat trickled down my temple as a needle penetrated my abdomen to dispense antibiotics, anti-inflammatories, or perhaps even the nanos. It could've been anything.

Well, almost anything. The sheer number of back-to-back surgeries took me to toxic levels of anesthetic, so when the latest malfunction of my body required the minor but immediate touch of a surgical blade, it was done without.

I squeezed my eyes shut, wondering if people would still want immortality if they knew how much it hurt.

CHAPTER 1

MY NEW LIFE

Shortly after I'd healed from that procedure, I walked the hallway, counting my steps on the worn laminate. It took twenty steps to get to the corridor I needed, but my calculations determined it should've taken seventeen. I was never going to progress at this rate.

"Where's your wheelchair?" my physical therapist asked as I fell into step next to him, my muscles stretching and pulling to keep up with him.

"I don't need it."

"Yesterday's bioscans showed you aren't ready for sustained weight-bearing exercise yet."

"Shuffling down the hall isn't sustained weight-bearing exercise."

"That's not for you to decide," Thai said as he faced the biometric locks. The door slid open, and he motioned for me to precede him. "I'll send for your wheels."

Pretending I hadn't heard that, I stepped into the natatorium room. Compared to the rest of the laboratory, it was large, perhaps four meters by five meters. Since the pool was a transparent tank accessed by awkward elevated platforms on each end instead of a watertight hole in the floor, it was obviously an afterthought. Someone had painted an undersea world on the tile walls with far more enthusiasm than skill, so I found myself surrounded by twisted and grotesque sea creatures.

In the changing room, unsecured cubbies held swimsuits and goggles. Likely because of the combination of security cameras and free access to goods, no one seemed interested in stealing anything. I hadn't even heard of a single incident of minor theft in the guise of petty thrill-seeking or practical joking.

Not yet, anyway. Then again, I'd only been able to leave the medical suites for the past six months or so. Six? I wasn't certain. Time was hard to get a hold of underground, especially since I'd spent so much of the first year unconscious. It was the year 2123, maybe early spring. I'd migrated from hospital bed to wheelchair in late fall.

Maybe.

Thai rapped on the dressing room door. "Maria's here."

I let her in and stood nude before her, arms out and legs spread so she could apply the sealant to the breaks in my skin from my latest round of surgeries. I no longer slept with the multi-armed surgical robot poised over me for emergency operations, but she still had her way with me regularly. I called her Kali, after the four-armed Hindu goddess of destruction. No one but me thought that was funny.

The cold fluid Maria applied smelled of citrus, so I always expected an acid burn that never came. When my torso was done, she helped me into the swimsuit before she continued sealing the rest of my broken skin.

"What day is it?" I asked her.

"Thursday."

Wow, what a meaningless answer. But given how similar my days were, any response she gave would've been just as useless.

"All done," she told me, capping the bottle.

"Thank you," I said with automatic politeness rather than a sincere appreciation for the service she performed. I didn't like anyone who expedited my frigid bath.

Thai affixed the sensors to me while I stood by the narrow reservoir, shivering.

"Is the pool heater on?"

He nodded. "Any hotter and we could cook with that water. I've been getting complaints all morning. I shut off the lap current for you, too."

He went to the computer and checked the leads were transmitting before motioning me to get in the pool.

I set my eyeglasses on the bench and climbed the grated steps, gripping the handrail in case my legs failed me. After the fuss I'd made about being strong enough not to need a wheelchair, I had to be certain I wouldn't drop into Thai's waiting arms.

I barely had enough room to sit on the platform, and I smoothed my hair down so it didn't touch the ceiling. Hugging my knees to my chest, I faced the water and fought my revulsion.

Thai climbed up and crouched next to me in case I deigned to ask for help. I wanted him to tell me I could switch to the treadmill or any other dry-land, low-impact device, but he didn't. I hated him some days, I truly did.

Yet I knew he wouldn't force me to get into the pool. After analysis had revealed the victims of the stasis experiment had some level of awareness of their century-long immersion in the icy fluid, the lab feared my psychological response to additional forcible immersions.

What pissed me off the most about the situation was that getting in the water was my choice. Swimming and other aquatic exercises were the most beneficial ways to improve my condition at this point, and that should've been enough reason to just buck up and get in the pool. The sooner I got out of here and returned to a traditional existence topside with the rest of humanity, the better.

Yet I shrank back from the edge.

Don't you dare quit. Don't give them a single reason to slow down your recuperation schedule. You get in there, dammit.

I sucked in three deep, fast breaths and launched myself into the icy abyss.

The water suffocated me. My eyes opened, but I couldn't see past the bubbles traveling up my body like rats escaping a sinking ship. My limbs flailed instead of responding true, and pain shot down my right leg like chain lightning, burning away any control.

My sense of direction was off. I didn't have the body fat or lung capacity to float to the surface, so I kicked and clawed with my remaining limbs toward the weak sunlight.

I hit the clear wall.

I couldn't breathe. I aimed for the sunlight again and again collided with the tank. My trigger finger flexed of its own volition once, twice, three times. I closed my eyes, feeling the familiar tug as the grim reaper made another grab for me.

A hard surface broke my fall. I'd hit the bottom. Finally having a reliable frame of reference, I righted myself and pushed with my good leg. Thai caught me from behind, and his powerful kicks propelled me to the surface like I had a rocket assist.

Thai thrust me out of the water to Maria, who bent me over the edge of the platform. I coughed, and water shot out my nose and mouth. My right leg thrashed errat-ically as the misfires continued.

Thai got me down to the floor level and held me still for the stab of three injections that left my right leg numb and limp.

Coughing, I snatched my glasses and shoved them onto the bridge of my nose so I could see the natural spectrum lights. "That one needs to be the brightest one, so nearsighted people know where to aim," I snapped, pointing to the one directly over the tank. "I haven't died in weeks. Were you trying to ruin my streak?"

Thai wheeled me to my room for my scheduled nap after physical therapy. The wheelchair knew where to go, but he felt guilty about not getting into the pool before I had time to panic. Overly helpful now, he lifted me to my feet and released my arm slowly, making certain I could sup-port my own weight.

"I got it," I repeated, straightening out of the slouch my body resorted to, ever trying to curl back into the fetal position's illusion of safety and warmth.

My room was a small, well-lit cell with a warm bed, a nightstand with an affixed table lamp, a chair of pale wood that matched the floor, and a tiny attached bath-room. The nightstand had two drawers for my clothes, which were all plain, soft, and loose to allow for my ban-dages and damaged skin. They chose muted neutrals for my clothes—creams and dove grays—instead of the stark black and white with harsh pops of color everyone else wore.

Oh, and my room came with a Big Blue, of course. Now that my condition had stabilized, the bioscanner's constant presence usually didn't register. It served as my medical watchdog, sending an alarm to the medical suite when an anomaly required immediate attention. It was tall and spindly, the frame the same porcelain white as most other medical equipment here, and it had a blue light that reminded me of the blue lights flanking runways at night.

Yawning, I sat on the bed. Blue rolled into position, the top arm extending to sweep its light over me while I reclined. "See, Thai? The transfer from one babysitter to the next was successful. You can return to your other tasks now."

He rolled his eyes and parked my wheelchair on its charger. After the download light signaled my ride was accepting the updated schedule, he left.

Triggered by weight sensors on the bed, Pachelbel's *Canon* played softly over the room's speakers. Like the books in the library, the loop of classical music had been curated rather predictably but was thorough enough to provide variety.

Before closing my eyes, I cast a longing look at the sliding door. I couldn't lock it since I resided in patient quarters. I didn't have anything to steal, and it was in everyone's vested interest I not be harmed, but I still hadn't lost my old world need for a secure portal.

The door slid open without warning to reveal my counselor.

I missed my damn privacy, too.

"How was your swim?" Sam asked, his rotund body blocking the view of the corridor.

"Fine," I said, frowning. "This couldn't wait until our afternoon appointment?"

"Just wanted to make sure. Thai said you had a rough session today."

"I'm fine," I said, but I could still taste chlorine and feel the ache in my lungs.

"Wow. That music is awful," he said with a wince, shutting it off. "I'll see about having it deleted."

"It's not necessary."

"This place looks like you just moved in," Sam told me as he surveyed the cell with disapproval. "You at least need a plant. You can get a spectrum light from the shop."

"I don't want a plant." Adding personal touches suggested either resignation or willingness to stay here for an extended time.

"Well, do your environmental controls work?" he said, tapping on the small wall screen by the door. "Cleaning services says yours are never active when they come in here."

The wall next to me cycled through scenery animations: mountains with a bubbling crystal stream, a white sand beach with cresting green waves, a cityscape with rivers of traffic under a full moon. I doubted any of those places looked like that after the Clan Wars had finished what the fall of the United States had started.

Sam glanced at me and switched to more fanciful images, including a space station interior with a view of Earth through its window and an underwater shipwreck on a tropical reef. I noticed he quickly skipped past the water ones.

He stopped at a wooded glade inhabited by a fairy society. Tiny wings beat the air, and laughter tinkled amid the birdsong and rustling leaves. A warm, capricious breeze brought the scent of pine and rotting wood to my room, and I pushed tendrils of my hair off my cheeks, annoyed.

"Really?" I asked him as he locked it in with his code so I couldn't shut it off.

"You're far too serious, Little One," he teased. "The levity will do you good."

At least he hadn't thought to mess with the starry sky program. Not that I'd ever admit it to him, but I did like the field of stars overhead. I'd lived in places with too much light pollution to appreciate the sky, but my room's ceiling animation provided phenomenal star-gazing. It was complete with seasonal shifting of the constellations and meteor showers, too.

"You still haven't told them what name you want."

I felt my frown deepen. "I don't want to pretend to be someone else. My name is a part of me. I like being me."

"You'll just be a different kind of you."

"That means being someone else."

"If you don't choose a name, they'll choose one for you."

I sighed. "Tycho Walker."

He shook his head. "The Texans you've met in the past may remember Walker was Miranda's maiden name."

"My maiden name never came up in conversation."

"There will be resistance."

"Why? The chances are astronomical I'll cross paths with anyone from my last life. And even if I do, they aren't going to recognize me as twenty-seven-year-old Miranda Donovan. Thanks to the extensiveness of the regenerative medicine, immunomodulation therapy, and tissue engineering, I have the physiology of a fifteen-year-old."

"I told you to stop using big words and technical terms. You're sixteen. You need to speak like a sixteen-year-old."

"I'm supposed to be fifteen, and I'm choosing to be a precocious one."

"You're sixteen years and three days old," he said, checking his palmer.

"What a deliciously random age to be," I commented.

"There's a formula we use."

"To ratio the age of my original parts with the age of new tissues?" I asked. I hid a yawn behind my hand.

"Must be a complicated formula to keep up with the changes."

"They decided to do the calculation once and let your age evolve from there, so tomorrow you'll be sixteen and four days. But we can discuss it later. You should sleep."

The door grated shut behind him, leaving me alone in the magical glade.

Why did it have to be fairies with their easy camaraderie and stupid flower petal hats? At least a proper acorn helmet would provide some protection if they flew into a tree.

I folded my glasses and set them on the volume of Voltaire on my bedside table. "Nap, daytime."

The room darkened as if a cloud had moved in front of the sun, and the forest noises became muted.

Not muted enough.

I muttered a curse and burrowed into the bed. I fell asleep before deciding whether it was less comfortable to lie on my side with my face in the artificially scented breeze or on my back listening to fairies giggle like they were on drugs.

CHAPTER 2

MAD SCIENCE

I woke groggily. The automatic glance at Blue's screen showed it reporting the length of my scheduled naps needed to be adjusted so I wouldn't wake in the wrong part of my sleep cycle again.

It was also automatic to look above the basin after washing my face, but my room lacked a mirror. The only way I saw myself was as a ghost image in glass or a distorted reflection in a doorknob. I didn't complain. Even as I washed myself, I avoided the sight of my skin. Too many bruises and signs of surgery showed on the average day. On the rough days, bits of flesh blackened, suffering from a failure of attached nerves and blood vessels while the medical staff waited for petri dish tissues to mature enough to harvest.

Even my gold eyes had failed me, and I now required glasses. Because of my nightmares about going blind, I'd told them how much I would appreciate them raising the priority for repairing my eyes, but they didn't seem to take my wishes under consideration.

The cold water on my cheeks refreshed me some, but I still yawned as the wheelchair carried me on its programmed track toward my standing appointment with my doctor.

In the atrium, the workers tidying one of the tree planters glowered at me as I passed.

Starved for sunlight on my skin and the feel of other natural wonders, I'd crossed the stone border without thought the day before to run my hand across tree bark. That intrusion into the plant bed might've been tolerated, but I'd found a blade of grass and had wedged it between the sides of my thumbs to make a whistle. I might as well have yelled at the top of my lungs about the planters not being properly tended. The sound had carried surprisingly far in the maze of hallways radiating from the atrium.

"You've got to let it go," I told the gardeners. "I said I was sorry."

I almost wished I had a more pleasant manner so I could smooth relations with them, but it was a blade of grass. Anyone who thought nature could be so beaten into submission a weed would never appear was a fool. Anyone who would hold it against the staff for missing a ten-centimeter blade of grass while weeding was an ass.

But I knew I'd ask Sam what I could do to get them to stop regarding me as a villain. I liked the cleverness of the atrium, so I wanted to explore it more. The designers even made the effort to make the underground lab more like the Earth's surface with the lights changing in intensity as they moved across the reverse side of the semitransparent ceiling.

Some would call the fake sunlight and other environmental manipulations successful. The animalian occupants of the atrium thrived in their tanks among the botanicals. Most people I saw down there seemed to be thriving, too.

I lingered, inhaling the scents of the mock orange in bloom. Some of the plants must've failed to receive all of the correct environmental cues because they went dormant or blossomed seemingly on a whim.

The hourly chime broadcasted my tardiness. Exasperated, I tabbed the switch to keep the wheelchair rolling.

"You're late," Dr. Isidro said, the stabbing motion of his stylus emphasizing his displeasure.

"I was smelling flowers in the atrium."

I regretted the admission when he stuffed a sensor up my nose and into my sinuses to look for pollen. He prepped a saline flush.

I grimaced at the feel of the nozzle flaring my nostril. "Where's Chase?"

"Dr. Chase," he corrected. "I'm covering your appointment today."

Great. Isidro barely recognized me as a human being.

"How do you feel?" he asked me.

Even after all this time, I still didn't know how to reply to that question.

Compared to when I'd regained consciousness after Greyson, I barely qualified as possessing nerve damage anymore, but only because nothing that remained was life-threatening. I had no feeling in one of my hands, uncontrollable tremors and numbness in my right leg, screaming headaches, the constant feeling I needed to pee, an agonizing and unpredictable digestive system, and so on. Combined, it sucked, but I was stable.

I rolled my eyes, and the brown eyes of his assistant Deni crinkled over her white mask at the impossibility of the question.

"Well, Dr. Isidro, Blue's readouts are more precise than my vocabulary," I said.

When I was as free of pollen as he could make me, Isidro sat at the narrow desk and made his notes. His back wasn't completely turned, but Deni and I recognized it was time for me to strip, so she pulled the curtain across.

Nude, I stretched out on the gurney, triggering the overhead bioscanner to sweep its light over me like it was scanning me to be copied onto a sheet of paper.

Deni adjusted my position, urging my right leg to straighten and holding me steady through the cramp.

Isidro's far newer bioscanner slid into position above me and came alive with a scream of alarms at my condition. It fell silent as it recognized me and loaded the baseline Isidro wanted.

I murmured, "Going to give me a heart attack, yelling like that for no reason."

Deni's eyes blazed with humor, but she hastily brought her finger to her lips with a pointed glance Isidro's way.

"Den, four-six," Isidro said.

"Close your eyes," she told me, reaching for the wall screen next to me.

Before my eyelids met, I saw my silhouette awash with neon colors, illustrating my body's malfunctions. The amplified and detailed feed from Isidro's bioscanner became a sidebar of psychedelic chaos. They supposed it would demoralize me to see that, but it fascinated me in a morbid sort of way.

"My ears are ringing worse than usual today," I said, realizing I did have something to say after all. "Left perhaps more than right but definitely both ears. I noticed it on my way to breakfast."

"Noted."

The scan took forever. Every day, it took forever, and they wouldn't let me nap through it because it skewed the brain scan. Each day brought me closer to the day I would leave, but my mouth tightened as I realized no one had ever said anything about benchmarks that would equal my freedom.

When the scan ended, I dressed and asked Isidro, "Can you give me an estimate of how long I'll be down here?"

"Functional is good enough for ordinary people, so it's good enough for you," Isidro said.

"Functional is a fairly nebulous term," I said, ignoring Deni's warning look.

Isidro set down his stylus and leaned forward to fix me with his reptilian gaze. "We're only willing to invest so much time into you. You understand this whole facility was not developed just to handle one little girl. There are other projects in this lab."

"Hey, the sooner you finish with me, the sooner you can return to doing whatever you were doing before I was killed, kidnapped, and brought here."

"Kidnapped?" he said, glossy black eyebrows shooting toward the heavens. "Texas won the bid on your remains. It was perfectly legal."

"They still killed me."

"You were already dead," he said.

"Dying, not dead, and I was fighting my way back to health," I corrected. "You haven't answered my question. When can I surface, Hades?"

"You? Topside? To do what?" he asked. "You're fifteen."

"Sixteen. My birthday was three days ago."

"You're still underage. If we let you surface, you'll end up in a foster home."

"So, say I'm eighteen."

16

"We could say you're fourteen," he warned. "You look it. Unless you want to bring the conversation around to medicine, your time's up."

"I don't appreciate your getting snappy with me. It's a legitimate question. And honestly, it's not like I asked for this."

"I didn't ask for you either, but here you are. Don't let me hear you've been out of the wheelchair again. Continued non-compliance will earn you restraints."

He left, his angry strides making it plain he would've slammed the door behind him if he could.

"You be careful," Deni told me, her eyes wide with alarm. "You don't want him angry. You really don't."

"What could he do that could be worse than what I've already been through?"

"Pray to God you never find out."

"Melodrama doesn't suit you."

She glanced up at the security camera and moved so her back was to it. "I think it's a crime against humanity what they did to you."

"Excuse me?"

"Can't you see they're redefining what it means to be a person?"

Redefining? How could a person be anything but a person? Cyborg? I wasn't one of those. The few implants I had showed readily on the glimpses of my bioscans, and they were tiny and located in my extremities. A person with a pacemaker was more a cyborg than I was.

She cast the surveillance camera a furtive glance before leaving the room.

I grinned at the camera and blew it a kiss. "Hello, Big Brother."

Had she been referring to the roll-back of my age from adult to teenager? That wasn't a crime against humanity, just a personal annoyance.

Sixteen. I cast an uneasy gaze down my body. I probably couldn't even pass for that. I wasn't having periods and didn't seem to be developing any female curves beyond the nubs I already had, so I was lucky they hadn't moved my arbitrary age to fourteen.

God only knew what the average modern teenager thought about, but I had the vague suspicion it involved things trendy and vapid for which I was both clueless and had no patience whatsoever. No matter which time and place I lived in, the one constant element was my well-earned reputation for being serious, scholarly, and altogether boring. I couldn't even tell a joke without it falling flat.

Going to high school during the day and being held accountable to a parental figure at night? It was preposterous. Would the lab even consent to it? It was preferable for me to be so autonomous I didn't have to explain anything to anybody, including any sudden disappearances for medical care. But that was only possible if I resembled an adult.

In my room, I remembered Sam's gentle insistence I make the place look homier.

They couldn't mean to keep me there indefinitely. They were going to let me go as soon as my repairs were complete. Granted, no one had said that, but it was understood. Why would they keep me here when I was whole and healthy?

They kept asking me for an alias, after all, so they could build a new topside history for me in a different name. They weren't just asking so I would be lulled into the false hope they would someday let me go.

Right?

CHAPTER 3

No Diamonds?

I woke past midnight, confused by the scents and sounds. Fumbling for my glasses, I said, "Running lights on." Strips of dim lights glowed along the bottom edge of the walls.

I was still in my room in the lab, but I wasn't alone.

Fairies. Crap. I reached for the controls, too disturbed by my dreams for the pretense, but the system was locked. Sam had done that to me.

I dressed and left my room with my book of Voltaire, limping and lurching until my legs woke up. They'd finished painting the corridor, so the door sign for the library was back up, although now the sign for the chapel was above it instead of below. I snorted at Father Brannigan's handiwork but frowned at both signs being on the same door. What kind of world was it when there was so little interest in books and God that a library and a church were relegated the same room?

I perused the titles on the old metal shelves. Whoever had curated the collection seemed to have drawn from a vintage list of A Hundred Books You Should Read Before You Die, which explained the thick layer of dust on them when I'd first found them.

I didn't mind reading the classics. Some of them I'd enjoyed the first time I read them in college in the twenty-first century. Suspecting I would remain in the lab for perhaps a year's worth of repairs, I'd arranged the books alphabetically by author and had started reading them in order.

Jason would've chuckled at the perversity of it, applauding my rebellion. Not the reading. The part where my preference was in no way communicated by which books I read.

Pushing the thought of him out of my mind, I scanned the book spines shelf by shelf. Nothing missing and no new titles. I didn't expect to see any deviation, but I had to acknowledge the possibility of a disruption to my ordered shelves even if it was just someone returning a book.

My right leg shook, and my hand went to it, searching for the locus of the misfires. Irritated at my body's disloyalty, I sat, counting out a minute in my head. I would give my leg sixty seconds of rest, no more.

"It's an unfair position for you to take," Father Brannigan said from the other side of the bookcase, and I quickly reached for the noise-canceling headphones on the small table next to me. Some of it was politeness, but most of it was that he made a lot of biblical references that drove me to look them up in the digital Bible on the stand when I had more important goals to pursue.

I fumbled with the ill-fitting headband, cursing the old man's insomnia.

A new voice spoke, this one gravelly but not unpleasant. "No, I completely agree. Miranda's situation is more than a little tragic."

My head snapped up at my name.

Mauss, the chief of security, continued. "But you can't call her that anymore."

"She is definitely still the victim of a tragedy, Abdon."

"I mean you can't call that gem Miranda Donovan anymore."

A long silence followed, and I was curious how the padre would refute that.

"Lawfully, Miranda died at Greyson," Father Brannigan allowed, "but she was resuscitated. She is still the same woman—"

Mauss burst out laughing.

Father Brannigan paused. "Same mind."

"Oh, she's got a great mind. It's only a fraction of her whole being, though. You of all people have to understand why I won't accept her the way she is. Reading the Bible cover to cover every year, I've found nothing saying I'm in the wrong."

"Tolerance—"

"And patience," Mauss supplied. "I manage civility most days. That has to be enough for now. Listen, I'm running late, so can we finish this conversation later?"

"Late? You're never late."

"The new guy isn't read in yet, and Javier is starting to get sick, so I told him I'd take his shift."

"I'll say a prayer."

"Thank you. It'd be much appreciated."

I should've donned the headphones. Now I was intrigued with no way to get answers without admitting I'd listened in. I doubted I could've broached it without my irritation showing anyway. I wasn't tragic. I was alive, which was more than a lot of people could say.

Well, if they weren't dead.

Jason's penchant for accuracy had ruined me. I couldn't have an internal monologue without correcting myself anymore.

I had to stop calling myself immortal if I wanted accuracy. I died with the usual ease. Remortal? Quasi-mortal? What was the word for someone who wasn't allowed to stay dead?

I returned the Voltaire to the shelf and tipped my head civilly at the padre at the door.

"I'm here for you," Father Brannigan told me, his creased face showing patience. "You know that, don't you?"

"Yes, sir."

Indicating the canvas of a man fighting a dragon, he said, "The fight of good against evil isn't limited to one faith."

That made me pause and ask, "So you serve the dragon's faith, too?"

His mouth tightened.

I hadn't meant it facetiously, so I left without apology, disappointed he was unwilling to consider the question of religious perspective even momentarily. Apparently, he was only willing to serve as a spiritual leader for human-centric, monotheistic religions.

I yawned widely enough to pop my jaw and trudged away from the library/chapel. My leaden legs resisted my attempts at a longer stride. Focusing on that, I didn't realize I wasn't heading to my room until I found myself in front of the doors that sealed the ordinary part of the lab from the end where the real work happened. The contents within were secured with retinal scanners, finger-print readers, and digital locks.

I'd thought I was the only patient. It wasn't a conscious thought, just an absent awareness I never met anyone who acted like he wasn't staff no matter where I went in the enclosed world.

Well, Puck must've been here, so there had at least been one more like me. He'd been dying of a brain disease when he approached me at a Confederation airport and said God told him to warn me the lab was closing in. He'd barely spoken the warning before two lab personnel gunned him down.

Even before I met him, my Hernandez roommate and I had come to the unwilling conclusion whoever began my repairs from the cryo had put in too much effort to let me go. My time among the vicious Hernandez merely delayed the inevitable.

Healed by devils instead of angels still meant being healed.

But it still meant dealing with devils, too.

Reluctantly, I let the fear turn me away from the double doors. I needed to mind my own business.

I couldn't let it go, though. Puck had suffered from damaged cognition, yet he'd escaped the lab for a while, tracking me on Hernandez lands before we met at the airport. Was someone down here sympathetic to the plight of people like us? How would I ever know who it was? A lot of people made overtures to me, so in some ways it was the friendliest neighborhood I'd ever lived in. My lack of trust didn't make people want to stay around me for too long, though.

It was draining, too, to be suspicious of everyone, to always be on guard. Maybe if they hadn't been involved in giving me to the Hernandez as a bribe, maybe if they hadn't murdered Puck, and maybe if they hadn't killed me in the Greyson locker room—no, I shouldn't trust anybody.

It was a lonely existence, though, especially now that I had more downtime from medical procedures. Instead of spending money on visual simulations with the associated scent cartridges, they should've built a robot dog to keep me company. No way would they tolerate a real one shedding and peeing on the trees in the atrium. It wouldn't be fair to a real dog to keep him down here anyway.

In the central corridor, I passed a man bathed in the scent of the outside world, and the sensory novelty excited me so much I turned to see where he went.

The edges of his face were sharp, the paleness of his eyes unnatural, and the shape of his body angular and hard. However, his walk was fluid, like he was used to moving over rough ground. I trailed after him, hanging back when he ducked into an occupied office for a chat and a laugh with the people working late.

Near the cafeteria, he went through a set of double doors I'd never passed through, having always assumed all the security measures on either side were operational. Hesitantly, I pressed on the door, and it opened, so I stepped through the doors and into a short corridor.

Just in front of the double doors at the other end of the hall, the man whirled around as if my presence finally registered, and electronic circuitry on his face glowed. It must've been just barely under the skin for it to show up since he looked ordinary under regular light. The wiring covered one side of his forehead and cheek and then disappeared down under his collar to emerge on his hand below the cuff of his shirt. One of his eyes glowed alien and white in the dark.

"What are you doing?" he asked me.

"Staring rudely, I imagine."

His smile flashed, but his seriousness was unmistakable when he said, "You're not supposed to be down here, Little One. Turn back before Mauss finds out you're here."

Unsettled by his circuitry, I complied without comment.

I returned to my room, frightened by more proof of procedures that never should've been attempted. Did the strange light reveal to him the computer chips they implanted in me, too?

The door to my room opened, making me jump. The room flooded with light.

The way Mauss eyed me made me take an involuntary step back.

He said, "Since you don't have the mental capacity to remember which areas are off-limits, I'm keeping you in lockdown from seven p.m. to seven a.m."

A curfew? Was he serious?

"It's for your own good. If you keep poking around, you'll someday see a sliver of someone else's secret, and do you know what people do when they see part of a secret? They jump to conclusions. They get everything wrong, they get paranoid, they stir things up, and they make a mess. Over and over, I've seen it."

"Wow, I don't think you could've said that with any more condescension," I said. "And you know seven to seven is total crap. I'm not a child. If that set of doors led to a dirty secret, there'd be a lock. You're just using that door as an excuse to punish me."

"For what?"

"For me killing your team at Greyson when it was plainly self-defense."

"Self-defense? Neither carried a weapon, and both stood at least two meters away from you. You murdered them. Five p.m. to nine a.m. now, and you're being fitted for a locator ankle bracelet, so I'll always know exactly where you're at and when you're somewhere different from where you're scheduled to be. Go ahead. Open your filthy mouth again."

After a long silence that showed my understanding of the situation, he strode out, locking the door behind him.

Stomach clenching, I saw my right hand curled like it held a gun, index finger light on the trigger. I flattened it out and pressed my palm against my leg.

No, it had been self-defense. I wasn't a killer.

CHAPTER 4

BLIND CURIOSITY

Two weeks later, I woke with a chemical aftertaste at the back of my throat. It was a distinctive flavor like I'd breathed the smoke of burning plastic through my mouth, and it appeared only after I surfaced from an anesthetized surgery. But the feel of the sheets, the temperature, the impression of space, the stupid fairies, all of it communicated I'd woken in the same bed I went to sleep in. Why wasn't I in the surgical suite?

I couldn't see. Underground, the world would've been tar black if it weren't for all the lights we lived by, but this was a different kind of darkness. I touched the bandages over my eyes, my heart sinking as I recognized the shape and the ache from when I'd woken on Hernandez lands.

They'd replaced my eyes, no doubt once again transplanting yellow-irised ones, correcting my vision to 20/10. My original eyes had been blue and nearsighted, but even if the lab could've grown me another set of those, they wouldn't have. Their version of implied consent included upgrades because who wouldn't want to be a better version of themselves?

It set a bewildering precedent to drug me while I slept. This was no emergency surgery, and I showed up where and when I was supposed to, so such measures were unneeded. Now that I was ambulatory and aware, were they expecting me to fight them on the repairs? Like I knew some of them weren't exactly necessary?

I swallowed with difficulty, fear and fury at the violation forming an ugly knot of emotion in my throat. I felt for my wedding ring to calm myself with the reminder of my husband, but both the ring and the husband were long gone.

My own demise at Greyson didn't come with any insight into what came after release from mortal bonds. Perhaps that was because of the triple dose of tranquilizers they'd fired into me. I'd supposedly coded countless times here, too, but again, death had happened beneath my consciousness. Did I have to die while conscious to glimpse the afterlife?

I chose not to believe my husband's death meant the absolute end of him. He'd been a good man, known for his moral fiber and his fight for those less fortunate. Casting him off to another plane of existence felt rather cruel, but placing him in Heaven where he could watch over me was a scenario that created its own difficulties.

For a moment, I filled myself with the memory of my first sight of him. He'd been a golden blond who radiated strength and confidence like a god as he sat in the sun.

I took a deep breath and focused to make my message as clear and firm as I could.

Look away, Paul. You can't change what's happening here, so just look away.

Realizing I might be drawing his focus to me because I thought of him when I needed comfort, I held tight to the love and grief for one last moment. Then I released it out into the universe.

Goodbye, Paul.

A week later, still blinded by bandages, I sat on the shelf in the shower and sponged myself clean. I visualized my optic nerve accepting the new tissue and the tear ducts feeding the necessary moisture to my new eyes. Then anger scattered my usual self-healing attempts until my mind was a seething mass of discrete bits of data forming unwanted connections between people and events.

I needed the distraction of my books. They hadn't let me use a computer of any kind because they wrongly suspected I was tech savvy enough to have a hacker's skill set, but perhaps they would allow me one that could play audiobooks. Anything to suppress the relentless flow of puzzle pieces falling into place that revealed more of the lab's ugly secrets.

I dressed and cautiously made my way down the corridor. Like any mouse in a familiar part of the maze, I knew how to get to where I needed to be, but temporarily deprived of my eyesight, I was a newborn colt. I didn't have a cane, but people got out of the way of my stiff-armed wall groping and shuffling feet. They'd warned me of unexpected obstructions and offered assistance, which I shrugged off. I didn't need help. In the cafeteria, the workers loaded a tray with a balanced meal and kept the table closest to the end of the chow line empty for me.

I expected at least one accident from not being led around and not being told the peas were at the twelve o'clock position on my plate, but I managed. With my senses of smell and hearing, I could even tell when someone I was in regular contact with was nearby. It would've been easy to say deprivation of one sense triggered the honing of the others, but honestly, the overzealous cleanliness of the lab always made any organic scent stand out.

I approached Domino, the hulking goon who strode the corridors like he was the only one standing between order and complete chaos. He didn't wear cologne, but his was a distinctive scent of man sweat and wintergreen candy.

"Where are you headed?"

He wasn't so much greeting me as interrogating me. He was new, and I'd already lost too much time debating whether he or Mauss was the bigger dick to me. Although to Domino's credit, he was the same with everyone, while Mauss singled me out specifically.

"History, as scheduled," I told him.

"With Ramon Garcia?"

"Yes."

"Didn't anyone tell you? He's no longer here. They aren't going to replace him."

I frowned. Two days ago, Ramon had asked me roundabout questions about my treatment here like he suspected physical or sexual abuse. When I denied suffering from that kind of abuse, he'd seemed shocked, like I'd just said that a crowd of people had walked by a twenty dollar bill on the ground and no one had picked it up because it wasn't theirs.

"Did he get fired, quit, or what?" I asked Domino.

"None of your business. The hours you used to spend with him are your own."

"Mr. Domino?"

"Yeah?" he asked, his tone making it plain I was wasting his valuable time as if his impatience wasn't transmitted by the clicks from his tongue flicking his mint against his teeth.

"When I have questions about Texas history, who am I supposed to ask? Isidro says I'm not to pester people with subjects outside their field of expertise."

I could feel some of the tension leave him when he realized I wasn't going to ask any more questions about Ramon. In fact, his relief was so tangible, I knew the teacher's leaving had been more complicated than his quitting or being fired.

"Ask anyone you want," he said as he strode away. "Well, anyone but Isidro."

Hair standing up on my nape, I made my way toward my room.

Just color within the lines, and everything will be fine. Mind your own business and do what you're told. Nothing more, nothing less. It'll be fine.

Sam called out to me, "You look troubled. Do you need to talk?"

"Just the person I wanted to see. I want environmental controls returned to my control."

So much for keeping my mouth shut.

"You didn't like the Japanese garden?" he said. "Most people do."

"I don't want anything on that wall. How often do I have to tell you that? None of those sights, sounds, or scents will ever fool me into thinking I'm topside."

"Living underground has its challenges for people who are used to living topside," he repeated patiently. Normally, he didn't pace, but his voice came from a different direction. Was he doing it to me on purpose as petty revenge for being contrary? "You may think you prefer a windowless room, but I promise you it's a lot healthier to take advantage of the animations."

"You know what would be healthy for me? Being able to fall asleep secure in the knowledge I won't be drugged and operated on before I wake up. That would do more

31

for me than the artificial reality of those environmental packages, don't you think? I'm starting to suspect I've got no recourse and no patient advocate. I mean, Isidro and Chase can do whatever they want, can't they?"

I heard the frown in his voice. "They had an unexpected opening in the surgery suite and saw no reason to wake you just to put you under again. You did know an eye surgery was coming up, so when you woke, I'm sure you were disoriented and confused for all of five seconds before you reasoned out what had happened. You've got the maturity not to unwrap your bandages and poke at the repaired area, and Blue's monitoring you, so they returned you to your bed. Can't you see the trust in that? I thought it was a big step for them."

"Don't make it sound like I'm being unreasonable. If someone operated on you while you slept, you'd be pissed, too."

The thunk of bamboo against rock disappeared, and a rush of relief went through me. Whoever had thought up the inclusion of the rhythmic sound of the deer scare in the Japanese garden animation was a sadist. A dripping faucet would've tortured me less. The blessed silence from the wall speakers ended with the *keeer-r-r* of a red-tailed hawk's cry.

"You're nothing but porcupine today," Sam complained. "You must have at least an idea of how much biotech is being used to repair you. They're entitled to—"

"Their rights? I'm referring to mine. When biotech laws protect the governments and corporations more than the individual, something's desperately wrong."

"Those laws are built on ones that were passed in your own generation," he reminded me. "And they *are* fair since the money and resources being invested comes from those governments and corporations. It's not like you're being given a bill for all this."

"What happened to me wasn't my fault. Why should I pay for it?"

"It wasn't our fault either. Why should we?"

I ground my teeth. Sam should be grateful Jason wasn't there. Jason didn't believe in physical violence, but he had no problem hacking their records until they had no money to live on and no proof they'd been educated enough to get a job. After Jason found out Kairo had broken my nose in an attempt to keep me out of Jason's cockpit and ruin my chances at Hernandez citizenship, Kairo's computer mysteriously developed a hidden partition shielding an accumulation of revolutionary material. The Domestic Protection Service not only snatched away his flight assignment but threw him in jail for terrorism.

At the first whiff of the scent of a field with a creek, I said, "Can't you at least get rid of the bird-of-prey noises? It's disconcerting."

"Studies say it's a reassuring sound because it tricks a part of the brain into thinking there's open sky overhead. It stays."

"You're a terrible counselor."

"That you're a whiny brat instead of a shell-shocked mess proves otherwise."

"I'm this good because of me, not you."

He'd already left.

CHAPTER 5

COMMAND PERFORMANCE

Several weeks later, while I was in that gray state between being asleep and awake, the tone to my door chimed. It wasn't the polite use of a doorbell so much as a warning someone had opened the cover to the new keypad at my cell's entrance.

The door slid open, and booted footsteps thumped against the laminate. "Wake up. They want to talk to you."

"Not interested," I murmured. I was having a low-energy day where I wanted nothing more than to curl up with a book until my round of appointments.

Domino crossed the room to jab me in the ribs. "They are. Go shower and dress, and I'll take you there."

"Maybe later."

He hauled me out of bed and shoved me under a stream of cold water as a brutal reminder my life was not my own to live.

I hit the dispenser tab for the shampoo, but apparently I'd lost my chance to be accommodating. With one hand still wrapped around my upper arm, he pushed the washcloth over my skin with the other. Under Domino's heavy hand, I smelled fresh and was dressed in record time.

Glancing over me as I pulled my hair into a ponytail, he said, "You brought it on yourself, but I didn't know you were made of glass."

I pulled a light sweater over my short-sleeve shirt to hide the swollen, soon-to-bruise mark where he'd grabbed me. My red skin was almost abraded in some areas, but my clothes hid those spots. I could feel them, though, tight and raw.

"I didn't mean to hurt you," he persisted. "You should've said something."

"I'm always in pain," I said dismissively.

I walked toward the door, but he stepped in front of me, careful not to touch me. "When I tell you to do something, just do it because I'll make you if you don't."

"You made that clear."

His eyes narrowed. "Just don't push me. That's all I'm saying. If you don't push me, I don't have to hurt you."

I stared at him, amazed by his smidgen of conscience. Didn't he know down here a person's morality was defined by what he thought he could get away with?

His hair was blue, I realized. Well, finally believed. Domino's short hair and eyebrows had definitely gone from his natural golden brown to a sapphire blue. It brought out the blue and green flecks in his hazel eyes and made the gold speck in his right shine like the star Aldebaran.

I couldn't look away from that hair. Some of the individual hairs were indigo and some were a cerulean blue, making it look like a naturally occurring human hair color variation. It was exquisite, although I doubted he would take that as a compliment.

"Stop staring at it," he gritted out. "You've got weird yellow eyes now. Do you see me staring at them?"

"Stare at what? They've been gold the whole time I've been here. And if you don't want people to stare, don't dye your hair blue."

"Who says I dyed it?" he asked, a dusky flush creeping up his corded neck.

"So it's a case of spontaneous repigmentation?"

His mouth thinned, his irritation overcoming his regret for causing me pain.

"For your skin tone and eye color, it's actually a great choice for you as far as personal color theory goes," I offered. I tactfully refrained from mentioning which colors he should use for his purse and shoes.

He pointed at the door, and I scooted out ahead of him.

The conference room was nothing more than a white room with a glass table and chairs on beige carpet tiles. The handful of self-important people in pale suits sat at one end of the rectangular table, and I took the chair at the opposite end.

Taking a position in the corner near the door, Domino stayed, too, perhaps more for their protection than mine.

It became immediately evident my constant attempts to get someone to give me a firm answer about what it would take for my release had been brought to the suits' attention. I hoped my suggestion I be returned topside as an emancipated minor had also been passed on.

For the next two hours, the administrators took turns telling me how I was part of something important, so much more important than dates with teenage boys or chocolate or sunshine. They assured me I was advancing science. Because of me, space exploration was a real possibility. What they learned from me would also make it possible for people surviving terrible accidents to regain full use of their bodies and live a full hundred years.

Wasn't that worth a few years' confinement in an underground lab where I was guaranteed safe from harm? No one was going to shoot me in the head like in my first incarnation. No one was going to break my nose or kick me breathless like in my second tour. That was all part of the past, not this beautiful future I was so vital to.

"What is this?" I asked warily. "Why the sudden interest in my willingness to be a part of your agenda?"

Mr. Sarcasm spoke over a colleague, his voice cutting and impatient. "You've reached a point in your recovery where it's more than reasonable to expect you to contribute. The unique gifts within your genetic code don't entitle you to a life of leisure while there are tasks you are capable of performing."

I raised an eyebrow. "A life of leisure? So that's what I have here. I wear a tracker like I'm a felon, and I'm locked in my room when I don't have scheduled appointments. My desire to leave the lab in my current condition is rejected, which means I'm here against my will. Conveniently, now that implied consent can't be used, you've decided I'm underage and still have no rights to refuse further surgeries or make any other decisions. I'm curious what excuse you'll use when I reach eighteen. Will I be convicted of an imaginary crime? All this is because you want me to surrender my rights for the record. Does that mean you're actually accountable to somebody?" I asked mockingly, getting to my feet.

Domino blocked my exit. "You ungrateful bitch, you'd be dead if it weren't for these people."

"Just like nature intended," I reminded him.

"If it weren't for humankind's attempt to master nature, no one would live to be thirty. There would be no antibiotics, no—"

"There would be no water or air pollution, no massacre of hundreds of thousands of species indigenous to this planet, no unnatural disruption of the ecosystems or anything else. Humankind is what ruined this planet for every living thing on the planet, and you want me to support efforts to make it possible for people to last longer? If you think the population problem is critical now, wait until you prevent everyone from dying. And what would I be saving them for? There aren't enough resources to go around as it is. There's plenty of infectious disease to go around, though. Plenty of famine, too."

"That's an exaggeration based on eco-terrorist propaganda."

"Perhaps," I said. "But I think it's interesting the Texan government is sterilizing people hand over fist to control overpopulation while the exact same government is sponsoring this lab's efforts to make death optional."

"Your stubborn refusal to see the value of the work going on here makes me sick," he ground out.

"You're kidding yourself if you think all this will amount to anything good for humankind."

The Boss spoke. He had claimed to be Director of Operations during the introductions, but he didn't seem to have difficulty letting everyone else run his meeting. "I asked to speak to you because I believe you have reservations about what you think goes on here."

"Let me guess. I'm delusional about what's going on, and everything that's been done to me is actually to protect me from myself. You completely robbed me of my rights and expect gratitude when you give me somewhat of a right that's dressed as a privilege. And you people wonder why I don't trust a single person on the planet. Did you just write off my cynicism to a chemical imbalance in my head, not years of experience?"

"Trusting no one gets you nowhere," Domino said.

Everyone turned to look at him. His arms were crossed over his wide chest, his gaze unflinching despite the frowns for his interruption.

"I'm just saying," he said.

"We aren't the ones who kidnapped or shot you," the Boss told me, bringing the conversation back around. "We aren't the ones who put you in suspended animation either. We're the ones who got you out of there alive. We protected you from the media onslaught that would've occurred if that experiment had been made public, too. We even tried to right a wrong by rebuilding you after your death."

"Which one?"

He ignored that. "Your kidneys were originally healthy. We know that. We know exactly how much degradation your body sustained, and one of our primary missions has been to repair it. Our goal has always been to restore you to the condition you had been in before you were shot, teach you everything you'd need to know about the new world, and release you."

"It's acceptable to me to be released as is. Let me go."

He hesitated. "It's not that simple anymore. Thanks to the unprecedented issues arising from your physical resurrection, a basic bioscan would reveal you're carrying around amazingly sophisticated technology, technology that isn't made accessible to the ruling family let alone the—"

"So make it available," I said, my heart racing. They had no plans to release me. None whatsoever.

"The Texan government doesn't know we have it because we don't trust in their motives. At the moment, all they know is we haven't perfected suspended animation, and that's true enough. Everything else we've done revolves around saving the people in those cryopreservation tubes."

Part of me wanted to believe him, but I wasn't that naïve. Absolute power combined with absolute secrecy bred little honesty, especially to the subjects of the experiments.

"How many people have you saved from those tubes?" I asked nevertheless.

"I could tell you, but it would be better if you saw them yourself. You'll realize the scale of this project and appreciate the difficulties we're dealing with. I want you to work for us, and not because I think you owe us," he said with a sharp glance at Mr. Sarcasm.

"I already work for you," I pointed out. "I'm a lab rat."

"Let me rephrase it. I want you to work *with* us. I think it would be good for you to become a part of our community in a way that encourages you to develop conventional adult relationships instead of the patient-doctor kind. And I know you're feeling—"

"You don't know anything about the way I feel."

"Well, I know you're a brilliant woman used to having an extremely demanding workload, and all you do down here is read what few books we have in the library. You're back to Dostoyevsky, aren't you?"

I willed my expression to go slack before he saw my wariness. It was *Crime and Punishment*, and if he knew what it was about, it would be removed and replaced with something less inciting, like *Little Women.*

"You've read everything in there," he told me. "You went alphabetically by author the first time through, and you're going alphabetically by title this time. I'm only pointing this out to show you we know your mind is actively seeking ways to entertain itself. Would you like to mull over the retraining paths we have repeatedly offered you?"

I continued to regard him without emotion. Given I was now limited to what could be taught by an off-network computer without any interaction with other students or instructors, my retraining options were beyond boring. I didn't want a degree in business or anything else dooming me to work in a cubicle. And it wasn't like I could learn more about how to fly while living in a cage.

He said, "I'm offering you the opportunity to help us get people out of the cryo experiment in one piece. You know what they're going through, and you can help them acclimate. Help us give these people what we couldn't give you."

"That's not what we discussed," Mr. Sarcasm said, almost launching from his chair.

"She wasn't going to be satisfied with sweeping floors."

I waved my arms expansively. "You've got everything you need to get these people from zero to sixty again. Counselors and therapists, tutors and sociologists, and doctors and more doctors. There's nothing unique I can offer. Those people won't want a teenage girl holding their hands while telling them they've been given an incredible opportunity to rebuild themselves any way they want. You may not believe this, but the people who were kidnapped don't necessarily give a damn about that."

"All the more reason for you to help us with them. We need you. Those people need you, too."

"No."

"We could move you to better quarters," he told me. "Special order different food, too, as long as it fits within your dietary restrictions. If there are books or recordings you want us to acquire, you just have to make a list. Even hardcopy books."

"I must not have said it with enough conviction behind it, so I'll say it again." I leaned forward and spoke emphatically. "Hell no."

"Why not?"

"You must be joking."

The hourly chime sounded, and I glowered at them all. "Now I'm late for physical therapy. Do you know what happens when I'm late?"

Heavy boot steps signaled Mauss's approach.

"It wasn't me," I snapped as soon as I saw him. "They called me into an unscheduled meeting."

"Consider this a police escort," he said, with cold eyes that belied his pleasant tone.

CHAPTER 6

A Walk in the Park

As soon as Mauss and I were out of sight of the leadership, his talons wrapped around my upper arm so he could drag me down the corridors.

"What about my Miranda rights?" I asked.

No response. If anything, that just made him mad.

"Hey, that was funny," I told him. "Ouch, damn it. I'll need that arm later."

Thai had his back turned when we entered the room, so Mauss released me with a petty shove that sent me sprawling.

"Careful, Little One," he said with a twist of his lips as he pulled me to my feet. "We can't always be there to catch you when you trip."

He and Thai greeted each other, and mercifully, the security boss left.

Thai pointed me toward the changing room. "Full treadmill suit."

Fifteen minutes later, I was finished being encased in the skinsuit impregnated with sensors. For my sense of modesty, I was allowed a T-shirt and shorts, but they bunched up and interfered with results, so I approached the machine with every tiny bump and crevice revealed. It was ridiculous to be shy in front of these people anyway. They knew my body better than I did.

Thai checked the readouts and stepped out from behind the console to crouch in front of me and adjust the fastening on my shoes.

"Don't you think I know when it's too tight?" I said, half teasing.

"My machines know more than you. Not much more," he added with a grin. "Where would you like to go today?"

I gave him a sardonic look.

"Great Wall of China it is," he said cheerfully.

I closed my eyes, unable to take the steps onto the conveyor belt. I knew I had to go through with this, knew I had to take advantage of every opportunity to get stronger—

Stronger. Huh. They wanted me healthy, not strong. The gym and pool were off-limits outside my scheduled times.

"What benchmark do I have to meet to use a treadmill without all this crap?" I gritted out, forcing my hand to let go of its death grip on the rail.

"The committee will decide that when you're further along. You're well ahead of schedule, but you're nowhere near optimum."

I stepped onto the machine, going to the front to get hooked up.

Thai showed me the bulbous helmet now wearing a fancy paint job that made it look like a mushroom cap with a ladybug on it.

"Cute," I commented as he strapped it on me. "What's the old mushroom joke? I'm kept in the dark and fed crap?"

"Knew you'd like it."

He regarded me expectantly, and I gave him the thumbs up. "Full blow."

The sensor hood had made me hot, so he'd cut it off the suit and devised a helmet that blew air through my hair to cool me even as it scanned my brain function. It gave me such crazy hat hair it never failed to make him laugh.

Chase chuckled when he saw the improvements to my headgear. "Isidro will have a fit."

"She wants a normal treadmill," Thai said as he unpacked the mask from the sterile pack.

"She wants a normal life," Chase corrected absently, tapping parameters into Thai's machine. "A sure sign she's deluding herself about what one's like."

My nasty retort was lost as Thai tightened the mask to my face. The mask bothered me the most. I never felt like I got enough air despite the machine's feedback proving otherwise. It shouldn't have upset me so much. I'd never had difficulty with the oxygen mask from my flight gear.

"Breathe in. Slowly. Deeply."

The air flowing in was tainted with the taste of sterilizing fluid and plastic. My hands jerked reflexively toward the mask to pull it off, but I stopped them even before Thai could catch them.

"Do we have flow?" he asked.

"Yes," I said. "Confirmed airflow."

"I see a fresh blood break under the skin on her upper right arm," Chase called out.

"Mauss escorted her," Thai said, his voice carefully neutral.

Chase's mouth flattened. "He picked the wrong place to work."

"His security measure leaves her ankle swollen and abraded after the treadmill."

"I'll talk to him," Chase sighed, standing with slumped shoulders like he'd just volunteered to bash his head against a brick wall. "You're loaded and good to go."

Thai returned to the console, and Chase approached me. He tapped my clenched fingers, and I forced them to relax.

"You've got this," he assured me. "Get good lung inflation. Don't hold your breath. Remember to concentrate on your diaphragm."

I signaled my understanding.

He thumbed a tear away from the corner of my eye. "We're starting you on a lengthier warm up to keep you calm enough to breathe properly. It'll help with the feeling of suffocation."

The belt under my feet moved, and I shuffled my feet to keep up. The Chinese countryside appeared around me. I'd walked about half a kilometer toward the Great Wall when a brace clamped around my calf, making me jerk and stumble.

What fresh hell was this?

"Stay calm and just keep walking," Thai said. "It'll move with you. We need to correct your gait for proper weight distribution. You're favoring your left leg too much."

The second brace shot out and took hold of my opposite foot, securing it and turning my heel inward slightly. I lifted my heel, but it lifted easily. I attempted to take a step and found no restriction other than an inability to land with my heel too far out.

46

Nothing to worry about. Just another muscle memory exercise.

"How are you?" Chase asked me.

Calming, I signaled I was functional, and he left me to my work.

The whirr of a third brace made me hastily straighten my back and square my shoulders. The third brace retreated.

"Yeah, you've got it figured out."

I focused on the Great Wall before I gave in to the temptation to look down at my legs out of scientific curiosity. I didn't want to see the robotic assists connected to me. If I looked at them too long, they might become a part of my self-image forever.

My shoulders soon sagged, and this time I didn't fight the brace clamping over my back. When my muscles fatigued from holding myself correctly, I still needed the help and that was that.

The people in that experiment needed help, too. What would I have given to be spared the misery of waking up from cryo suspension more dead than alive, having no answers to my questions, and having no one from my own time to relate to?

No, my circumstances had been different. I had awakened in a plane crash on Hernandez lands and had been saved by a man who didn't know what to make of me. We'd spent the whole time I was there either debating what kind of experiment I'd been in or the best way for me to earn citizenship from the Hernandez.

Down here, despite what Isidro said, I felt like the world still revolved around me, and I was sick of thinking about myself first, even if it was for my own protection. It would satisfy me to focus on someone else and perhaps make another's life even a little bit better. I might even make a friend.

What if I reached out and the patient died instead of recovered? Could I handle that? Could I handle that repeatedly? The lab regarded my recovery as an anomaly, so how many had died before me?

Why did they even want my help? I had no bedside manner, and the first thing I was likely to tell another victim was not to trust anything the lab said.

My sigh tasted like plastic and sterilizing fluid.

Back to square one. Back to being distrustful, lonely, bored, and selfish. What an existence. The Great Wall of China was nothing compared to the wall I built around myself.

Suddenly, I couldn't breathe. I felt surrounded, trapped. I tore off my mask and clung to the rails, kicking free of the braces.

"Little One, no," Thai yelled, running toward me. "Be calm."

I lost my balance and went down with a cry. The braces kept trying to grab the misplaced limbs and snapped and bit my flesh while I fought to escape. Abruptly, they went slack, dropping on me like leaden anchor chains. Metal screeched as the housing toppled, pinning me to the treadmill's belt.

Everything went mercifully still, and I closed my eyes, trying to calm down long enough to figure out how serious my injuries might be. Probably not too bad. I didn't feel that sickening twist in my stomach that warned something was horribly wrong.

"Emergency team lift in Therapy Room Two," Thai shrieked, making my heart leap in panic. "Medic to Therapy Room Two."

Booted footsteps made me cringe, but it was Domino's voice that said, "Cancel team lift. I'm here." He crouched down, and his calm, steady eyes found mine. "Don't move."

He looked to Thai for guidance, but my physical therapist shook as he pushed his hair back. "I don't know how, but she hit the emergency release on the arms."

"I don't care what she did. I just want to get it off her," Domino said, wedging himself between the wall and the treadmill. Holding my gaze, he said, "You tell me if you feel sudden pain."

"Don't you drop anything on me."

"I won't," he promised.

"What the hell happened?" Isidro said as he charged in. "Do you have any idea the amount of money and time we've invested in this project?"

That man didn't have a sympathetic bone in his body. His precious, expensive, custom robot had just tried to eat me.

"Help or get out," Domino told the doctor.

CHAPTER 7

SOMETHING WICKED

A few weeks later, a pair of pale, merry eyes peered around the partition separating Father Brannigan's world from mine. Again, I could smell the outside world on him, and it was everything I could do to keep from cornering him and sniffing him up one side and down the other.

"I found these for you," the man with the hidden face circuitry told me. He handed me a pair of books, one on American folk heroes and the other a random novel.

My gaze shot to his.

"They probably suck," he said apologetically. "I come across books sometimes, but they usually smell moldy. These didn't, so I brought them for you."

"Thank you," I said, delighted.

"Well, I feel bad about Mauss putting a dog collar on you. If I'd turned you back as soon as I knew you were behind me, it wouldn't have happened."

"Why didn't you?"

He shrugged. "I didn't see any harm in it. Sorry, kiddo. I should've known better."

"Don't worry about it. Hey, what's your name?"

He grinned, backing away. "Can't. Don't follow me again, okay?" he said before silently retreating.

I hugged the new books, a rare flare of happiness alight in my chest.

An hour later, Domino burst into the library with a force that made me jump.

I snapped, "What—"

He clamped his hand over my mouth and dragged me around the bookcase, slipping on the Marcus Aurelius volume and almost toppling us both. Unsettled by the management's notice of my library's structure, I'd given in to the compulsion to reorder the shelves again, this time by topic. I'd started to devour one of the new books before finishing the task.

"There's a threat," Domino said into my ear before dumping me on my ass and hoisting my left leg in the air so he could jam the security override key into my ankle bracelet.

From my vantage point, I saw writing under one of the bookshelves.

AMF wuz here

My teeth gritted at the slangy *wuz*, and I just knew AMF was the bastard who'd folded down the corners in some of those books. Some people had no respect. No one made books in the old way anymore, so all the books here were antiques deserving of better treatment.

Domino caught the anklet before it hit the floor. In a low voice, he said, "Do you have a hiding place?"

Scrambling to my feet, I shook my head.

"Get out of the library and find a place to hide," he told me. "Don't go to your room."

Did that mean I was a specific target? Heart pounding, I pulled off my shoes and socks for stealth and purchase on the laminate flooring. Following him to the door, I murmured, "Wish I had my gun."

"Not as much as I wish I had mine. I don't get to wear it for three months after arrival. Apparently," he said with a smile that didn't reach his eyes, "some people go batshit crazy when locked underground."

He listened, then risked leaving the room. After a moment, he motioned for me to come out. He pointed toward the atrium, but I didn't know if that was the direction to go or the direction of the threat. Looking exasperated, he pushed me in that direction, and I padded down the hall.

The power went out, and without the backup generators firing, the corridor became dark and silent. Even the individual battery banks of the emergency lighting failed. Someone planned this well. I heard primal, far off cries in response to the blackout, but the darkness didn't bother me.

Perhaps the medical suite held better nooks and crannies, but I stopped in the atrium where any noise I made might be lost among the sounds of birds and animals.

My nostrils flared at the tang of fresh bird droppings.

High or low? I wasn't confident any of the shrubs or trees could either support my weight or hide me well, especially if they got the lights on.

The bases beneath the tanks must've been full of pipes, motors, pumps, and other accouterments. I was probably skinny and underdeveloped enough to fit around them, but wedging my body in there meant there would be no quick, easy egress.

A crack of sound made me go still. What was that? It was like the pop of a whip in experienced hands, but the tone was deeper. I hoped it wasn't the pop of a rivet. I didn't relish the idea of being buried under tons of dirt as the walls gave way.

What the hell was going on?

More cracks.

Jesus, it was gunfire. I pulled my cloth belt from its loops and whipped it around the trunk of a palm tree, wrapping the ends around my hand. I used the belt to climb, slipping down enough times that I questioned the sanity of my plan.

Linemen. I'd never seen a lineman hug a pole. Trusting the belt more and leaning back, I ascended to the crown. Without taking a moment to catch my breath, I turned and pushed off with all my strength. By not accounting for the flex of the palm, I hit the big tank too low and scrambled to hang on to the edge, but it was too slick. I fell and forced myself to go limp before impact. I hit the ground with a fleshy thump but without snapping my ankles or blowing out my knees.

I froze for the measured count of five, listening to discover if my racket resulted in someone's appearance, and then I approached the tree again.

Don't risk it again. How many more shades of agony do you need to experience? Stop wasting time and just hide in one of the bases.

The second ascent was rapid, and at the top, I attempted to leap the breach at a higher angle. I reached the top on the tank just as a man's distant scream ended abruptly. Had the cry come from the surgical suites? If so, I had time to get to a more concealed position.

Crawling low along the edge where the tank was sturdiest and frequently pausing to listen, I made it to the far side.

When I ran out of tank, I reached up, feeling for the ceiling brace. I wrapped my fingers around it, the heavy translucent panels scraping my knuckles. I gave the frame more and more of my weight, breathing more easily when the metal didn't flex.

Hanging from the brace, I inched across the ceiling. Blood trickled down my hands, and I wished for the foresight to wrap my hands in pieces of my T-shirt.

My arms felt like they were coming out of their sockets, and fearing the moment my muscle fatigue turned to muscle failure, I quickened my pace.

I found the next tank by jamming my big toe into the corner of it, and I bit my tongue with enough force to draw blood from my effort not to cry out.

With a grimace and a prayer, I made it on top of the nocturnal animal tank. Unlike the other tanks, the roof of this one was dark, so no one looking up through the tank would be able to see me when the lights came on. If I stayed flat in the center, I would likely be safe from a casual glance across the atrium, too.

Something big scuttled out of one of the corridors and across the atrium floor. A person scrambling on their hands and knees? Two more came from the same hallway, and I swallowed a curse. They made too much noise. But what would they know about evading gunmen? This place was supposed to be safe. No emergency exits existed to allow someone to sneak out with the lab's secrets, so they had to be careful about screening potential occupants.

Someone was opening the base of the tank below me.

Get away from me, you noisy bastard. You're going to draw the gunman's attention.

The other two fought in a whisper that was louder than if they had spoken in a low tone. Their scuffle resulted in the sound of glass shattering like a small beaker being dropped. Hasty footsteps revealed their flight, but they crashed into one of the planters and thrashed against the vegetation.

You stupid, stupid bastards.

They stumbled out of the atrium and picked up speed once they hit the corridor toward the cafeteria.

I went motionless at the sound of slow, deliberate boot steps, glad I'd made it off the ceiling brace in time.

The booted newcomer moved around the big tanks, and the squeak of hinges told me the bases were checked. He wasn't using a flashlight, and he wasn't shaking down the bushes either. Night vision goggles? Did that mean infrared? The plastic I sprawled on was warm, but I didn't have a gauge for how close it was to body temperature. I was never warm enough.

I sensed movement by my tank and pushed my hair behind my ears. I waited, chin lifted so I could listen better.

"Nice try."

I recognized Mauss's cold, amused voice.

My heart felt like he'd punched through my ribs and squeezed it with his fist.

A woman cried out, "No, don't—"

A bright flash and muffled pop ended the conversation, and the methodical search for the next victim continued.

CHAPTER 8

SHAKE AND BAKE

Long after Mauss had finished checking the atrium and moved on, I waited. I stayed still and silent, ignoring the pain in my toe and my bony hips pressing into the unyielding surface. The animals were subdued, too, and I wondered if it was because they could smell the blood like I could.

Was the predator still in the area?

Where was Domino? Hopefully, the time he'd spent finding me to issue a warning didn't cost the man his life. Standing next to him in the library while we listened for the threat had been a warm, comfortable moment of feeling like we were on the same team, maybe even like we were partners.

Time passed. The quiet eventually gave way to the sound of someone shuffling along the edge of the atrium, hesitant and clumsy in the dark. The sound of crying came from another direction, accompanied by harsh, low warnings.

The animals stirred, rustling and chewing.

The first of the power cells hummed. Not wanting to reveal my hiding place in case I ever needed it again, I moved over the ledge of the vivarium's top and hung by my fingertips for a moment before dropping to the ground. The lights came on, momentarily blinding me.

A glance over my shoulder showed the mess I'd made in the planter. Good. Hopefully, people would see it as my hiding space, not the route to it.

As the cameras panned the atrium, I limped over to the woman spilling out of the tank's base. Her left eye was pierced with a large caliber bullet. Not that I knew anything about ballistics, but Mauss seemingly had been satisfied with the one shot's god-awful spray of fluid and chunks, so a large caliber was logical.

The victim was an anesthesiologist I recognized from my surgeries, but I couldn't think of her name. I forced myself to turn away before I rifled through the woman's pockets for not only her ID but for a clue why she had been singled out in case she was more than a target of convenience.

I was nearly to my room to clean up when Domino called out to me.

"Are you okay?" he demanded as he strode up. The fresh lump on his temple oozed blood. It looked like he'd been pistol-whipped.

"Better than you by the looks of it," I said, presenting my ankle. At his blank look, I said, "My locator anklet."

"That was Mauss's thing, not mine."

Past tense, so either the turncoat security chief was dead or gone. Suited me either way.

I wondered if—

No, no wondering. Make a chessboard. Contemplate Nietzsche. Rub your head and pat your belly. Do anything and everything you can to distract yourself away from this.

"What happened?" I asked. "I heard gunfire. Was that Javier shooting at him? Mauss's gun had a silencer. Or was there another gunman?"

Oh, my God, shut your fool mouth.

Sloppy black writing marred the corridor wall opposite my door. I caught only the last line before he pushed me into my room: *Christ's Love Only Needs Effort.*

"Hey, what's that?"

He ignored my questions in favor of tabbing his comlink. "Little One's safe. I'm sealing her in her room."

"Can't you seal me in the cafeteria? I'm hungry."

Why did I open my mouth? I made certain he saw my aggravation while he closed the door to my room. My sigh was lost in the grating noise of the big locks aligning as the thick security doors added another layer of protection.

With nothing else to do, I peeled off the remainder of the torn toenail, showered off the grime, and cleaned out my scrapes and cuts.

A new Bible had been placed on my bedside table, and I frowned at the intrusion. Someone must've meant to be helpful, but for all they knew, I could be Jewish or Hindu or anything else.

Mauss read the Bible, though. I used the tip of my stylus to lift the cover. Sure enough, he'd inscribed it. His hard-to-read lettering proclaimed I needed to read it in its entirety as soon as possible. At least I thought that's what it said. Few people in the digital age had legible handwriting.

I put the Bible under the clothes in my bottom drawer and went to bed with a collection of Shakespeare's early works instead, refusing to let any of the day's events sink in.

Sighing, I set the book down. I needed to deal with the emotional side of what had occurred. Inadvertently suppressing the memory of my husband's passing had resulted in irrational fears and odd habits that almost cost me my slot in flight school. Thankfully, Jason had gotten me sorted out.

The chief of security had an all-access pass and the equipment to go around exterminating whomever he wanted. Go ahead and be scared. You know he hated you, and you didn't have your pistol or a way out of the lab. Don't be shy. Go ahead and piss yourself.

I smiled slightly.

I'm serious. If you had hidden in the base, Mauss would've found you and cheerfully murdered you. They would've resuscitated you like always, but dying hurts like a bitch all the same.

But why was he killing everyone else?

No. No whys. This is the part of the incident you need to shut down. Deal with the emotions. You've already moved past denial he would've terminated you, so let the rest of it happen.

What was there to say? I was a coward for not jumping down to beat his ass once I knew where he stood. It was shameful the way I regarded the dead woman without dignity or respect, and it was shameful I felt pride in outwitting a killer she hadn't. I was stupid for not picking up a weapon. I was naive for believing the lab was capable of keeping me safe. I was afraid, too, of the other monsters this place must be spawning.

But most of all, I was angry. There should've been protection from threats like this. No one man should've been able to remove safety features like battery-powered lights and glow-in-the-dark tape without anyone noticing. Where was the psych evaluation showing Mauss capable and willing of this?

My anxiety manifested physically, and after I had trembled and cried to the count of a hundred, I considered the matter dealt with and returned my attention to my book.

Days later, my head was spinning with Elizabethan English from concurrent readings of Shakespeare so the plain speak of the administrator in my doorway didn't quite register.

"What?" I asked, grimacing and jamming my hand against my cramping stomach.

"You're needed in the conference room," the Idealistic One repeated. "Immediately."

"Thanks for just walking into my room. Very polite. Shows how respected I am as a person."

Nonplussed, she retreated to the corridor, saying she'd wait for me in the atrium while I dressed.

As I sat in the same chair before the table of suits, I uneasily noticed the lineup had changed.

Had Mauss removed people from office or had people higher up on the food chain replaced them in the wake of the shootings?

The new man in the center said, "Thank you for agreeing to meet us. I'm Alan Tuncay, and I've taken on the tasks of Director of Operations. I wanted to personally address any doubts you may have about the lab's ability to care for you in the wake of such a terrible event."

"I've been locked in my room for four days without food. I have doubts you can keep a hamster alive at this point."

The shocked silence ended when he spoke low to the woman next to him. "Shouldn't the Blue in her room have gone into alert as her values dropped? Why didn't Dr. Goddard respond?"

"Dr. Goddard isn't on her team," she said in a strained voice. "Chase and Deni monitored her room feed."

"They're both dead?" I asked. She had definitely used the past tense. "Mauss killed them, too?"

Tuncay asked, "Why didn't you use the intercom?"

"Why didn't anyone fix it when I reported it broken three months ago?" I retorted. "And for the record, I did attempt to get someone's attention, but Morse code on the door yielded nothing. Are you people used to the sound of patients pounding on their doors?"

More wide-eyed silence as the man looked to either side for an explanation. No one met his eye.

Time dragged.

I left the room and went to the cafeteria.

Domino poured himself a cup of coffee, frowning at the light color of it.

"You forgot about me," I snapped. "You locked me in and no one ever freed me."

Thanks to his hair's forest-green dye job, his narrowed eyes were slivers of jade. "I reported to the proper authorities you were locked up safely but needed a medic for minor wounds. They told me someone would physically check on you within the hour. When I did my rounds, your blast door was open and your inner door was shut like it's supposed to be. Forgive me if I thought it was acceptable for me to investigate the dead people at that point. Get away from me before you piss me off."

My low blood sugar robbed me of the ability to grin and bear it, let alone apologize. Given what Mauss had done to those people, I at least needed to thank Domino for removing my ankle tracker and warning me. Too bad I was so weak from hunger I couldn't kowtow properly.

I turned away in a huff and snatched up a plate to load.

"Annalise? I didn't know you were back."

I realized the woman had spoken to me, and when I turned to correct her, her eyes widened.

A man grabbed her shoulders and pulled her back as he gave me a smile that didn't reach his eyes. "Sorry, Little One."

"No need to be sorry. It isn't the worst thing that's happened to me all day," I said, catching the cascading muffins before they fell off my tray.

"Everything okay here?" Domino asked with an edge to his voice.

I waved him off. "Nothing more than a case of mistaken identity, so return to your weak coffee and your murders, you jolly green giant."

I ate past the point where I felt like I was going to throw up. I bared my teeth at the workers when they tried to deny me the chocolate cake slice and other verboten items meant for the general populace and not the carefully tended human test subject.

I hadn't even finished the first slice of cake when two med techs flanked me and dragged me toward the medical suite.

Isidro induced vomiting until I was limp and sore. His hostility lingered as he checked my restraints and snaked the tube up my nose and down into my stomach. "Get Bob to run the numbers on a liquid diet for, oh, let's say the next week. She needs the reminder she's on a special diet."

Tears rolled down into my ears.

He added, "And I don't like the look of her flesh wounds."

"Blue says there's no sign of infection and they're healing well. They were kept clean."

"They're ragged, so open them all up and reseal them. We're going for zero scars, people. And don't forget the stimulator pads. Chase let you slide, but I expect zero muscle atrophy while she's in restraints."

Determined not to feel any of the humiliation and rage and confusion that threatened to choke me, I closed my eyes. I turned my thoughts to my physical being, encouraging my immune system to initiate repairs on the raw tissues in my throat and my abdominal muscles to rebuild their action potentials for normal firing. I didn't understand human beings from the neck up—including the contents of my own head some days—but from the neck down, it was a beautiful, orderly collection of integrated biochemical processes. No matter what Isidro did to me, I knew I would recover.

The sting of the needle in my arm introduced the burning sensation I recognized as a mild sedative meant to take the edge off my dreams so I didn't thrash.

I drifted off, but while I slept, my traitorous mind became bored with cheering on my biological repairs. Questions, connections, and hypotheses formed unchecked, and when I woke, one thought burned clear and hot in my mind: Mauss's actions were only the beginning.

CHAPTER 9

PALE HORSE

Eyeing the chiming intercom the morning after my release, I tucked a bookmark in my Milton. It should've been my new book on American folk heroes, but someone had swiped it from the library, perhaps as an effort to encourage me to break from my American past.

The intercom chimed again as if to emphasize they had fixed it. While I'd been strapped down on Isidro's gurney learning my place, my room had been thoroughly cleaned and painted in a soft, calm blue. They'd also replaced my furniture with newer pieces. Hell, a fresh flower arrangement had even been on my new desk along with three romance books chosen more for looking new than anything else.

But did all the upgrades encourage me to forgive them for making me go without food for four days? Not so much.

I padded over and tabbed the cold silver switch. "Yes?"

"Good morning. It's Director of Operations Alan Tuncay. Would you be available for a tour?"

"While I like the way you said that as if I have a choice when we both know I don't, I do resent being put on display for the amusement of a VIP."

"No, I meant I would be showing you around, not showing you off."

"I'm not interested."

"You will be," he said. "May I stop by at ten?"

"Yes," I said cautiously.

Given that I was politely invited instead of told, I would make an effort with the new regime. If freedom from the lab was too much to hope for, perhaps I could petition for an easing of my restrictions. If nothing else, I might be permitted an emergency pack of crackers in case my door got stuck.

After I ate what I was supposed to—no more and no less—I stopped by the supply room to pick out a new outfit.

"Wow, these run big," I said, returning my choices to the counter with a sheepish smile. But how was I to know what clothes to get? Someone else did my laundry so when my clothes showed stains or wear, they disappeared from my drawer and new ones magically appeared on my bed.

The woman called up my file. "Your last batch of clothes was several sizes smaller."

"Texas sizes must be all jacked up compared to Hernandez ones then. What do you have in the size you have me listed as?"

"Let's measure you to see what your proper size is, and then we can bump it up for bandage clearance or comfort. You wouldn't happen to know your height and weight, do you? It's not necessary, but we might have something flattering to your proportions."

"Yeah, 175 centimeters, and, ah, 52 kilos," I said, recalling what I'd weighed when I was this skinny among the Hernandez.

Her tape measure stilled, and she glanced at me. "I'm 175," she said, looking down at me.

"What?"

I was now more than four fingers shorter than I used to be. I knew they'd had to do extensive work on my fragile bones, but I didn't appreciate them cutting corners like that. I liked being just tall enough to reach the cookie jar on the top shelf.

The hourly chime warned of my deadline, and I snatched the clothes she held out and returned to my cell. After donning gray slacks and a nice white shirt that covered the bruises from my restraints, I twisted my hair into a chignon, holding it in place with a smooth, debarked stick from the atrium.

Tuncay's eyes widened at the sight of me. "Good morning, Ms. ahh..."

His mouth opened and closed several times while I gave him the opportunity to come up with the correct response.

"Donovan," I supplied icily. "My name is Miranda Donovan."

"I know," he assured me. "I wasn't sure if you preferred Little One or if you'd switched over to Tycho Walker."

As if they hadn't already told me they didn't want to let me return topside where a different name would be necessary.

We traversed the lab, and after Tuncay and I walked through the double doors that had been sealed moments before, I saw rooms devoted to research in biochemistry, anatomy and physiology, microbiology, and materials and computer engineering. So far, I was unimpressed with the sight of microscopes, reflux set-ups, laminar flow hoods, and other boring equipment that could be seen in any freshman-level college science class. Was this the façade they showed VIPs who insisted upon a walkthrough?

In an elevator large enough for a gurney and pristine enough to operate in, he presented me with his back while he worked the biometric and alphanumeric security station. The elevator hummed to life and carried us toward the center of the earth. It was perhaps four floors down when it jerked to a stop and opened its doors.

My pulse jumped. So used to the sterility of the upper part of the lab, I recoiled from the dark, dirty foyer. Corpses of spiders and roaches littered the industrial laminate flooring. I batted at my hair, already imagining bugs crawling on me. Every sound bounced off the battleship gray metal walls and struts. Opposite the elevator, an oversized panel was inset in the wall. Was that the door? I saw no handle.

Tuncay's shadow was twisted and sharp edged as his hand shot out to prevent the elevator doors from closing. "Well, come on."

On trembling legs, I stepped past him. He returned to the elevator, and I whirled. Was he going to abandon me there?

He locked the elevator doors open. "We need the light," he explained, pointing to the empty ceiling of the foyer.

He crossed the room and went through the long, complicated security measures next to the door.

I picked my way through the insect bodies so I didn't have to listen to that crack of exoskeletons giving way from my weight. "Are you guys worried about an earthquake tearing down the lab?" I asked, looking at the utilitarian struts. "Don't you need a fair amount of flex to survive a decent p-wave or s-wave or whatever you call them?"

"Texas might rumble every once in a while, but it's nothing to worry about. The lab is a series of joined cells that will fracture at the junctions as necessary, not one giant structure."

"And what about a source of uninterrupted power? Geothermal?"

His smile suggested his appreciation for my interest. He didn't need to know I was asking random questions to keep him talking while I coaxed my nervous stomach to settle down.

He discussed the construction of this part of the lab, and I listened to him with half an ear, still brushing off imaginary insects from my nape. Why had I agreed to this? I wasn't ready to be here. I already had preconceptions of the nightmarish collection of pseudo-coffins for cryopreservation. Would it be worse to find out I'd imagined it accurately? I suspected it wasn't going to be the clean, scientific setting I was used to, if nothing else.

Prepare for the full-blown, worst-case scenario. Don't step through that door thinking only a handful of people were put in cryo. Prepare yourself for seeing a dozen. Maybe even two dozen.

I shook my head at the idea. Cryo must've been an expensive proposition, especially in 2014, when I'd been kidnapped to be a part of it. The upper end was probably eight or ten victims.

Clicks gave way to a grating sound as the big door eased open. I stilled, caught in the calm before the storm. Cold curiosity heightened my senses even as it shamed me. Clammy air scented with metal poured through the dark crack.

Tuncay fumbled in his pocket and drew out a flashlight. He ensured it worked before stepping through the doorway.

I trailed after him, asking, "What's your carrying capacity?"

"Fifty. Not all are currently in use."

My stomach dropped. Fifty. Jesus Christ.

"Because you dismantled some to learn how they functioned?"

He shook his head, flipping a switch on the wall to illuminate a unit. Mercifully, it was empty.

"We know how the icers work. They just don't work well enough to completely suspend someone. They slow biological activity by combining low body temperature with a proprietary trick or two."

He said it like I was a competitor intent on stealing their secrets for my own use. Proprietary tricks indeed.

The stasis tube was predictable in shape and size. The transparent, central tube for imprisoning the person had a framework holding it upright, and countless tubes and wires connected it to a chest-high control panel up front. Behind it, a low mechanical hum came from the floor to ceiling cabinet holding the power supply and other support gear.

He reached over and popped the hatch on the unit, giving me an unobstructed view of the tube's interior as the front half lifted up. "You connect the prepared subject to the central life-support system here and here to ensure the availability of oxygen, essential nutrients, sedatives, antibiotics, and anti-icing agents. This other set functions for waste removal. Then you bring the temp down, keep it stable at the optimum temperature, and let the subject sleep away the years. Of course, I'm oversimplifying things."

Seeing as it sounded he was regurgitating facts he'd learned in a brochure, I doubted he could explain the tech in any more depth, so I didn't pursue the engineering side of it.

"You said prepared subjects," I asked, stepping inside the tube. It was something I had to do. "But what does that involve?"

"Well, according to the journal of the man who started this experiment, part of it was choosing the correct people in the first place. He preferred adults in their twenties to balance physical maturity with less environmental and lifestyle-caused damage. He also chose people who had the body-fat percentage at the high end of normal, considering it sort of an emergency energy source. Muscled people or ones with low body fat percentages failed much sooner."

I rested my hands on the top edge of the housing like I was used to hanging around the icers, which I supposed I was. "I fit the sought-after physical profile, but so did a lot of other people in the twenty-first century. Not to be callous, but why pick me instead of a criminal or homeless person no one would miss?"

"Homeless people didn't have the level of health he required. He also rejected the idea of human trials with hardcore convicts, pointing out the obvious problem of what to do with them if the experiment succeeded. Maladjusted people with histories of antisocial behavior or violence? That was the last thing he wanted to deal with."

"Unconscious people in giant test tubes aren't much trouble to manage."

"He was thinking about afterward. He argued a certain kind of people would stand the best chance of recovering from the loss of so much time. Mentally, I mean. Introverts would tolerate the solitude of the initial rehab and be more comfortable keeping a low-key existence. Their extensive schooling would leave them more open-minded in general, so better able to accept what had happened to them."

"And it would also result in less training required for the subject to function and make a living in a more technologically and scientifically advanced age," I said. It made a crazy sort of sense. "So he stalked the local universities, tracked a candidate for a week or a month, kidnapped him, iced him up, and moved on to the next one?"

"Not that simple, even in theory. He needed the medical history, too, as well as a situation where there wouldn't be too much of an investigation into the subject's disappearance."

"You keep on saying *he*, but there had to have been more people involved in setting all this up. Even my shooting took two men."

"Please elaborate."

It must've been in my file, but I told him about the two men arguing in the parking lot that night. One of them had approached me and told me we were going to change the world before he shot me. The bullet grazed my temple and left me unconscious. I woke up on Hernandez lands more than a century later.

"Would you recognize the men who took you in that parking lot?"

I shrugged, stepping out of the tube. He opened the opposite door and motioned me into a dark corridor with a cluster of three icers.

"Is that one of them?"

The sudden illumination of the icer next to me drew my attention, and I looked into the face of a nightmare.

The murky brown fluid failed to hide the skeletal body of a dark-skinned man, his bare skin laced with fungal or bacterial growth. He was hairless and his bones stood out like those of a concentration camp victim. Dark, growthy holes indicated where eyes used to be.

I dropped to my knees and splattered the metal grates with the masticated apricots of my morning snack.

"Is that one of the men?" he asked. "He's the only one we don't have any data on."

"No," I croaked. "They were Caucasian."

How could Tuncay not react to the sight of the man in that tube? Didn't anything touch these people?

"One minute you're unaware anything like this exists, the next, you're puking your guts out," he said. "It was the same for me. Imagine the doctors who cut away the dead parts of the victims' eyes and mucous membranes until they find living tissue again. Imagine being the counselor who has to tell these people what has happened to them. It's a miserable, horrifying job, so maybe you could be more patient with the people who do it."

"Pull the plug," I whimpered, jamming my fists in my eyes. "Let these people go."

"I can't do that when we've got the capacity to save them. The people with no idea what happened to them deserve better than being discarded like trash. The ruling elite believe so as well. Funds have been authorized to reestablish these people in society, doing whatever they want to do. Within reason."

I shook my head. "You don't know what it's like. It's not like moving to a new city and not knowing a soul. It's so much deeper than that. Please just let these people die without pain. I wouldn't wish this on my worst enemy."

He raised his eyebrows. "You want to kill everybody down here? Some are in much better shape than others. Do you want to set a benchmark of deterioration? Well, where do you draw the line? So much toxin build-up per twenty-four-hour period? Every single one of these people settled into a different baseline. Different temperatures, different intakes and outputs, and different rates of deterioration for different parts of the body. So tell me how to choose who lives and who dies."

I took in his slick suit and manicured nails. He seemed to make a good living off other people's misery.

I shook my head. "I can't be a part of this. I won't."

He motioned for me to follow him. "I want you to see something."

"I've seen enough."

"It'll be the last thing, I promise. If you turn down my offer, that'll be the end of the discussion."

CHAPTER 10

DEAL WITH THE DEVIL

Tuncay shut off the icer's illumination and headed down the corridor, the scant light of the cryotubes' displays lighting his way. The people who worked down here must've had more light than this, but it seemed he wasn't brave enough to see all of his monsters in the full light. I certainly wasn't.

After walking through several pods of icers, he shone his flashlight on the engraved nameplates on the left side. He stopped and wiped off one of the plaques.

It was mine. I didn't need to take a closer look. Because I'd been unconscious when I went in and unconscious when I came out, I lacked an emotional response to this particular unit. He had to know I didn't need to see my nameplate on one to believe this had happened to me.

Or was this a threat?

"Topside authorities haven't been able to find Mauss," Tuncay told me.

What did that have to do with anything? "So you're offering to return me to cryo to protect me? To hide me until he's in custody?"

"What? No, I want you to help us find Mauss. Luckily, he didn't gun down your team until after they were finished with all of your essential repairs, so I'm sure you can handle the task of finding him. Your file says you love puzzles. Solve this one, and I'll show my appreciation."

My team? He targeted the people who repaired me? I caught myself before wishing Isidro had been among the victims. Mauss's rage confused me, though. If he wanted to kill me, it could be argued he had a reason. Killing an anesthesiologist because I was her patient was insane.

I said, "You're sort of all over the place. I thought you wanted me to work for the lab in a traditional capacity." The quaver in my voice revealed far more of my unease than I would've liked. "And then you said you wanted my help with these people."

"No, that's what the last administration offered you. When I read your file, I doubted mopping floors and reading to bedridden patients would be enough of a challenge to entice you. The reward for your help with Mauss will be substantial: freedom."

My pulse surged. It wasn't like it didn't benefit me directly to have him locked up. I just had to ensure my freedom was contingent on my honest attempts to find him instead of a guarantee I could.

Was the offer even real? If he just meant freedom from such a tight schedule and freedom to have a sliver of cake once a month without getting my stomach pumped, well, that wasn't worth getting involved. Locked down in the lab, I was safe from topside threats, including Mauss's return.

I said, "So, to clarify, by freedom you mean you'll let me return topside?"

"Well, it's either your freedom or his."

He flipped on my stasis tube's light to reveal a naked Latino perhaps thirty years old. His dark brown eyes stared at me from above high cheekbones, and his wide, full lips were parted as if he were about to accuse me. He wasn't particularly handsome, but he was lean and well-built with his long swimmers' muscles.

My eyes locked on Jason's unseeing ones.

Tuncay said, "Are you really so surprised to see him here? Your death at Greyson caused an international incident."

"What?"

"A Clan Hernandez visa holder dying on Farragut lands would've been bad enough, but there were formal accusations that the Hernandez knew you were a danger to everyone in the air because of your illness and sent you there anyway. *He* caused that when he hid your kidney underperformance from the Clan Hernandez. *He's* the one who didn't admit the deception even to you when he found out you were flying on Clan Farragut land at Greyson."

"Are you kidding me? I hid my illness from as many people as I could, including him. He thought he was masking drug use."

"The difference is that your morality testing proves you wouldn't have climbed in a cockpit if you had known the truth about how far along your kidney disease was. You honestly thought you had recovered to the point where you were flying safely and legally. He knew for a fact you didn't have the health needed to fly, but he made sure they cleared you anyway. As soon as you died, he ran away and hid."

"Hid?"

"For almost a year that man hid like a rat—"

"Don't talk about him like that."

"—but they caught him when he attempted to flee to Europe. His conviction was immediate."

"So this is his punishment for hiding my secrets, most of which are also your secrets? That doesn't make any sense."

"He went to the Defense Minister, who is a family friend, and told her he knew about a failed stasis experiment you'd been a part of."

"What?" I said, astonished. "I was too desperate to have him work with me to even hint at an explanation I wasn't sure I believed myself."

"I'm not accusing you of saying anything. I'm telling you what happened. He saw the footage of your demise in which self-declared Texans claimed their authority over you preceded your Hernandez work visa by decades. The Clan Wars were mentioned. Your partner told the DM if you were Texan, she must've known about the time travel or suspended animation one way or another. He wanted to be a part of it in exchange for lightening his imminent prison sentence. Asking for your tube spoke of your closeness."

Jason was a self-serving bastard who would easily use forbidden info to better his circumstances, but this was cowardly. It didn't fit.

I reached to the icy tube imprisoning my partner, but Tuncay stopped me, saying, "It's like ice. Your skin will stick. Do you want me to get a set of gloves?"

I shook my head. This couldn't be happening.

"He's supposed to be in there for five years," Tuncay said. "With such a short stint, he should emerge with minimal degradation. You could free him early, but look, his manipulation of your lab values to get you that flight assignment didn't just hide you weren't healthy, it actually prevented you from knowing just how close to death you really were. He might as well have killed you himself.

No one would think any less of you if you chose to free yourself instead. He'll never know about it."

"And what's my punishment if I don't cooperate? If Mauss finds out I'm searching for him, it'll renew his interest in killing me."

"Look, I don't know how things were run before I got here, but given the mess I walked into, I have to guess it was severe. I wasn't put on Earth to torture or punish strays from the twenty-first century because they don't want to perform a task they think is dangerous. I personally would stay here where it's safe and tell the topside cops to earn their pay. If you returned to your room and did nothing more than read your books and go to your appointments, I know Dr. Isidro in particular would be ecstatic."

He shrugged. "But testing shows you have a remarkable gift for connecting seemingly random pieces of information, and we do need Mauss caught. I don't have the clout to free both of you, but I thought I could shave the time spent down here for you or someone you love."

The edges of my mouth turned down. "I don't love Jason Chavez. A lot of days I didn't even like him. He was my mentor."

"Oh, of course," he said smoothly, clearly not believing me. "Sorry I wasted your time including him in the discussion."

He sent Jason into darkness with the flip of a switch.

I followed Tuncay through the maze. He got turned around, and as much as I enjoyed watching him start to panic, my throat still burned from stomach acid, so I pointed him toward the elevators.

Once we were in the main part of the lab, he was surer of his path. He took me all the way to my room and told me he'd give me two days to think about it.

Alone in my room, I stripped and got into the shower to get rid of the feeling of spiders and moldy dirt in my hair. The narrow confines of the shower stall didn't provide much more room than those icers.

Jason was in one. Jason was here. In one. Was he as unconscious as he'd appeared? They already knew the process only slowed down physical processes. Puck had been positive he saw me as he looked out his icer and into mine.

I turned around, letting the hot water cascade over my hair. The brain was simple to comprehend, but the mind still held a lot of mysteries. For one, it didn't always see time the same way a clock does. Dreams that felt like days only lasted minutes. How long would his five-year stint feel like if he did occasionally drift up to some level of consciousness? What if it was happening often?

When I woke from my cryo sentence, I was crazier than when I went in. I emerged with my husband's death suppressed, and then when the facts surrounding it did surface, I remembered killing him. Only through Jason's careful questioning was I able to recover the true memory that Paul had been killed in a mugging hundreds of miles away. A hundred and five years of survivor's guilt turned me into a murderer.

Jason had done some terrible things, and he said he wasn't sorry, but his stimulus-starved mind might've reinterpreted those events. Five years, and I'd already been here for at least a year, possibly two already. If he'd had a long trial, maybe he still had a giant chunk of his sentence to go. Or maybe it was settled immediately, and he'd spent almost two years beneath my feet having nightmare after nightmare. I had to get him out of there.

I turned my face under the water so the surveillance wouldn't catch me crying.

What if Mauss did to me what he did to that woman who hid under the atrium tank? She'd never stood a chance and must've died terrified. That bastard had sounded like he wanted to laugh when he found her. He had *liked* killing her.

Jason might emerge unscathed. Five years wasn't so long. Tuncay had lied about understanding I didn't love Jason, but I believed him when he said I wouldn't be punished. Given how Isidro felt about maintaining and protecting my body, I was confident it'd be easier on everybody if I didn't go. Isidro in a bad mood was something to behold.

And if Mauss killed more people, I could tolerate knowing I refused to get involved. It wasn't my problem. It wasn't my job. It wasn't even my clan. I was far more Hernandez than I was Texan. Let them clean up their own mess.

I shut off the water and stood dripping, feeling the cold air surround me, chill me.

Going after Mauss might be my only shot at earning my freedom from this place.

"Dammit," I muttered, reaching for my towel. "Jason, you owe me big time."

Of course I would bail him out. He had a life, a family. After working with him, seeing his passion for flying, I knew he still had so much to offer. If he got brain damage, I would never forgive myself.

CHAPTER 11

LUCAS

A few days later, I woke to the low hum and rattle of an old air conditioner. Disoriented, I realized I was wearing a long T-shirt of cheap, synthetic material and was sitting up in a big bed with thin white sheets, a flat pillow, and a bedspread selected more for durability than looks.

Above a generic, old dresser, a modestly sized television screen showed a professional soccer game with Spanish captioning. Another bed, tidily made, was to my left.

And sitting at the table by the curtained windows? A man cleaning a gun.

"What the hell?" I said, clutching the sheet to my chest.

It was the pale-eyed man with the face circuitry, the man who had gifted me those books. He smiled engagingly and set down the firing pin he was cleaning. "Hi."

"Hi. What the hell?"

He chuckled. "This is a hotel room. We're topside."

"Why?"

"You and I are tasked with hunting down Mauss. Didn't they even tell you that much?"

"Are you kidding me? How are we supposed to do that? I'm not a detective. I thought they meant to keep me down there while I did it."

"Are you done sleeping, or do you want to sleep more?"

"Done."

"Good. That bag is yours, so go ahead and use the shower, and make sure the clothes fit. They included a medical kit and instructions on how to take care of your surgical sites."

I'd had unscheduled surgery within an hour of agreeing to work for Tuncay, probably to remove whatever implants they didn't want any emergency room to find.

He said, "I can buy whatever you're missing before we start."

"Start? So you have a plan?"

"They gave us a list of places to check for him," he said. "Oh, and they issued lenses for your eyes because people will remember them. Do you know how to put them in or do we need to stop by an optometrist?"

"Where are we?" I asked.

"Austin, Texas."

My eyes widened. "When are we?"

"What day is it, you mean? May 30, 2123."

"And who are we?"

He laughed and dug in my bag. He opened the wallet and tossed it in my lap. "Tycho Walker."

"Tie-ko," I said. "Not Tie-cho."

He nodded. "Good to know."

"And you are?"

"Lucas."

"First or last?"

"Pretty much only."

"And what is it that you do?"

"I'm a problem-solver," he said, indicating a high-powered rifle on the table beside his pistol.

Was that the polite term for assassin? Great. "Why would a place with less than a hundred people need an in-house gunman?"

He scratched his chin, looking like he was picking his words carefully. "Well, I'm technically part of the security team down there, but mostly I run errands and do odd jobs."

I raised an eyebrow.

"I can cover a lot of ground fast and without leaving tracks," he explained. "I can talk my way through topside bureaucracy, too."

I believed him. I found him surprisingly easy to converse with, like he was a friendly stray cat that made the rounds but didn't ask anything of anyone.

I peered through the crack in the heavy curtains. Under the stormy sky, a city was revealed, complete with honking traffic and people in business attire dodging puddles. A sliver of the Colorado River was visible between the buildings.

"It's real," he assured me. "Who would make an animation that crappy looking?"

He seemed to expect more of a reaction, but I had none yet. A thousand new sounds hammered against my eardrums, all signs of the movement of people and machines, but the environmentals in the lab proved how much reality could be faked. I didn't believe the smells of the cleaning products and age in the hotel room, and I didn't believe the coarse, plasticky feel of the curtain in my hand.

However, I did believe my need to pee was real. "Where's the bathroom?"

As soon as I got cleaned up, we left the hotel, and the city opened up around us.

"I'm topside," I said, tears stinging my eyes. "I'm actually topside."

"You need to stop saying that," he told me. "It makes people wonder what you would consider the ground floor if you call this the upper deck."

"Is it just you and me? No rule police?"

"Well, let's just put it this way. Since you don't know when you'll be recalled, it would be wise to do what Dr. Isidro expects of you."

Four weeks later, I knocked on a hotel room door. A month ago, it would've been the polite three knocks, but this time it was a sustained rapping against the faded red paint until the door was thrown open.

"I was sleeping," Lucas complained, stark naked.

"It's time to go to work," I said, averting my eyes. Not that he cared if the whole world saw him without clothes on, but I was raised by prudes and his casual nudity embarrassed me. When the light was low, I also feared I'd catch a glimpse of his hidden circuitry.

I pushed past him and flipped on the lights.

He ducked in front of me, blocking me. "You don't want to go in there."

"Please tell me you didn't bring home another skank. Don't you know women weren't put on earth to be blow-up dolls for men?"

"Women are entitled to have one-time sex without someone calling them a skank," he told me. "And honestly, my sex life is none of your business."

"It is when you make us miss the train. Get ready."

84

He winked at me and disappeared around the corner. From my spot in the tiny foyer, I heard the shower start and the female laugh join the male one.

Resigned to the delay, I slumped in the chair and reminded myself why I put up with him.

Lucas was not the man they should've paired me with. After a mere two weeks of my constantly pecking at him about punctuality, neatness, and the lab's rules, he got a suite instead of a room with two beds. After another week of my banging on his door for every noise he made while entertaining or when the TV was loud enough for me to pretend I thought he was entertaining, he laid down the law about my not pestering him outside a real emergency when it was dark outside.

So my time was my own a lot more than the lab must've intended.

The obvious impulse was to run, but I had reasons not to, the first being I hadn't actually seen Jason before I left, so I didn't know if the lab had freed him like they said.

I'd also spent time as a fugitive and then living on the fringes of Hernandez databases, and it sucked. Despite my use to that clan, I still hadn't been authorized the medical care I needed nor were there repercussions when I was assaulted. No, I wanted my release from the lab to be a government-sanctioned, legal agreement where I had entitlements like anybody else.

On a more pragmatic note, Lucas was a man hunter, and he'd grown up traveling Texas at length, so he definitely would have the home-field advantage in tracking me down. And when he captured me, that ankle tracker would go back on my leg, perhaps for the rest of my days.

The final reason why I didn't simply catch a ride and attempt an escape was complicated.

Mauss was still out there. Domino hadn't been mistaken in thinking Mauss might single me out. When the security boss had left the lab, he carried a backpack with hardcopy files and photos of me, a download of all my digital data, and my wedding ring.

One day, my counselor had shown me the personal effects that had been stored with my cryo unit after I'd been shot and kidnapped in 2014. There wasn't much: a cheap necklace, my blood-spattered clothes, and a ring. After I confirmed it was indeed my wedding ring with its peculiar lopsided silver groove in the gold, he told me they would release it to me when I no longer needed it. While I didn't have the burning urgency to cling to my past and return that ring to my finger anymore, I still wasn't going to tolerate Mauss possessing it.

For reasons neither Mauss nor the lab shared with me, I was special to him, so it was natural for Tuncay to use me as bait as much as a detective. Lucas thought we were wasting our time looking for Mauss since the top-side cops came up empty, but he had no problem going through the motions. One of the few things we had in common was preferring to be outside in a hailstorm than underground in that lab.

A prescription bottle peeked out of his bag. The label indicated it contained potent painkillers for his occasional headaches, so I swiped a capsule and wiped the bottle down before returning it where I'd found it. With any luck, if he realized he was short a dose, he would think his playmate had stolen it.

He emerged from the bathroom, tucking his tight white T-shirt into his leather pants. His companion stepped between us, barely glancing at me as she trailed her hands across Lucas's chest. She had a cross tattooed on her nape, the crooked line of the crossbar making my mouth tighten. How did it not bother her?

"The next time you come to town, leave your bitch of a kid at home with her mama," she told him, making us both stiffen. Damn my youthful appearance.

86

She left before either of us could recover from our shocked silence.

"Forget her," I told him. "We discussed the schedule repeatedly. You said you'd try not to make me nuts. You said you'd do your best to be ready for work by this time each day if I did my best to leave you alone between the hours of eight and six."

"You need to learn how to relax."

"Perhaps," I said, getting to my feet.

"Where're you going?"

"I'm completing my end of the mission so I can relax. Do what you want with your end."

With that, I left the building. He fell into step next to me, steering me toward the parking lot instead of the train station.

He gestured at a motorcycle. "Isn't it beautiful? Now we don't have to worry about missing the train all the time."

"Yeah, it's nice," I said flatly, heading up the sidewalk.

"You barely looked at it," he accused. "I bet you couldn't even tell me what color it was."

"It's a sapphire blue Keoni J-1000 with the sport package exhaust," I said without inflection. "Been downed at least once. Most of the plastic is aftermarket and one side of the fork is scraped up."

He burst out laughing.

"I'm not getting on that bike," I told him. "There isn't enough room for both of us and our gear. You want to forge ahead, knock yourself out. I'm taking the train."

"No, you aren't. The blue one's mine because it's man-sized like me. The little black and silver Keoni is yours because you're littler," he said, pointing at the smaller bike hidden behind the blue one. "I even got you a license."

Curious, I took the fake ID from his hand. It gave my name as Tycho Walker and my age as eighteen, and it permitted me to drive a motorcycle.

"I take back all the nasty things I said about you," I said, grinning.

"We need a destination. We can go anywhere there's a road."

"We head northeast," I said, looking over my new ride. It was a sexy piece of hardware for certain. Sleek but slightly curvy. Subdued coloration but not boring. It had been downed once or twice, too, but it made up for that by being loaded with all the honey. It wasn't a fighter jet, but it was still awesome.

"Why northeast?" he asked.

I straddled the Keoni, pressing my lower belly against the fuel tank. It was a good fit. Damn good fit. Tabbing the ignition, I was rewarded with a sweet, soft purr. A cautious sniff of the helmet revealed it was new, also black with a subtle gray design, as were the matching gloves and jacket. I donned the jacket and headgear, settled my knapsack between my shoulder blades, and pulled on the gloves, noticing with approval they reached past my wrists like my flying gloves had. Lucas must've been busy with more than the girl to get this ready before morning.

"You going to answer me?"

"No."

I pushed my sunglasses into position, dropped the bike into first gear and released the brake. The way motorcycles drove hadn't changed much since before I went into cryo. It was easier than I thought to get reacquainted with the idea of the throttle and clutch at my fingertips and shifting with my foot. After weaving in and out of obstacles in the parking lot and circling around to Lucas's position, I felt comfortable enough.

"Not bad," he told me as he tightened the chin strap on his flashier blue helmet. "You're welcome, by the way."

"You owe me this for being a pain in my ass for the last month."

He hid his amused blue-gray eyes behind a pair of sunglasses and mounted his bike with a familiar ease. "That's funny. I thought I was rewarding myself for putting up with you being a pain in mine."

CHAPTER 12

SPINNING OUR WHEELS

We decided to stay in Dallas another day, using the time to touch base with Domino and determine what conditions would be like along the route I meant to take. Lucas moved us to a suite at a hotel with a security garage for the bikes, and then we hit the nearest diner for a big dinner.

Naturally, Lucas got into a conversation with the server, which engaged the men at the next table, and we ended up being invited to the local firefighters fundraising party. Lucas happily accepted. When I declined and offered to do the shopping before I returned to the hotel, he gave me his shopping list and a cash card along with his thanks.

I watched him drive off, pleased by the turn of events. When I was confident he wasn't coming back, I hurried to the store.

I checked the list against everything in the cart and made space for more items. I had no money of my own and Lucas was reasonably accommodating about letting me pick up a few extra things, but he did check the receipt so I had to be careful. Oddly enough, he required far more justification for the first aid kit and duct tape for repairs than a box of tampons in the unlikely case I ever reached menarche.

A young woman with smudged black lipstick was shopping nearby, and I approached her with my game. She thought I was crazy, but the idea of my screwing over my parental unit did appeal to her, so we worked something out.

It was simple. I picked out twenty bucks of supplies I didn't think I could get away with buying, plus a cheap shirt on clearance. She handed me a nice shirt she wanted that cost twenty-five dollars. I paid for her shirt along with the other things on Lucas's list; she paid for my contraband things and the discounted shirt along with the rest of her items. Then we swapped. My receipt would show Lucas the purchase of a single shirt, and when I wore the clearance one, he would assume it was the one on the receipt.

Back in my room, I furtively repacked and hid the illicit items within my other possessions. If Lucas got killed or I had another reason why I had to evade or hide, I was going to have some basic survival equipment on me. At least while I was topside. I knew it would all be confiscated when I was returned to the underworld, but hopefully I'd have enough warning so I could stash it somewhere topside instead.

My final hiding task of the night was to wrap the plastic bags holding food tablets and water purification tablets around the screw in my antiperspirant container. I checked the mechanism, shook the container to make certain it didn't rattle, and then returned the container to my toiletries kit with satisfaction.

Ever aware I might be digitally monitored, I used the hotel's computer mapping feature to call up the area where we were heading and nowhere else. After down-loading a copy to my palmer, I held a piece of paper to the screen and painstakingly traced a map to add to my collection. If I ever had to run, I would have to dump the bike, the palmer, and anything else electronic so I couldn't be tracked that way.

By then, my hand was cramping from holding the pen, and my lower back hurt from holding the position so long. I was almost done. I eased the stitching in the back piece of my motorcycle jacket and slipped the map into the plastic bag between the installed safety plate and the small metal sheet I'd found in the garbage. I tightened the stitching and glanced around the room to confirm every-thing looked as it should.

Not quite.

I dug through the supplies from Lucas's list and opened a bag of sugary, caffeinated candy. I took two out of their wrappers and tossed the sweets in the toilet to be flushed down with my next piss. I dropped the wrappers on the nightstand.

Perfect. Lucas would respond with a grin and relax when he saw proof of my tiny, poor life choice of eating candy that would keep me up all night. If he had to report on me, the counseling team would no doubt agree it was a healthy, expected rebellion.

The polite knock on the door between our suites made me jump. The polite knock repeated but with a variation. After the third time, a final variation, I opened it.

Lucas pulled the trigger on the gun he'd made of his hand, shooting me in the face.

"But you had the secret knock," I protested, my heart leaping.

"Doesn't mean it can't be replicated or coerced. Let me show you how to answer it."

Once he felt like I could be trusted to open a door, he said, "Any change in the flight plan?"

I shook my head. "I still mean to start at Vinita." It was in what used to be Oklahoma, but when the new borders were firmed up, it became part of the expanded Texas.

His nose wrinkled. "I don't want to go up there if we don't have to. It's mostly ruins, so the law's thin up there."

"So tell me where you want to go. We'll go where you want to."

He shook his head. "Domino said the only reason to deviate would be if you said so."

"And you trust his judgment? Just like that?"

He looked at me like I was crazy. "Yeah."

"What makes you think he's not using you to advance his own agenda?"

He chuckled. "Because I don't see how going to Vinita with you can possibly help him go up there." He pointed upward.

"Heaven?"

He laughed again. "Space, girl child. He wants to be a lawman in space."

"Then what is he doing underground?"

"How else are they going to know if he can handle enclosed environments full of crazy scientists?"

I imagined Domino on a space station, his blue-haired bulk twisting through tiny spaces while he used his penetrating gaze on a handful of people to make them act properly. Was there even a nation that could afford to build a space station big enough to warrant a lawman? Hell, I didn't know. Until I was locked underground, I hadn't cared about anything in those skies past the reach of my fighter jet.

"What time do you want to leave?" Lucas asked.

"First light," I told him. "I don't know how long it'll take for us to find shelter up there."

The following morning, we traveled for an hour before Lucas indicated a lone fuel stop on the side of the freeway. The motorcycles' primary energy source was the solar packs, but he believed in topping off the liquid reserves whenever we could.

As he fueled both bikes, I loitered near the register watching for his signal the first bike had confirmed the quality of the fuel. Only then would I authorize payment for the liters we needed.

Someone grabbed my ass, and I whirled around to see a trio of drunk men. I stepped between them, but they pushed me back and trapped me against the window.

"Let me pass," I demanded.

"You leave when we're done with you," one said, showing me the gun in his belt.

The other patrons pretended they didn't notice what was going on.

"I'm warning you, you won't like what comes next," I said.

Their feral smiles promised me it was quite the reverse.

"Hi," Lucas said, pressing the barrel of his pistol against the back of the leader's neck.

I didn't hesitate to snatch the weapon from the shoulder harness of the guy on the left as Lucas took the leader's belt gun. The third man swept his gun from side to side, uncertain whom to target.

Unable to help myself, I advanced, safety off, finger light on the trigger, pushing the gun barrel into the left man's mouth until he gagged.

"Little One," Lucas murmured. "No."

"We were just having some fun," the leader said, motioning for his friend to lower his gun.

"I'm having fun," I agreed.

"Little One," Lucas repeated, his voice soft and calm. "No."

"Look at me," I told the man I was penetrating. "Look into my eyes."

The man flicked his eyes to mine.

"Apologize," I demanded, easing the weapon from his mouth.

Lucas smothered his laughter.

"I'm sorry," the man said hoarsely.

"Say it like you mean it."

"I'm so sorry."

"Leave. If I see you again, I'll do my best to blow your dick off. I'm not a good shot, so you'll likely take shots to your gut and legs. Do you understand me?"

He nodded and retreated.

"I'm paying for our fuel," I announced loudly. "And I'm cutting to the front of the line because you people want us gone as much as I want to be gone."

I stepped through the hole and dealt with the cashier. On my way out the door, I looked back at everyone in there. "Thanks for nothing, you bastards. May strangers be as kind to your females when they find themselves in a similar situation."

When Lucas and I were far enough away from the fuel stop to be alone for a few minutes, I pulled over and stumbled off my bike. I yanked off my helmet, shaking and crying.

Lucas approached me. "You're safe," he assured me over and over in a soothing voice, but he was careful not to touch me.

"Those people did *nothing.*"

"Don't judge them so hard. They might've if it had escalated."

"If I saw someone being groped and cornered and scared, I would've acted instead of waiting until it turned into a kidnapping or gang rape," I snapped.

"I told you it would be dangerous once we left the cities. Why didn't you yell for me? Didn't you trust I would come help you?"

I yanked the gun out of my jacket and thrust it at him. "Here, take this."

His mouth twitched. "You made him piss himself. Did you see that?" He burst out laughing.

"It's not funny."

His amusement faded. "Maybe not. You looked pretty intense."

"I can't be scared?"

"You didn't look scared or pissed. You were cold as ice. I don't think any of them thought you would've had a problem pulling the trigger."

"And you?" I said warily. "Because if you report that to Sam, I'll be in the lab before nightfall."

"I don't think that's necessary. I'll tell Domino what happened, but I don't think he'll make an issue of it since you gave up the gun before I had to ask for it."

I gave him a pleading look.

He said, "Don't think Domino's like the rest of the lab. He understands extenuating circumstances, and he appreciates a person's ability to stand tough in a hairy situation."

"Yeah?" I said, wiping away tears.

"You look like a kid again, all pale and snotty."

"I'm sorry," I told him. "I should've been paying more attention to my surroundings. I should tell you I don't get bad feelings about people. They have to be an overt dick for me to realize I should be wary."

He nodded. "I was told you were book smart and not people smart. I'll teach you some stuff that'll help."

"So what do we do with those?" I said, pointing to the gun.

"I'll wipe them clean and dump them in the nearest police drop box."

Relieved, I nodded. I didn't want to get caught with stolen property or anything like that.

He glanced in the direction we came from. "We should get going."

I hurried to my bike.

"Do you want to return to the route the lab gave us?" he asked me.

"No. We're staying on mine."

CHAPTER 13

ROAD TO HELL

Vinita was a dried-up husk, long abandoned. We surveyed the area and motored on. Lucas was gracious enough not to say "I told you so."

Tulsa was next. Or as Lucas called it, Tesla, which entertained me. While avoiding road kill, I hit the curb with enough force to rupture my motorcycle's fork seal, so we ended up staying overnight while he repaired it. I expected him to be pissed, but he took it in stride.

After my scare at the fuel stop, I had no difficulty sharing a room with him in the sole hotel in the inhabited end of town. A rough crowd partied at the other end of the hall, and my last sight before falling asleep was his squared-off fingers curled absently around the drab gray sling to his breakdown shotgun.

In the parking lot after breakfast, he checked his repair job while I strapped down our gear. Something was wedged in my fairing: a photo of a grinning Mauss sitting on my motorcycle, the motel we'd just checked out of in the background.

I pressed the audio recording chip in the corner, and his cold, amused voice rose over the sounds of the party.

"It's about time you showed up. I've been here for weeks playing with myself, but now I get to play with you. I wonder how soon it'll be before you meet God. Do you think you'll make it to the Promised Land? Maybe you should just go home, gem. But whether you choose to stay or go, you should know that in any millennium, God-liness only improves national governments. To obfuscate knowledge impedes legitimate lawmaking, yet one understands Christ's love only needs effort."

The photo fell from my numb fingertips.

Frantic, Lucas spoke to me, but I couldn't hear past the pounding in my ears. Wow, did I hate being right sometimes. We'd been on my choice of routes less than a day and already gotten a ping.

Lucas rushed me into the motel. Domino had to be called, the photo had to be analyzed, and the locals had to be interviewed by the cops.

Sinking onto the nearest bed, I wondered if anything was expected of me. What does a worm do when dangling in the chilly water, pierced through by a hook so barbed there is no escaping it? Contemplate God?

Sapulpa.

Nothing but coordinates on a map and ancient concrete proved it had ever been there in the first place. I was never so grateful to see nothing. I wasn't ready for another sign of Mauss.

"Tidy," Lucas commented. "No one can slum here if there's nothing like a structure. If you had to, where would you hide?"

I glanced around and pointed at a bit of vegetation.

"Wrong. It's the first place someone would look. Since plants grow there, that also means there's moisture that likely makes it a rest stop for critters. You may fall asleep alone but wake up with company." He pointed out a depression. "There. With half-decent camo, you could hide there."

"That's awfully exposed."

"You'd be surprised."

"Why are you telling me all this? It's like you want me to escape."

"Domino says you won't. Mauss is a city gorilla, but I'm more of a country gorilla. If he gets us separated, this country gorilla stuff will help you in areas where there are no cops to run to."

"Gorillas live in jungles, don't they?"

His confused look ended with a burst of laughter. "Not apes. Freedom fighters and rebels."

"Guerilla," I said, realizing. "Oh. Well, I don't think it will come to that. Let's move on."

Oklahoma City.

I expected at least Oklahoma City to give us a decent meal, but it had long since been reduced to craters and collapsed buildings. We saw traces of people, but we never did manage to meet any of them.

Lucas came to a stop near the airport, motioning to the water covering the road ahead of us. "Overseer's swollen."

"Lake Overholser," I corrected because I couldn't help it. "Fed by the North Canadian there. Almost a kilometer of the road covered, but the water looks shallow, slow moving. It's passable."

He grunted. "Don't trust appearances of ice or water, Little One, especially if your vehicle doesn't have a

100

snorkel. We go around. Are you comfortable plotting us a route down to the I-40? Rockwell looked passable."

"Rockwell?"

"Between the hospital and the park. Two klicks back, if that."

"You do know your rubble," I said. I called up the ancient line map on my palmer to get my bearings and switched over to a focused satellite view to see what the terrain actually looked like. "Yes, that'll work."

"Let me ask you something," Lucas said, surveying the shattered skyline with binoculars to check for signs of people on our new projected route. "Don't you think it's weird they maintain the roads from one ghost town to another? This place is trashed, but we still had good solid road through all that debris. But look at these places. No one's ever coming back. Still the clan puts out the funds to keep the roads clear between them."

"They also keep the airfields in serviceable condition," I said thoughtfully. I hadn't realized I'd noticed until Lucas's comment sank in. Hell, a fairly new patch marred the concrete not two meters from me. "For as few people as we've seen, there's been a lot of air traffic in and out of these places. Military."

"You sure?"

"I know Ploughs and Battle Axes when I see them," I said dryly.

His fingers tightened on the throttle. "Let's get out of here."

As we picked our way south to the highway single file, I saw Lucas suddenly jerk his head around and start shaking. I goosed the throttle to get beside him and saw he was laughing.

"Sorry," he told me. He pointed to a sign so old some of the letters were all but worn away. "I saw Pollo

Elementary, not Apollo, and actually wondered why the Americans would name a school after a chicken."

"Get moving before I smack you upside your cabeza," I said.

Outside of town, the land opened up before us, and I motioned for him to pull over again. He regarded a couple of decorative boulders I pointed out.

"Left one is for ladies," I said.

"I'm good," he said, motioning for me to go ahead.

I trotted away from him, my trowel and wad of toilet paper in hand.

"Stop with your damn crap holes," he yelled after me. "There're no park rangers out here. No one cares."

"I care," I yelled.

"Wide berth," he reminded me. "Make sure no one's behind it first."

Behind the boulder where I was out of sight, I measured my paces and dug hastily, cursing the stubborn Texas soil. I yanked down my pants and squatted over the hole. Shielding the move with my body, I slid the sealed plastic cache from my jacket's armpit pocket and shoved it in the hole. I shifted as if I needed to rebalance myself, deliberately knocking dirt on top of it.

"Little One, come on already. You already gave the turd a burial. You don't need to stand over it saying prayers."

"Just a minute. Almost done."

I squeezed out a bit of piss and then wiped myself before I refilled the hole the rest of the way. If someone were watching me and chose to dig up my hole, they would find used toilet paper and hopefully stop there. I tamped the ground with my boot heel, checked my pace count to the boulder, memorized the visual markers around the site, and hurried to my bike.

102

"Not the crap journal," he groaned when I opened a paper notebook. "That's just nasty."

"Tell Isidro that when you see him," I said absently, sneaking a glance at my odometer before writing the last three numbers transposed along with my shorthand for the pace count and site markers. "What's another word for squishy? He likes a more technical term."

"I'm leaving," he announced.

I grinned as I tucked the notebook in the inside pocket of my jacket. He made it too easy. Sometimes I fooled with him just because I could.

I pulled ahead of him, which spurred a race I couldn't win given the power of his bike and his years of experience riding it. My bike's smooth-running engine and all that speed while we raced under the wide Texan sky made it in no way a loss for me.

El Reno. Clinton. Elk City. Sayre. Shamrock. Texola.

Lucas lost his sense of humor. The original route we'd been given put us in modern cities with people, restaurants, hotels, and places to get fuel. My way was taking us through ghost towns destroyed during the Clan Wars or abandoned soon afterward. Hell, most of them hadn't been sizable cities before America collapsed.

In case Mauss had left signs in the fractured towns, we dutifully explored them, but the result was nothing more than wasted hours, minor injuries, and deteriorating attitudes.

Amarillo.

Lucas pulled his helmet off with a groan before scratching his scalp with his blunt fingertips. The ticking of cooling metal was as much an indicator of the long ride as his stiffness as he dismounted.

"This sucks," he commented, sticking his sunglasses on the bridge of his nose to block the harsh midday sun. He'd stopped his bike in the middle of the freeway on the highest overpass in sight, but we hadn't seen any traffic in hours.

I cautiously put my weight on my own legs. My back hurt, my wrists hurt, my neck hurt, and the rest of me had gone uncomfortably tingly about a million vibrations ago. Glancing around the remains of the downtown area, I thought of the awesome steak house just off the freeway my husband and I had once eaten at. It was just rubble blended with more rubble held together by whatever tough grasses could get enough of a foothold to survive the poisoned conditions.

Not that I'd be having steak if the place were still standing anyway. No one ate real steak anymore. The land couldn't support cattle's need for plenty of grain, water, and pasture. So much for the bright and shining future my generation had been promised and had promised our own children.

Lucas limped to the edge of the overpass and pissed over the side. "This better be worth it."

As far as I was concerned, this was still paradise compared to living underground. I'd always loved road trips, and I found myself enjoying this one despite our task and the desolate surroundings. The enormous amount of sensory input was making me feel truly alive for the first time in years.

I even welcomed the sight of the battered remains of Amarillo, the violation of the no-seem-um swarm refusing to be chased away by my waving arm, and the stench of the bloated roadkill nearby because it all meant I was outside the controlled environment of the lab.

Traveling with a gunman didn't exactly give me a sense of freedom, but at least I felt a sense of possibility again, and I often found myself smiling for no particular reason.

"We've seen no more sign of him. Are you sure we should be headed in this direction?" he asked.

"Hell, no. But the route we were given brought us to cities on Route 66 even if it took us three trains and a week to get there. I've got us on the even older American Route 66 as much as I can. I figured there would be plenty of small towns where people would either remember him or remember us to him. I didn't expect them all to be gutted."

"In this part of Texas, the tornados finished what the wars started. Ever read about Tornado Alley in any of your books? We're on the west edge of it."

"Well, if nothing else, the astronomers must be happy. Nice roads and no light pollution make for great stargazing."

"Not you, too," he said, nose wrinkling. "Domino's into that stuff."

"Blame my counselor. He's had the stars twinkling on my ceiling at night for years. It's very cool. I can magnify the sky and see galaxies."

He pretended to fall asleep, snoring loudly.

"Boring? Let me change the subject. Why did Mauss kill those people?" I asked him.

Lucas's eyebrows shot up. We didn't speak about it. I supposed we should've been discussing nothing else.

"For a man who loves his Bible, he murdered a lot of people."

He shrugged. It must've felt good because he did it several more times. "Little One, it doesn't matter to me why he is the way he is or why he does the things he does."

"You're not the least bit curious?"

"How would you feel if your gun had its own sense of right and wrong and fired when it felt like it was justified instead of when you felt like it?"

"Ah."

"No lectures about why I shouldn't do what I do? No questions about the body count?"

"Perhaps some envy. Life must be simple for you."

Nodding toward the suburb of El Reno where people purportedly lived, he changed the subject. "Let's go eat and ask around. Unless I get a bad vibe, I want to stay here tonight. Maybe tomorrow night, too. I need a break from being hunched over. The bikes are coming inside the room with us, too. I want to run a diagnostic on them. I'm not getting stranded out here."

"I'll rethink the route, too," I said. "Whether he wants to be coy or not, we should've seen another sign from him by now."

CHAPTER 14

POISONED APPLE

The El Reno diner was old but well-cared for. Lucas nevertheless surreptitiously wiped down the clean-looking table and our plastic menu with antibacterial towelettes before settling in.

"Spicy bean burritos," I decided.

He gave me an impressed look. "Wild child. I'll have the same."

Like usual, Lucas fell into conversation with the server, and inwardly I groaned. People like Lucas were the reason other people had to wait to order or be served.

He nudged my foot under the table, and I brought my attention around to their conversation. A young girl had disappeared from her bed and had been discovered a night later on abandoned railroad tracks. The child didn't remember any of it, likely due to the traces of a strong tranquilizer in her system. Her father had packed up the family and left town immediately afterward.

"Sounds like a good idea," Lucas commented casually over a cup of chicory coffee, but his grip on the cup tightened.

"That's the first trouble we've had in a while," the server replied, pushing her wiry forearm across her brow. I could smell her stale sweat. "Our sheriff is a good one."

"Was the girl injured?" he asked.

"No. Whoever took her just drew on her skin with a marker. I don't know what."

I forced myself to release the fork I held in a white-knuckled grip. Absurdly, I noticed the second tine was bent laterally.

Seeing our expressions, she said, "Sorry. How's about a piece of pie on the house? You'll have to split it, but free pie is still free pie."

As soon as she left, I cut off whatever Lucas had been about to say. "We need to find out more about that girl."

"You think it's Mauss?"

"I don't know yet. I need more information."

"As soon as I get you settled in the motel room, I'll find out."

With the motorcycles in our room, it wasn't easy to pace, but I couldn't sit still and I was too jittery to run the diagnostics. It seemed like he was gone for hours, and when I concluded he'd been ambushed somewhere, he knocked at the door.

"Wasn't easy," he told by way of a greeting when I let him in, "but I got a copy of the police report."

I took the palmer from his hand and read the screen, damn near each line striking a chord. My knees on the verge of giving way, I sank onto the corner of the bed.

"So this means something to you?" he asked. "Because I read it, and I'm not feeling anything that makes me think Mauss was here."

I shook that off. "It was him." I explained how I knew.

Lucas floundered. "But that's just…"

"Reaching," I supplied. "I don't know. It's possible he just heard her name while he was deciding what kind of sign he was going to leave us."

"Who would get a clue like that?"

"It was in the book I was reading the day of the shooting. That folklore book you gave me, remember? I'm the only one who goes there, so it would've been natural to assume the open book on the table was mine when he went there to kill me."

"Go through it again. It might not sound stupid this time."

"It's a reference to the nineteenth-century train engineer Casey Jones. He was from Jackson, Tennessee, and his train was headed to Vaughn, Mississippi."

"And someone left a girl named Casey Vonn at the Jackson Road railroad crossing. That's coincidence. I want to talk about the bomb drawn on her back. Do you think whoever took her is telling us he's going to set off one on a train or at a train station?"

"What her kidnapper drew was a cartoon cannonball. Casey's train that night was a passenger train called the *Cannonball Express*."

"What night?"

"The night of his death. When he realized a cargo train couldn't be pulled off the main track all the way, Casey did everything he could to stop his train. His was the only death in that wreck."

"So he sacrificed himself for the greater good. Is this supposed to be some kind of message? He wants you to sacrifice yourself for the greater good?"

"Yeah, probably. Although I don't know why he thinks my demise will improve anything."

"So now what?"

"No idea."

"What other American heroes were in that book?"

"I'd just started reading it. Casey Jones was the first one. I remember childhood stories about Pecos Bill and the like, but I'm sketchy on the details. I'll make a list anyway. Mauss wasn't an American scholar, was he? Because a hundred years ago, these folk tales were already so old most people didn't remember them."

"He never said anything to me about liking this stuff. It's probably all from that book. We need a copy of it," he decided. "Maybe. And maybe we need to pass this info to the transit authority in case he does mean to threaten the railway."

"Don't we need to tell Domino?"

His furrowed brow smoothed, and he relaxed. "I need to call him because this isn't our decision to make."

"You know, if you feign stupid long enough, you'll stay that way."

We rode to the site where the girl was found, but nothing there stood out to me. It was just an old intersection of road and abandoned railroad tracks with the requisite rusty detritus, pavement cracking into gravel, and glass shards reflecting the sun.

Lucas's hands shook, and he stuffed them in his pocket.

"What's wrong?" I asked.

His incredulous gaze pinned me. "Are you kidding me? He tossed an unconscious eight-year-old girl out here like a piece of trash."

"Oh."

"Is that all you have to say about it?"

I didn't know what to say or do. She was physically unharmed, which was more than I could say about

Mauss's other victims since his count at the lab was seventeen dead and zero wounded. She was unconscious the whole time he had her, and her father had taken her away, not that Mauss would do anything more to her anyway. It could've ended far worse.

As the day wore on, Lucas's jumpiness and snappy remarks increased to the point where I wondered if I needed to request he be replaced. I didn't want to lose the man who gave me so much freedom, but I had a job to do.

I did manage to look shaken up about the girl, sort of a delayed reaction thing, and while I couldn't summon any tears, I did tremble and look like I was going to throw up so he stopped looking at me like I was a heartless bitch.

Under his regard, I mournfully picked at my dinner, rearranging it and mashing it with my fork, but when he looked away, I sneaked big mouthfuls of it. It was good, too, some kind of meat with root vegetables in a spicy sauce. I hoped it wasn't cat.

"Don't know how I'm going to get any sleep tonight," he muttered, setting down his fork. He hadn't been able to eat a bite. "You want cake?"

"What?"

"Comfort food. I'm ordering you cake."

Why would I refuse an offer like that? I took my fork to the slab of chocolate cake until nothing remained but brown smears. Then, feeling my mother roll over in her grave at my manners, I licked the plate clean.

"C'mon, let's go to the room," he sighed. "I still need to run diagnostics."

I covertly poked the parsley garnishes into my mouth before scraping the rest of the food into to-go boxes while he paid the bill.

It was annoying to have to toss and turn when I could've fallen asleep without effort, but with Lucas rolling around, I didn't have a choice but to pretend to be distressed like he was.

Around midnight, I woke to the sound of him picking at his food, his gaze far away.

I used the bathroom, and when I emerged, he said, "How're you doing?"

"My stomach's upset," I said honestly. I was positive it was the cake that did me in, traitorous avalanche of sugar and fat that it was.

"Your seal is still leaking," he said, indicating the fluid collecting in a plastic tray under my bike and the assorted parts on the tarp. "I saw a 24-hour place a few blocks from here. I want to see if they have the stuff I need, and then I want to leave here at daybreak."

"I'll go with you to the store," I said, pulling on my jeans.

He relaxed. "I didn't want to leave you here alone."

His bike had a slick shell instead of a passenger seat, and I clung to him with arms and thighs as he shot through the erratic traffic.

"Ease up, possum baby. I have to breathe," he complained.

I squeaked as he made a sharp turn, sending my ass sliding sideways. He was going to kill me long before Mauss had another chance.

The store had the epoxy he wanted. As we approached the line at the checkout, Lucas was knocked into me by a couple cutting in front of us. We exchanged raised eyebrows as the two argued about a bakery clamshell with a pair of cookies until the man snatched it from her hands and thrust it onto the rack of gum and candy.

I pretended I didn't see them, but I could smell the sweetness of the vanilla. My stomach churned uncomfortably at the thought of more sugar, but my eyes kept returning to the colorful sprinkles and dribbles of white

112

icing on the sugar cookies. It was the lab's fault. If they had given me a monthly cookie, I wouldn't regard every sweet topside as a chance of a lifetime.

"No," Lucas told me. "I already got you cake."

"I wasn't asking."

"I can hear your stomach growling."

"It growls for kale," I assured him, but when I opened my mouth, a tiny squirt of saliva shot out.

He shook his head, but his lips turned up at the corners. "I just can't resist doe eyes from a little girl," he teased, for once looking like a doting father as he added the cookies to our basket. "Thank God they don't sell ponies here, or I'd be buying you one of those, too."

Out in the parking lot, he popped one of the cookies into his mouth whole before putting his helmet on, but I clutched the plastic-housed verboten delicacy to my chest, savoring the idea of the remaining cookie as a bedtime treat. I drooled the whole way to the motel.

I woke feeling decidedly odd. I opened my eyes through the painful crusties and tried to push the hair off my face, but I couldn't. Someone had affixed a Bible to my right hand with industrial-strength tape.

"What the hell?" I croaked. A chain of paper dolls was taped to my left hand, and I had to use my teeth to tear them off. A residue of glue and paper remained. "Not cool, Lucas. Not cool."

He was sprawled uncomfortably on the other bed, fully dressed, like someone had thrown his body there.

I sat up and gasped at what else had been attached to me.

"Lucas," I said sharply. "Wake up."

He didn't respond.

CHAPTER 15

LOCKED DOWN

I scrambled to Lucas's side and checked his pulse at the carotid. The heat of his body as well as the steady throb under my fingertips promised me he was alive.

A pair of empty medication blister packs was taped to the mirror in our room along with another photo of Mauss. This one showed him in a food service setting mixing crushed tablets into the sprinkles that were about to be used on the cookies we'd bought. I could see the head and shoulders of two other people from behind and recognized the garish clothing. It was the couple who'd just happened to butt in front of us in line and ditch the tainted cookies where I'd be tempted by them.

Full of dread, I pressed the recording in the photo's corner.

"Did you sleep well?" Mauss said, laughing. "Maybe you should've learned from the last time you went off diet and ended up with a tube down your throat. Well, you'll be happy to hear I had the motorcycle fixed properly. You can't play the game if you keep breaking down. Are you in over your head? Maybe you should just go home, gem."

Teeth chattering, I wrapped myself in the bedspread and pushed and poked Lucas with increasing violence until he woke.

"Ease up, Little One," he complained, his voice thick and groggy.

"We were drugged," I said. "Mauss spiked the cookies."

He surged out of bed, half falling to get to his bag. "You didn't see this," he told me, breaking out a single dose syringe that he stabbed into the vein in his arm.

It wasn't even a minute before he was wide-eyed and sharp again.

"Adrenaline?" I asked.

"Sure. That's it."

He snatched the photo off the mirror and played the message. After a moment of shocked silence, Lucas said, "I'm never eating a cookie again."

I'd backed into a corner, shaking. If I'd eaten both cookies, I might've died from an overdose.

Lucas checked my motorcycle and grunted. "Factory fresh parts." He initiated the diagnostics just to be certain but didn't look like he expected any trouble. After all, like Mauss said, our mission depended on our ability to drive around.

"He was here," I croaked.

"Yeah. Time stamp on the pic is thirty-six hours ago. I'll tell Domino."

"He was in our room."

"He's gone now."

"A man who wants to kill me was in our room while I was unconscious," I yelled at him.

115

"If he wanted to kill you, don't you think he would've? He had the chance," he said reasonably.

"Sure, for an unknown girl you're all teddy bears and compassion. For me, someone he does actually mean to kill, you're a dick."

"She was eight. You're sixteen. Sixteen? Seventeen."

"I don't remember," I snapped. "I'm too fucking freaked out."

"Well, you're old enough to—"

"To what? Be afraid of cookies that had their safety seal intact? Call Domino. Tell him I want a gun. And a food tester. And a gun. Did I mention a gun?"

"He's not going to give you a gun. He gave you me."

"Fat lot of good that is, cookie man. I honestly had no intention of asking for them. Those cookies are totally your fault."

"Hey, I didn't force feed you."

"Look at that picture, Lucas. Look at the girl's neck. She's got a crooked cross tattoo. It's that skank you screwed the night you picked up the motorcycles. Black hair instead of blonde and a ton more cosmetics, but look at that tattoo. It's her. You let her in, and you let her learn us."

"Learn us? What could she possibly have learned? That you can be a bitch and I like sex doggie style?"

I blanched. "I didn't need to know that."

"I'm sure you already knew you can be bitchy," he told me with a ghost of a smile. "Look, we got our asses handed to us. It happens sometimes. We have to just shake it off."

"I'm going to shake you all the way to perdition."

He made a soothing noise. "Jumpy and paranoid is just how the psycho wants us. It would help if you weren't such a sore loser."

116

"This happened because you weren't taking it seriously. I don't want to die. Do you have any idea how much it hurts? Resuscitation is even worse, trust me, but dying really sucks."

"Just stop it. We don't know he wants to kill you. He's singled you out definitely, but we don't know why. Preparing for the worst is just good planning, not a guaranteed outcome. Don't let him get into your head."

"Why are we still arguing about it? Call the big, blue-haired ox and find out what he wants us to do. And while you're at it, ask him what I'm supposed to do about this."

I unwrapped the blanket to show him I still wore my usual sleeping T-shirt but now had a brand-new set of panties, courtesy of Mauss.

"What is that?" Lucas said, tilting his head. "It looks like it's made out of metal."

"It *is* made out of metal. It's a chastity belt. It's what prehistoric assholes slapped on their women to make sure they weren't screwing."

"Well, that's unsanitary," he commented. "How are you supposed to go to the bathroom?"

"There are barbed holes."

Lucas finally looked as horrified as I felt. "Take it off. Take it off now."

"Don't you think it would negate a prehistoric asshole's purpose if the woman could just take it off?" I said, pointing at the lock. "This has to be cut off me because I'm not hanging around in it until Mauss deigns to give me the key."

"Lie down and let me get a look at the lock."

Unsettled as he was, Lucas had me draped with thick layers of towels and blankets until only my head and the lock were exposed. With his headlamp, magnifiers, and tiny metal implements, he looked too much like a surgeon, and I clenched my eyes shut.

"Some men find them sexy," I gritted out, dealing with it instead of pretending it wasn't happening like I desperately wanted to. "The whole control and denied orgasm thing. Some women find it sexy, too."

"Why did you have to say that? It's bad enough I'm afraid to eat a cookie, but now I'm going to be afraid every woman who wants to take her clothes off in front of me is wearing one of these."

"But I don't think he meant it that way. I fall within the range of a typical female reproductive age, but I guess he doesn't know my body isn't making the needed hormones for me to get pregnant. Still, he's left no doubt as to his position on prophylaxis. Do you think if I'd been pregnant, he would've used a metal coat hanger on me instead?"

"You have got to shut up. I couldn't be a whole lot more freaked out, and you casually talking about that is not helping."

I scratched my nose with the Bible taped to my hand, and belatedly realizing the sacrilege, I switched hands. "Sorry. You could turn on the TV."

"No, I think I'd prefer to be mentally scarred in silence, thank you."

I laughed.

Being quiet and still was terrible. Under the thick layers, I sweated until it trickled down my skin. The tiny clinking and scraping noises as he worked on the lock were as unnerving as the intimacy of his physical presence bent over my lower torso.

An accident, I decided. Through a freak accident, I was pinned beneath debris, and Lucas was painstakingly sorting through a bunch of wires to clip the live one so he could move the metal and free me. It was a stupid scenario, but I could accept it.

Lucas leaned back and turned away. "Try it now."

"Halleluiah," I said as I lifted my hips and shimmied out of the barbarism. "Thanks."

He dug out a knife and solvent and motioned for me to give him my hands.

"Check it for marked passages," he said as the Bible was freed.

"You're such a useful person to have around," I said with admiration as I gave him my other hand. His patience and skill was going to leave my hands with nothing more than redness and irritation from the solvent.

"Don't say nice things about me," he said.

"Why not?"

"Because I'm sitting here wishing I never met you."

I grinned at him, and he reluctantly returned the smile. Then he laughed. "This is turning into one crazy day."

I went into the bathroom and stripped so I could see my back. The highly placed mirror wasn't accommodating, and I went out to Lucas.

His eyes widened at my nakedness.

"Shut up," I told him, spinning around. "Did he write on me?"

"No."

"Be sure," I said, lifting my hair.

"No, you're clean. Hey, check me."

I wrapped myself in the blanket and checked his taut, pale skin carefully. I saw nothing beyond the constellation Orion in his freckles and scars.

"I feel ogled," he commented as the exam dragged on.

"You wish. I'm checking if there's a symbol written in something less obvious than washable marker."

He dug in his pack and handed me a small UV lamp.

"How do you fit so much in your pack?" I asked him. "You've got three guns in there, don't you?"

"Years of practice," he said. "Turn around. Let me check you again." He tipped the light this way and that and then repeated it with the UV like I'd done on him. We were both clean.

"I need to talk to Domino," I told Lucas.

After he finished briefing Domino, Lucas took a change of clothes into the bathroom, leaving me his palmer.

"Look, is this about those two people I killed at Greyson?" I asked Domino in a low voice. "Does the Bible-thumping extremist want Old Testament justice? Death for death? I know he blames me, and he knows I won't be tried in any courtroom."

Domino's voice held more than a little surprise. "No. He didn't like or trust them to get any job done. I know he blames them for botching your retrieval. He also agrees with why traditional laws can't be applied to you, so again, no, this isn't about them. If he said it was, it's misdirection."

"Really? Because that's the only thing he's got against me."

The silence lasted so long I checked to see if the connection was still open.

"Look," he said eventually, "he doesn't believe it was self-defense, but he doesn't care they're dead."

"Domino, these are definitely personal attacks. Those photo messages are directed at me, not us. The Bibles he leaves me make it seem like I'm supposed to be praying my ass off because he thinks I'm guilty of a specific sin."

Another long silence.

"Domino?"

"Do you want to come in?"

"No," I blurted. "No, I can do this. Lucas and I are shaken up but recovering quickly." Lucas had emerged from the bathroom, and I thrust the palmer at him. "He's asking if I should be taken to the lab. I said no."

Lucas promised Domino we were still good to go while I snatched up my bag and locked myself in the bathroom. Alone and momentarily safe, I shuddered and hugged myself as the water warmed from the icy temp Lucas preferred. Occasionally, I caught the scared look on my face in my reflection.

Jesus Christ, Mauss was good. I mean, were we hunting him or was he hunting us? How was he even finding us so fast?

I jumped when Lucas knocked on the door. "I'm going down to the lobby to check for any surveillance footage. When you're finished, Domino wants you to compare the photo messages to see if we missed something."

"Like what?"

"He mentioned speech pattern. He said you'd know what he meant."

I listened to the pair of photos again. Mauss called me 'gem' both times. He'd done that in the lab, too, often with a fake smile. I'd always thought he meant it sarcastically, but I filed the word away for later thought and moved on to the second anomaly, the one Domino wondered about.

The way Mauss said that last part of his message from the first photo was odd. It was awkwardly formal or forced, like he was reading a manifesto instead of speaking extemporaneously. I said it aloud to see if it sounded as awkward from another speaker.

"In any millennium, Godliness only improves national governments. To obfuscate knowledge impedes legitimate lawmaking, yet one understands Christ's love only needs effort."

121

No, it still sounded deliberate. I remembered that last part from before, too. It had been the graffiti on the wall outside my door the day of the lab murders.

I dug out my palmer and typed the words one per line. I saw the intent instantly as I read down the first letter in each.

I AM GOING TO KILL YOU, CL—

I deleted the file and turned on the television loud enough to wake the dead. Anything to drive the thoughts out of my head.

When Lucas returned with a frown for the lack of useful surveillance, he saw the pair of photos face down by his bag. He shut off the television, giving me a questioning look.

"I didn't find anything," I said.

CHAPTER 16

THE PLAGUE

A few days later, we were still in Amarillo, but we had moved to the highest security hotel available. It was more like a fortress or jail than a hotel, but the sheets were soft. Mauss was slipping further through our fingers with each passing hour, but ours was a necessary delay.

"I still say it was him," Lucas said.

"Mauss did not give you the flu," I said.

"He could've," he countered irritably, punching his pillow into submission before slumping into it. "He could've got it and licked our door handle, and since I touched first, I got the big dose of the plague while you got none."

The glare from his bloodshot eyes indicated he considered it on par with him taking a bullet for me.

"Will you take off that stupid mask?" he said. "It's—" His words gave way to a coughing fit. He spat a glob of mucus into a tissue and checked the color.

Even from where I stood, it looked tinged with green. I took an involuntary step back.

"It's been three days," he told me. "The doctor said I wouldn't be contagious anymore."

"I'm not taking any chances, Typhoid Mary."

In preparation for a supply run, I tied my shoes and checked my appearance. The unyielding gaze coming from my narrowed eyes made me look like I'd survived alone in a warzone for years. It was too hard, too cold. Without moving my head, I looked upward and grinned widely before letting my expression relax. Now I saw nothing in my eyes beyond youthful confidence.

"And you didn't answer my question," I said. "Did you want juice or more of the electrolyte drink instead?"

"I don't care," he said crossly. "Just don't bring that nasty crap again because I'm not drinking it. I want the stuff with the bear on the label."

"I told you they didn't have it. Look, whatever. I'll see what I can do. Was there anything else I can do for you?"

He again gave me a long list of items he needed, all brand- or flavor-specific products I didn't find the last time I went to the stores after the trip to the medical center confirmed he was suffering from nothing more sinister than a nasty influenza infestation.

The red spots high on his chalky face made me think he was still running a fever, but his graduation to whining told me he was starting to feel better. Thank God he'd become sick in a place large enough to have a medical center so the illness could be identified quickly and treated aggressively with the meds.

"I'll return within two hours," I said, switching his video feed from sports to history.

"I was watching that."

"You were falling asleep to it and waking with each whoop and holler."

124

He checked his palmer for the time and burrowed under the covers, grumbling. "Two hours. Check in every fifteen minutes. Be careful."

After a consultation with the pharmacist on duty, which led me to better tasting options for Lucas's meds, I stopped in the secondhand store across the street. I saw a pair of old books that were brittle but not moldy, and I put them in my basket without reading the titles. Anything new to read thrilled me. I still couldn't read for hours on a digital screen without my eyeballs getting tired and skittery.

I had time before I had to return to Plague Central, so I wandered the rest of the store, evaluating the castoffs for anything useful. Lucas wouldn't mind the books being put on the government tab, but I also had a cash card of my own to use thanks to creative money schemes I'd used behind his back.

I saw a motorcycle jacket my size, but the new one Lucas had given me fit, and the drab color suited me.

But my eyes kept returning to the way the jacket hung crookedly on the hanger. I managed to pass by the tilted pictures on the wall, but this one jacket listing to the side was going to kill me. I set down my basket, determined to reseat the jacket so it hung straight. It wouldn't, though.

My nose wrinkling at the odor of the jacket's previous owner, I pulled it on to make sure nothing was caught in the sleeves to weight it funny. The faux leather was worn and soft at the folds, but the jacket fit stiffly. I removed it and examined it closely. With growing excitement, I discreetly slit the lining and at the first sign of carbon fiber, I snatched up the garment and strode to the checkout counter.

In the hotel room, I read the book on rebuilding old car engines until Lucas fell asleep, snoring thickly. I slipped onto the floor where the bed would block sight of me, and I held the stinky jacket to my chest, profusely grateful for my treasure.

This jacket didn't have the optional rigid safety panels in the front. It didn't even have the law-mandated safety panel in the back, though the hardness there certainly made it seem that way.

It held three panels of body armor.

Lucas's palmer signaled an incoming call, and he shot out of bed, stumbling in his haste to get it. I pointed to where it had fallen to the floor and discreetly hid my contraband in my pile of laundry before sitting on the bed, watching him.

Lucas's terse conversation ended with him saying, "No, I've got the flu." Setting his palmer on his nightstand, he told me, "There was a sighting down in Plainville."

"Was it another girl?" I said, annoyed. Why did I even have to ask him to elaborate?

"No, facial recognition nailed Mauss on a traffic camera feed. He resuscitated a woman at a car accident. Even saved her dog."

I burst out laughing.

"Not the appropriate response," he told me.

"Can't you see the irony of it? That murderer is out there saving lives while we commit crimes in our effort to find him."

"Crimes?"

"Trespassing and fraud. I'm not eighteen. I'm not supposed to have a driver's license or get my own hotel room, but my fraudulent ID makes it possible."

"I hate it when people think you're my kid," he said grumpily, crawling into bed. "I'm not even thirty, and we don't look alike."

"We're both paler than pale," I reminded him. "What about Mauss? Where's Plainville?"

126

"Due south. His family used to have a house there. Domino's sending someone else since I'm sick."

I let that sink in, my fingers tightening on my pants. I didn't want to go underground where I was defenseless. "So we're done?"

"They haven't captured him yet," Lucas reminded me.

"You know, information like where he's from would've been useful to know."

"Little One, believe it or not, when he left the lab, all the topside law enforcement agencies were notified, and all the normal places were put under surveillance. We were called in because there'd been no sign of him. No one expected him to pop up where security feeds could tag him, and if they don't catch him down there, Domino expects him to drop out of sight and return to whatever his plan was."

"Clarify. So if they don't catch him?"

"We continue west on the path you chose."

Glenrio.

I pulled the bike over and barely got my helmet off before vomiting on the side of the road.

Lucas circled back as soon as he realized I wasn't beside him, and I held my hand up to let him know not to dismount.

I retched again with agonizing force.

He said, "We need to find a place to stay. If we push any harder while you're sick, it could delay us days."

Actually it wasn't just some kind of stomach flu. I was vomiting regularly now. My left arm was acting up, too, with tingling, numbness, all the warnings signs my nerves weren't staying connected or firing properly like they were supposed to. Hell, if I wanted to be honest with myself, it had been getting worse each day since my implants had been removed two months ago so I could be released topside.

I should've told Lucas earlier, but I kept waking up thinking I felt well enough to keep going. By nightfall, I felt like crap and promised myself I would tell Lucas in the morning, only to wake up and feel functional again.

As I vomited on the side of the road, I realized it was time to tell him, although I didn't know how. The lab could likely fix me up and have me out on the road within weeks, but they'd only let me surface again if they felt I was still necessary to the case despite my relative failure to find Mauss.

I took the water bottle Lucas offered and rinsed my mouth thoroughly, directing the discarded fluid toward a straggly plant that looked like it needed it more than I did.

"Not too much," he reminded me. "We need water, too. If I let you carry our water supply, you'd water every plant you could find and then let us die from dehydration."

I swished and swallowed to take away the burning in my throat. "What if you have a kid someday? Wouldn't you want him to grow up in a world lush with plants and healthy animals instead of this desolate wasteland?"

"I have an eight-year-old daughter. The psycho took her picture from my room the day of the killings."

"*What?*"

But that was all he'd say.

So much for calling for a retrieval. I'd stay out here as long as I could before the next girl we heard had been taken was his. I strode to my bike and donned my helmet.

"If you're sick—" Lucas persisted.

"I'm not," I said bluntly before I rode off.

In Tucumcari, we heard about another girl who'd been kidnapped, drawn on, and returned unconscious.

"They found her on railroad tracks just a few hours ago," Lucas told me as he squatted beside me, lowering his voice so the others at the crowded fuel stop couldn't overhear. "He may still be here."

I removed the diagnostic tool from his Keoni's primary port and stuck it in the secondary, watching the cops speak with a pair of truckers. "I don't think he'll take the chance of us getting ahead of him, so I imagine he left as soon as he released her."

I looked over at him, noticing how his pale eyes shone in the late afternoon light. If I didn't have brown-colored lenses with a UV block to protect my virgin eyes, my yellow eyes would've been glowing like twin suns. "A broken heart. Are you positive that's what he drew?"

"Not without seeing it."

"It might be John Henry. Was she black?"

"That's a dirty word that will get you knocked down in some places."

"Um, dark complexion?"

"Deep complexion."

"Does that mean you and I have a shallow complexion?" I said in irritation.

Lucas ignored that. "How did you know what color her skin is?"

"Because it would fit." I switched motorcycles, running the diagnostic cord around his bike to mine. "John Henry was a deep-complexioned steel-driver who died drilling holes for explosives for a railroad tunnel in the nineteenth century."

"Same era and another railroad. What does it mean?"

I shrugged.

"So why is he a hero?" Lucas asked. "Did he jump on explosives and save a bunch of people?"

"Perhaps legend more than hero. Depends on your perspective, I guess. He went head-to-head with a steam-powered hammer in a legendary contest of raw human strength versus a machine. He won, but his heart couldn't take the strain and he died immediately after."

"Man's will beats modern technology but at a cost?"

"Intriguing interpretation, but I just don't know," I said.

"Because it sounds like he wants to teach you a lesson."

"I don't even know if John Henry was in that book. I don't remember anything else about him, so I won't recognize any additional clues that would point to him or someone else entirely. Remind me why Domino can't just give us that book?"

"The psycho took it, and Domino still hasn't found another copy. It didn't make it to digital."

I grunted, irritated and saddened by the dwindling supply of my favorite medium. "Is it just me or is this weird for Mauss? Not that I knew him well, but with me he was almost as straightforward as Domino. Up here, he teases us instead of hammers us, and he uses nostalgic Americana to send messages instead of Bible verses. Doesn't it feel like he's playing a role someone else wrote for him?"

"I don't know what to tell you. I didn't know him long. Or well."

Looking at the bikes' readouts and seeing signs of heavy use, I said, "We could just have the authorities keep an eye out for the next girl and have them send us the clues. It would save us the travel time."

"Domino thinks he'll just drop out of sight as soon as he realizes we're not behind him. I wouldn't be surprised if he's already got the next girl picked out and is delaying until we're close before he takes her. Christ, I hate living like this, having my whole world revolve around this game-playing fuckbag and his need to lead us around the whole goddamned clan."

I scrubbed my scalp hard, debating the best way to handle Lucas's increasingly shortened temper. When he swore, it was definitely a red flag. "If you want to go blow off steam until morning, go ahead. I'll finish up here, eat, and then lock up tight in a hotel to see what I can find on John Henry. We'll meet here at daybreak."

Lucas spun around at the sound of a young girl's distress but relaxed when he saw the doll in the dirt and the girl's grubby hands reaching for it.

I asked, "Did Domino put your daughter and her mom in a safe house?"

"Don't bring her up. I need to focus," he said, tearing his eyes from the girl.

"Can you?" I asked. "You seem to be a bit on edge. Is there something you're not telling me?"

He shook his head and exhaled forcefully. "What about the psycho?"

"He must not be ready for the high noon showdown. I guess we're not sufficiently impressed yet. I'm as safe as I ever am," I said, gesturing to the police presence.

With a curt nod, Lucas got on his bike and took off with an impatient show of power.

I finished the diagnostics on my bike and rode to the eatery attached to the fuel stop, relieved Lucas was gone. I was having a rough day, and his deteriorating attitude wasn't helping any.

And perhaps I was a lot more tired of waiting around than I let on, and ditching my chaperone might be enough incentive for the psycho to—

131

Not *the psycho. Mauss.* Lucas had stopped referring to Mauss by name, which indicated things were coming to a head and the traitor was indeed targeted for termination. Lucas never called me by my name. It was possible my future was just as uncertain as the psycho's.

Mauss's.

"Potayto, potahto," I muttered. "Still gonna get mashed in the end."

Scanning the diner, I applied the lessons Lucas had taught me about reading people. Unfortunately, I could argue everyone in there looked both harmless and dangerous, so I gave up. But after I claimed a stool, I did find my gaze returning to the same man sitting at the other end of the counter.

His black cowboy hat shadowed most of his face, but his profile wouldn't let me go. He appeared to be in his early thirties, and his big body was held in a manner that made me think he was exhausted. He had longish, dark brown hair, a tiny silver hoop in one earlobe, and a thick pelt of a beard trimmed neat.

The server tried to get my attention but the Tex-Mex wearing the battered blue jeans, rundown cowboy boots, and tight black T-shirt was too much of a distraction.

The corner of his beautifully shaped mouth tipped up at something another server said, and recognition shot through me with the burning force of a lightning bolt.

The man had Jason's smile.

CHAPTER 17

FAMILY RESEMBLANCE

The man at the end of the counter obliviously ate his chili as I stared at him, but his head snapped up to the screen when the newscast mentioned resident outlanders assaulting travelers. He was passing through then. Now that I knew that, I saw the signs of a man who had grown up in the cities despite his comfort in clothes the locals were likely to wear. Like Lucas had said, a lifetime of good nutrition and medicine couldn't be faked.

I left my seat and went to him, debating what to say.

I stuck my hand out. "Tycho Walker. Bounty hunter."

The outrageous gambit should've been enough to get him to look at me, but it just made his hand tighten on his fork. "I don't need any help finding him."

"Sorry, I was joking. You're seriously looking for someone?" Then my knees almost gave way. Gripping the edge of the counter, I said hoarsely, "Jason Chavez is missing, isn't he?"

He finally gazed at me. His dark eyes widened and his thick eyebrows shot up into his hat.

"I'm older than I look," I said.

"My jeans are older than you look. What would a girl your age know about Jason?"

"He's not actually missing, is he? Why would you look here? He's an urbane man, and it's like the Old West out here."

"Just because you saw his picture or read about him, it doesn't mean you know him."

"Yeah, but I'm right," I said. He had to be Jason's brother. The marked resemblance both in features and manner ruled out another explanation.

"The H-E compound isn't too far from here."

"Really?" Harbinger-Ellis was the designer and builder of the plane Jason and I had flown. "I don't know why it didn't occur to me it was a real company with real buildings. Is Valhalla real, too?"

"God, you're not a groupie, are you?"

"Has Jason been to H-E?"

He shook his head. "They've been actively pinging for him, too. The bump I thought was him was the man they sent out looking for him. They need Jason's research."

With a chill on my spine, I left the diner and got on my bike. Tuncay had told me they'd thawed Jason the day before I arrived topside, and I'd been promised he'd shown none of the decay I'd seen in Puck or experienced myself. He should've surfaced somewhere by now.

Jason's brother shut off my motorcycle's engine. He was taller than Jason by more than ten centimeters even without the hat. He was also built better than his hunched over appearance at the diner suggested.

He said, "If you know something about Jason, I want to hear it."

"When's the last time you heard from him?"

"I got a message from him the day a student died at Greyson while he was there. You know of Greyson?"

I nodded. It was an advanced combat aviation school, and it was my demise he referred to.

Jason's brother said, "He just said he'd be home soon. We know he made it home a few days later. Then he locked everything up tight and took off before talking to any of us."

The forthcoming reply to a stranger could only mean he was desperately worried and willing to try anything up to and including a séance to find his brother. And why not? There'd been no sign of him in more than two years.

"What does the Defense Minister have to say about this? Wouldn't she care if one of her top aviators went missing?"

"She hasn't said anything."

"So she's involved," I said thoughtfully. "Does that make it better or worse?"

"I don't know, but her silence and lack of involvement is unexpected. Our family means a lot to the MoD. Your turn, Ms. Walker. What's the last thing you heard about his whereabouts?"

Christ, I hadn't been called that since before I was married. It was eerie.

"Tycho," I said. "I was at a research hospital, and when I saw him in passing and asked, I was told he'd volunteered for an experiment instead of going to jail for his role in the death of the Greyson student. I was under the impression he was being released then. That was a few months ago."

He shook his head. "She died from kidney failure. There weren't any charges, let alone a conviction."

My eyes locked on his while I digested what he'd said.

"As a member of his family, you would have better information than I would," I said. "I only saw the man for a moment or two anyway. Must've been a case of mistaken identity. Well, people messing with me when I thought I saw an aviation legend in our ranks."

"Oh, someone made a mistake," he said thoughtfully. "The only way we're going to know who did is by hearing the truth from his lips."

He took in my appearance again, this time with a look that suggested sudden comprehension.

"You're related to the woman who died," he said. "That's how you know about Jason and the inquiry into her death."

"What makes you say that?"

"I've seen the photos in my brother's file on her. That's why you looked familiar."

"She and I are of the same blood," I said in a tone that made it plain I wasn't going to elaborate.

In fact, the conversation was over as far as I was concerned. I should've gone to our hotel room as soon as Lucas had left.

"Goodbye, Mr. Chavez," I said curtly, starting my engine.

"No," he said simply as he planted his hands on my windscreen. "If you want to be done talking about that, then we're done. Doesn't mean we have to stop the discussion altogether."

"Yeah, buddy? I don't suppose you've become aware of the speculative patrons regarding my pretty face or my pretty bike. It's time for me to leave."

"My ride is over there. Move your bike next to it like we're traveling together."

Jason's brother drove a battered off-road hybrid that looked like it was made from five or six different vehicles.

He made a show of pulling out a sawed off shotgun and stared down the nearest group of people.

"Must be nice," I commented as they moved away from us. "To be intimidating, I mean."

"It's useful sometimes and a detriment sometimes. Beautiful women can be skittish."

"Dunno. I'm not afraid."

"You're a beautiful, reckless child, which is a whole different animal. Look, I think you're lying to me about who you are, but I'm okay with that. You've obviously been on your own for a while, and your lies are probably for your protection, not your amusement."

When I met his gaze steadily, he exhaled forcefully, pushing his black cowboy hat back on his head so I could see his face. His features were flat in the harsh light of the truck stop, but I liked what I saw. He looked weathered, capable.

He said, "So let's talk about this experiment you thought you saw him in. What were you doing there?"

I shook my head, knowing when someone didn't believe me. "Seems to me, you need to exert pressure on the MoD. If there's enough hue and cry about his disappearance, don't they have to release information about him?"

"Where's the hospital where you saw him?"

"I don't know. I was unconscious when I went in and unconscious when they transported me out."

The muscles in my jaw tensed at the familiar sound of Lucas's motorcycle.

CHAPTER 18

KISS AND TELL

Thinking quickly, I said, "That's the guy I travel with. I'm not supposed to tell people about that place, and you don't want to let him know you know I thought your brother was a resident. Ignoring this spy crap, the natural reason for a male and a female to find a quiet corner of the world is the oldest one, so kiss me and look like you mean it."

"I don't kiss children."

I surreptitiously flashed him the ID saying I was eighteen, and his demeanor changed. The force of his awareness touched me like a wave of hot velvet, and I felt the first fiery bite of desire.

"You're quite a family," I commented, crossing my arms across my chest.

"Yeah, well, your family's turning out to be damn interesting, too," he purred, planting one hand on the seat next to my ass.

"You have no idea," I murmured, genuinely amused.

His hands framed my face, holding me gently while his lips moved softly over mine. It shouldn't have been shocking, but it was. No one touched me gently. No one touched me at all unless it was part of my medical treatment. The heat of him devastated me as much as the feel of his mouth on mine.

His tongue slipped into my mouth, and I gasped. I felt his smile start, but it faded as he continued with the tender exploration of my mouth, drawing me into exploring his. I'd never felt such a soft, sweet consummation before, and I didn't want it to end.

Lucas's bike cut out suddenly. "Little One?" he prompted casually.

I jumped and tore my mouth from Jason's brother, staring at him in surprise, and not only because of the exquisite kiss. He'd managed to slip past my guard to the point where I'd forgotten about Lucas, forgotten about the lab, forgotten everything.

Jason's brother's expression was gentle, and I wondered if he thought it was my first kiss.

"Yes?" I responded, my eyes still locked on a pair of dark ones.

"Who's your friend?"

"Never learned his name. I liked the way he moved, so I followed him from the diner, thinking we could—"

Lucas's voice was suddenly firm. "You were wrong."

"I was blowing off steam, same as you."

"You want to end up dead on the side of the road somewhere?"

"I'm already dead," I snapped, shoving the cowboy back because I was suddenly feeling cornered. The heat and hardness of his body against my hands startled me, scattering my thoughts. Wow, had I forgotten what lust could do to a person?

I tore my gaze away from him to meet the scathing regard of my chaperone. I told him, "You're an idiot if you think you're going to survive this, too. That guy's wicked smart, and he's insane. He will kill me. If you get in his way, he will kill you, too. I'll be damned if I don't get to screw someone this hot before I die."

"Not a chance. You left a virgin and you're going to return as one. And stop being so pessimistic about our chances. It'll get us killed."

"Go to hell," I spat, starting up my bike. It died, and I stared down at the bike in disbelief.

A whistle made me look toward Lucas. He held up the remote kill switch.

Like that was going to stop me.

I dismounted and jogged away at a good energy-conserving pace. I could hear Lucas tearing into the other man.

"If I catch you near her again, I will call the cops, you sick fuck. What's the matter with you, thinking about a girl her age like that?"

"She's of age," he replied laconically, the wind carrying his words. "And she seems to know what she wants."

"She doesn't know what she wants," Lucas snapped. "Little One, if you cross that road, I will have you caged before you can blink."

I came to a stumbling stop but refused to turn around.

Lucas called out, "I'm sorry about laying down the law, but I have to. This area isn't as safe as I thought."

I could run, I thought wildly. *If I make it to those rocks, I could—*

"Not another step. Not one."

Unwillingly admitting I was outmatched, I lowered my boot to the ground next to its mate.

140

The bright moon showed streaky clouds that teased the dry earth with the idea of rain, and suddenly I felt teased like that, too. Part of it was loneliness. I supposed a lot of it was. I'd met someone sensual and interesting, and I'd stolen only a few minutes with him before the lab stepped in to end it.

But some of it was also due to the unexpected reminder of Jason. I thought I was past missing him. His show-stopping smile. His honesty about the things most people lie about and his lies about the things most people tell the truth about. His intellect and his love of flying that matched mine.

My hands went up to my temples, and I clenched my eyes shut. "Get out of my head."

"Are you okay?" Lucas asked as he approached.

I shook my head.

"Did he touch you somewhere?"

"No, nothing happened there I didn't want to happen."

He studied me closely, the worry on his face suggesting he recognized more was wrong than he first thought. A couple laughed nearby, and when I glanced at them and saw how scrawny they were, I jerked my eyes away.

I wanted to be tough and not let the disease and poverty of the outlands upset me, but I couldn't banish the guilt that my generation hadn't corrected its course before the United States had dissolved into this awkward confederation of clans. All the therapy I'd been through seemed like it had been for nothing. Perhaps I was broken beyond repair.

"Lucas, I can't do this. I thought I could, but I'm so overwhelmed. I'm sorry."

"No, I'm sorry I left you alone," he said. "But at least I got here before that creep did anything."

I let out a long, shuddering sigh that released some of the awful tension. "Let's get a hotel room and leave at first light."

"Little One, if you need to talk, I'll listen."

"Do you know my name?" I asked. "Do you even know the name you won't use or am I just an object you might be required to terminate and thus nameless?"

"I know your name."

"Use it," I said softly, my eyes staring down into the dirt at my feet. It was barren, gritty. "Please."

He ducked down and caught my eye.

"I'm not going to terminate you. They told me you could handle yourself better than most teenage girls, but I forgot you've been sheltered from the reality of the outlands. I'm sorry, but you have to get past the emotion. We have to catch this guy."

"Did it ever occur to you people there's a limit to what a person can take?" I asked him. "I've been torn apart and rebuilt repeatedly, both mentally and physically, and you want me to come face to face with the man who—"

"Not if I can help it," he said. "I don't want you anywhere near the target. Once I have a lock on him, I'm going to put you somewhere safe before I deal with him one on one."

"What?"

"Why would I want you to witness something traumatizing?"

"Two against one is better odds," I told him. "Haven't they been experimenting on you long enough for your compassion to give way to self-preservation?"

He brought the water bottle away from his mouth so rapidly an arc of the precious fluid splattered me. "Experimenting? What?"

"Your implants," I explained, brushing the water off my jacket toward the nearest straggly plant. "Or is it rude to ask about them?"

"My what?"

"The circuitry under your skin. I saw it. It runs from the fingers of your hand up your arm and neck and across your face. One of your eyes was white, too."

"That's not real. I get all painted up to go to a topside techno club sometimes."

"Like cosmetics and a plastic lens in your eye?"

That he was just another lab worker meant he wouldn't be able to appreciate what I'd been through. Appreciate, hell. He probably thought my real name was Tycho Walker and I actually was sixteen.

Looking past him, I saw Jason's brother watching us intently, seated on the hood of his vehicle.

I asked Lucas, "Can I speak to him for a minute?"

"Why?"

"From what he said, he's been crossing over plenty of territory himself. I want to see if he's heard of any Mauss-like occurrences."

"I'll handle it."

"You called him a pervert. I don't think he'll open up to you."

"He is a pervert, and yes, he will."

I glanced over at the man. "I can get an answer in about ten seconds. How long would it take you?"

Lucas's smile was reluctant. "Longer than ten seconds. Don't get too close to him, or I'll interfere."

"I'll make it quick," I promised.

Jason's brother's face showed nothing but wariness when he saw us approach, even when Lucas veered away to give us space.

"You're nowhere near eighteen, are you?" the man said. "Was anything you said the truth?"

I chose not to reply. "If I see Jason, I'll let him know his family is concerned."

"Are you in trouble? I don't believe what you said about yourself or my brother, but that doesn't mean I won't help you if you're honestly in a bind."

I thought about how to respond. Neither confirming nor denying what I told him sat well with me.

"Believe what you want," I said. "Believe whatever it takes to let you sleep at night. That's what I do."

"At least take my phone number. You may change your mind. Even if you just want to talk about the weather, call me."

"I can't," I said, my hands tightening into fists at my side. "It's not allowed. It's safer if there's no more connection between us than what he saw."

"No more connection between us than a kiss?"

My gaze shot to his. He'd said it lightly, but I couldn't dismiss the incident so easily. "I wish I'd never met you. I didn't need to know men like you existed. I didn't need to know *kisses* like that existed."

"Angel, it's going to be a long time before I forget you either. And if we ever do cross paths again, you better have legitimate proof you're of age," he added dryly.

Abruptly, I turned away from him with my heart throbbing, but seeing Lucas, I remembered what I was supposed to be doing.

I asked the man, "Have you heard of a man kidnapping girls, drugging them, and returning them with drawings on their backs?"

"No," he replied huskily. "I came from the south, if that helps narrow your search any."

144

I jerked my head at Lucas, and he escorted me to my bike. "Well?"

"If I got anything out of him, I would've told you," I told him flatly.

I couldn't resist a look back. Jason's brother stood there watching me. He didn't nod or lift his hand in farewell. He just watched me like I watched him.

It wasn't an uncomfortable feeling. Far from it.

Interesting.

Lucas whistled to regain my attention, and we left.

I still didn't know the man's first name, I realized later. I supposed that was fitting. He didn't know my true one either.

That night, locked safely in our hotel room, Lucas and I went about our familiar nightly routines, barely speaking to each other after his pronouncement I wouldn't be getting my own room for as long as we traveled together.

He shut out his light, and I wanted to smack him with a pillow. He should've known we weren't done.

"Are you going to report me?" I demanded.

"Are you still a virgin?"

"No, I haven't been one for a while."

He sat up and stared at me.

"But I didn't have sex with that guy, if that's what you're asking."

"Then there's nothing I need to say to them, but between you and me, you should've known better."

"Look, I'm the one who should be pissed, not you. If you applied that kill switch with me going any faster, I could've died."

"Could you trust my judgment any less?" he snapped.

"Could you have humiliated me any more?"

145

He closed his flashing eyes and exhaled slowly as if trying to calm down.

"Let's forget it," he said. "We're already going to be set back a day because you gave me a massive tension headache."

"How is your headache my fault?"

"I don't appreciate all this teenager drama over a guy who's old enough to be your father."

"Don't project your worries about your daughter onto me. I was fine."

"You set us back. We should be on the road again and you know it."

"So let's go."

"Didn't I just say you gave me a massive headache? Everywhere that carries what I need is closed. Maybe I can sleep it off instead."

I did have a single dose of the med he needed hidden in the decorative cap on my shampoo. It was a potent, fast painkiller. I could have us on the road in less than twenty minutes if his belly wasn't too full. I would've had to admit I'd stolen it from his bottle, though. That might make him wonder what else I'd stolen, and if he went through my belongings with an eye for concealed material, he'd find a lot. I didn't trust him to keep that knowledge to himself.

We slept with our backs to each other, both of us still pissed at the other but done with talking about why.

CHAPTER 19

MARROW OF THE BONE

I didn't sleep long, though, just enough to take the edge off. Too many thoughts rattled around in my mind to let me switch off.

Crunching antacids between my teeth, I considered Jason's predicament. If his brother were correct about Jason being held blameless, there would be no reason for him to be in an icer. But he was still missing, so where could he be that family couldn't be told? And if he was performing a sensitive task for the Ministry of Defense, where else would he be doing it if not Harbinger-Ellis?

Damn, I would love to have an excuse to get on the H-E compound.

I decided I could say I was following up on the rumor of a nearby airport because I wondered if Mauss was using aerial transportation to get around. I dug around the website from the H-E headquarters office in Austin, but there was no mention about any offices this far west, let alone a compound. I brought up a map of the local area. Perhaps I could put us on a route that would give me the thrill of driving by the plant. Nothing was there. I expanded my search and still couldn't find it. No large industrial buildings, no test runways, no sign of them at all.

There was a nature preserve, though. Switching to the satellite view revealed kilometer after kilometer of dusty wasteland, yet someone had fenced off a chunk of it as a preserve. Right. I needed to plot a route that way to confirm satellite images had been manipulated to provide false information to the general population so I knew I could no longer trust what the computers told me about an area. If the so-called preserve was nothing but a field, then Jason's brother might be the one lying.

Wanting to give him the benefit of the doubt, I returned to the H-E website to check their history and community service pages to see if I could find any kind of reference to that patch of land.

"Stupid puzzles," I muttered. "You've already decided the compound is there and hidden from general records for security reasons. You're never going to get through the gates. Let it go. I'm serious. Confirmation you're correct about it being there doesn't change the fact Jason is still missing, yet I can't help noticing you're still digging around this stupid website like a pig looking for truffles. Just let it—"

My eyes latched onto a familiar surname, and I stilled.

H-E didn't have a public museum, but they had several vintage aircraft on the premises of their southern office, including *Scheherazade*, the Battle Axe Jason's dad, Alexander Chavez, flew decades ago to win the North American Aerial Combat Competition. The short bio mentioned his wife Renee, and their five offspring: Shaun, Cristofer, Jason, Trey, and Risa. I dismissed Trey as too young to be the man I'd met, leaving Shaun or Cristofer. He looked more like a Cristofer to me.

I smiled, now having a name to put to the man with the melting kiss.

A man who'd been told Jason had nothing to do with my demise at Greyson.

I'd seen Jason in the icer. It had to be him. I knew what my damn mentor looked like.

But wasn't it convenient that the first I learned of him being in that lab was when they needed something from me and I'd refused to work with them?

A self-centered, rich, well-connected man was so devastated by my passing he volunteered to sacrifice himself in a kind of icy oblivion I'd never told him existed. He did that instead of doing his research from a white collar jail cell. Totally believable.

I was a damn fool.

Being the nearest lab representative, Lucas was lucky I didn't smother him while he slept.

But.

But Jason and I had been intimate once, and it had been the most passionate encounter of my life. It had come as a surprise to him, too, like his body had betrayed him so thoroughly it defied comprehension.

That wasn't half as disturbing as when he'd reached for me without realizing it. My roommate had asked if Jason had developed a tenderness for me, too. It had all happened far too soon after recovering the memory of my husband's passing for me to be comfortable with it, so I'd pretended I didn't notice.

Perhaps if Jason loved me, then he'd wished for oblivion after my death, especially if he figured out how he inadvertently hastened it. Maybe that actually was him I saw staring at me with those dark brown eyes.

Speaking of dark brown eyes gazing at me, I realized my fingertips were on my lips, which I imagined felt tingly and swollen from kissing.

"I'm going to Hell," I muttered through gritted teeth as I gave in to the need to do a search on Cristofer instead of figuring out a way to find out the truth about Jason.

The photos confirmed the man I'd met was the second son, but he was called Cris. He was two years older than Jason, and given the talent his parents had shown in the cockpit, he had been groomed to fly. But as soon as Jason had received his wings, Cris had turned in his to become an engineer and a consultant, mostly for H-E. He had a reputation for brilliance, defiance, wanderlust, and charity work. What an intriguing combination.

It was just as well I hadn't known any of that when I'd met him. When Lucas had retrieved me, I would've kneed him in the balls and made a run for Cris's arms.

A cramp seized my belly, scattering my thoughts, and I pressed my hand against the torment, thinking digestive thoughts to encourage my dinner to settle down. I sweated, too, despite the air-conditioned chill in the room.

The psycho needed to show himself, or at least lead us to cities with decent pharmacies. The latest round of antacids wasn't making a dent in my discomfort. Each time I ate, it was initiating a battle that only ended with a raw sphincter. And God help me if I needed to take a pain med. That just resulted in—

I stumbled, barely making it into the bathroom before I vomited. My knees hit the tile with a crack and barf hit my hair on the way down.

"You okay?" Lucas called out sleepily.

My arm shook uncontrollably. I held it against my body with my other arm while my gut emptied violently into the toilet.

"Little One?"

I thought of the two girls stolen from their beds, and I thought of Lucas's daughter.

150

"A bug flew in my mouth, and I accidentally swallowed it. Wouldn't you barf? Go to sleep."

Lucas and I woke at daybreak like usual.

"How's your head?" I asked him.

"Terrible," he told me, holding it like it would break off at any second. "You look like crap."

I scowled at his lack of tact and refused to admit I felt worse than I looked.

Our discussion over our breakfast options was interrupted by a knock at the door. I dropped to the floor and froze while Lucas lunged for his pistol.

A few minutes later, a pair of cops escorted him away.

"Do you have a communicable disease?" I pestered, trailing in their wake. "Is that why you're getting an armed escort to a medical facility?"

"I wish," Lucas snapped, pulling me forward. "Stay with me. I don't want you out of my sight."

At the clinic, they loaded a sample of his blood into a bioscanner, and then he was ushered into a room with chairs so old and cracked I wondered if they predated the Clan Wars. In fact, compared to the lab, this place was dirty and the staff's techniques were criminally sloppy.

I tried not to touch anything or do anything that would result in them touching me.

Lucas directed his furious gaze at everyone within range as he was forced to recline so they could tie a length of stained tubing above his elbow.

"You're donating blood?" I asked.

"Donating? I'm being harvested," he said viciously. "I'm AB negative. Someone must've told them where to find me."

He meant Mauss.

"Same old story," Lucas snarled at the technician. "You have a shortage. Well, guess what? Every town has a shortage. You'd bleed me dry if you could, wouldn't you?"

Shocked, I said, "What if you refuse?"

"I can't. It's a vital clan resource, and they can tap my arteries in jail just as easily. Don't you remember your Corinthians? We don't own our bodies. Texas takes that one to heart."

The policeman wrote in his palmer. "You're also being fined for not having a PIT implanted, which you must know is required for people of your blood type."

"A what?" I asked.

"Personal Information Transmitter." Lucas mouthed the words, obviously realizing the unexpected gap in my education.

The Hernandez had used them, too, but called them Personal Data Transmitters. I knew why we didn't have them. The lab administration wouldn't have risked communicating its position by adhering to the government mandate to implant PITs.

"What's your blood type?" the other cop asked me with sudden interest.

"Not AB negative," I retorted.

They had the Big Blue scan my ID and check a drop of my blood anyway. The bioscanner made a rude noise.

"I told you I wasn't AB neg," I said, using an antiseptic wipe from my bag to clean the skin where they'd touched me no matter how much it might offend them.

The tech shook his head at the cops. "She's blacklisted."

"I'm what?" I asked.

"You've got a medical condition that makes you unsuitable for donation."

Insulted, I demanded, "What medical condition?"

152

He shrugged. "Ask your doctor."

Damn Isidro. He'd no doubt made my file read I had the plague to prevent anyone from touching me. The man did like to protect me like he owned me. I was about to proclaim my fluids were as good any anybody's, probably better, but a look at the grungy chairs made me change my mind about donating.

"Don't they have synthetic blood?" I asked Lucas.

"If you've got the money, yeah. My blood is free." He examined the needle hole critically. "I'm going to bruise. Thanks, dickhead."

State-sanctioned blood theft. It shouldn't have shocked me, but it did. I understood the lack of resources, but I thought technology made up the difference. Instead, laws were rewritten to expand the legality of robbing people of anything and everything for the greater good.

I wanted to be fair. How I would feel if my child would die without a forced donation? Would I still be so morally offended by it?

But I didn't have a child, and what they did to Lucas pissed me off.

"Be happy for the blacklisting," he told me. "It also means they can't run a test to see if your eggs are any good."

"Eggs?" Ice flooded my veins. "They would steal my children?"

"Have you seen the miscarriages rates? The black market for quality eggs is so strong the government can't resist getting involved. They can't legally compel you to donate yet, but they can add you to a database of potential donors for when they get that law passed."

My hands covered my abdomen protectively.

"Theoretically, they'll pay you for what they take," he added with a sneer. "So that makes it okay."

"I'm not a commodity."

"You're not," he agreed. "That would be slavery. But they won't hesitate to slice off a piece of you after you go to the trouble of growing it for them. Cheaper than using the tech to grow it themselves."

My jaw clenched so tightly, my cheek spasmed, and I turned away.

I wanted to leave after the blood harvest, but they tapped a saline and dextrose IV bag for him. When it had finished draining into him, they released him with a six-pack of strawberry-flavored recovery drink as well as some pills. He was supposed to do nothing more than lie in bed for at least a week, with restricted activity for two months. He declined the option of having an excuse from duty written into his medical file for his employer.

"They used to just give you a cookie and orange juice," I commented, holding his goodie bag for him. "Even a sticker for your shirt."

"When they only took half a liter from people like me?" he said grimly, moving cautiously as he shifted his weight off the chaise. "Must've been nice."

My breath caught as I realized how weak he was.

"Don't panic," he told me, reading my face. "I'm calling Domino for immediate retrieval. I can't work like this. And don't worry. I'm not going to tell him this is your fault."

"It's not my fault."

"If we'd been on the road like we were supposed to be, Miss Teenage Hormones, we would've been out of their jurisdiction."

I gave him a helpless look.

Domino was meeting us in front of the police station down the street, but first we had to empty our hotel room of Lucas's weapons if nothing else.

Mauss had left a homemade Get Well Soon card taped to our door, and Lucas tried to snatch it down. He missed and collapsed against the door, his breathing shaky.

"Save it," I said, fumbling with the lock while I struggled to hold him upright.

"You save it," Lucas mumbled. "Check it for hidden messages."

"I know."

"Don't," Lucas said fuzzily, laying his icy hand on mine before I opened the door. "Let me—"

His words ended as the door opened from the inside. As we fell into the room, Lucas's weight drove me to the ground.

Mauss laughed.

"Run," Lucas gasped, his eyelids fluttering as he rolled off me. "Little One, run."

Mauss seized my hair and lifted me upright before spinning me into the wall.

I clutched the chair, dazed, as he dragged Lucas into the room and shut the door. Mauss took Lucas's rifle in hand and slammed the butt down once, twice.

Lucas stopped moving, his blood stark against the pale skin of his temple.

"It's God's will you remain alive," Mauss told me as he stepped over Lucas. "But He didn't tell me I couldn't give you a reminder I won't tolerate your crap."

Before I could ask why Mauss hated me so much, his slap snapped my head to the left. Before I could recover, his backhand blow sent my head snapping to the right.

Left and right my head snapped. I lost count of the blows, but when he stopped, my head spun so much I vomited.

I saw a flicker of surprise on his face, and he pulled me to my feet to stare me down.

My arm shook of its own volition, thumping errati-cally against my side. He wrapped his hand around it and felt the misfires as random muscles contracted.

He let go, and I fell in a heap. My head hadn't stopped spinning, and when I looked at him, my eyeballs skittered from side to side. I vomited again, and my hand slipped in the filth when I tried to steady myself.

"Give me my wedding ring," I said. The words were slurred, unintelligible even to my own ears.

"Not so healed after all," he murmured. "Not so whole. Well, that throws a wrench in the plan. Hey, don't pass out on me. Since you're not coming with me yet, we've got time for some fun before Domino realizes there's a problem."

I tried to crawl away.

He cut off my clothes and pinned me face down on the bed.

The blackness was a dark, cold, crouching monster filling my mind, and my desperate struggle to keep it at bay was failing. Mauss moved over me. His voice came as if from a great distance, but I'd lost the ability to under-stand him.

Pain exploded in my skull until everything shorted out and I became nothing.

CHAPTER 20

THE GOOD DOCTOR

I woke up strapped belly-down on a special table with a cutout for my face. It was the setup the lab used after taking the direct route to either my spinal column through my back or my hindbrain through my neck. The grogginess was wearing off in a familiar way, too. Most of all, that clench in my belly, that ever-present fear warned I was back in the lab.

The hum of the bioscanner nearby eliminated the need for me to announce my growing alertness. Sure enough, footsteps grew louder. The door opened, and a male voice said, "Right on schedule. You're quite the accommodating patient."

"That's not what Isidro tells me," I murmured, wishing I could rub my eyes. They felt gritty, like I'd been out for a while.

"Isidro has difficulty remembering the mind and the body are part of the same organism," the man replied. He lifted the lowermost bandage off my back to check an incision site. "I'm Dr. Finley Goddard, by the way. I've been requesting to be added to your surgical team ever since I heard it was a doctor short. I'm glad they finally made it happen. Your body is responding beautifully to my treatment."

I refrained from mentioning my body responded beautifully to everyone's brand of medicine down here. "I'll give you my name once I'm clear-headed enough to remember which one to go by. I don't mean to be a bother, but could you possibly scratch my right shoulder blade?"

It wasn't much of a scratch through his latex gloves, but it was enough to take the edge off.

"Feel free to use your real name. I would love to call you Miranda with reckless abandon. You can call me Finley, if you want."

"Is Lucas all right?"

"Lucas?"

"The man with me was hit in the head. I want to know if he's dead, fine, or somewhere in between."

He hesitated. "All I can do is tell them you would like to know."

Which of course meant I'd never be told.

"When will I be healed enough to return topside?"

"For what?" he asked.

"For tracking down Mauss. Do you know what he did down here?"

"Yes, but there are no plans to send you back up there. If anything, his ease in getting close to you made it plain you weren't safe. You're too important to risk again."

"Even to catch a killer?"

"To bait a killer, you mean?" he said, an edge to his voice.

I didn't like the way he reframed the situation. I didn't like him either, even if he had gentle hands.

Hopefully he was wrong when he said I wasn't returning to the surface. I had to get strong, the sooner the better. I inhaled deeply and slowly, willing my body to let go of the fear and be calm. Starting with my pinky toe on my left foot, I checked the status of every part of my body where I could register sensation so I could prioritize and visualize the repairs.

A week later I was allowed upright, and sitting up, I got my first look at Finley Goddard. He was younger than I'd expected, perhaps in his late twenties. Thinning black hair neatly trimmed. Thin lips, straight and sharp nose. Perhaps his most remarkable attribute was the quiet arrogance of a man who was used to taking on God and winning. How many lives did a doctor save in his career? I almost asked if he kept count.

He looked like he was about to speak, but a barely perceptible glance at the surveillance camera stopped him. His mouth tightened, and he stepped around me.

"You don't belong down here anymore than I do," I said in wonder, using the reflection in the nearby metal cabinet to watch him examine my back.

"Here in limbo? No, of course not," he responded, frowning over a slight swelling at the base of my neck.

"Limbo?"

He tabbed the comlink and spoke into it.

Isidro arrived with a scowl. "What is it now?"

Finley said, "I want to go in again. How soon can I get a few hours in surgery room four?"

Isidro's fingertips went over the area in question, bringing me to the point of pain. He backed up his tactile scan with a glance at Big Blue's display. "Even with the swelling, Blue says her functions are already within range."

"How soon?"

"I said no. The human body is a unique and complex system of organic mechanisms. You're never going to make anyone perfect. She's already in better condition than we ever thought possible."

"I can correct this," Finley said. "After everything she's gone through, we owe her the attempt to address her lingering neural degradation. She lives with discomfort and agony every single day."

"She's no different than anyone else here. Little One—"

"She has a name."

Isidro's heels drove angrily against the floor as he crossed the room. "I'm taking you off the team. You're showing the exact immaturity that prevented us from including you in the first place. This is medicine, not magic. We put in a reasonable effort, and we correct ninety percent of the damage we come across. The last ten percent always costs more than the other ninety in terms of money, labor, and frustration."

"I need a type nineteen surgical kit, a standard anesthetic kit, and one nurse. In fact, I don't even need the nurse, just a sterile room to work in."

"It's over, Finley. We've got other projects for you to work on."

"None this important."

"We warned you about showing her preferential treatment," Isidro gritted out. "Your having history with her doesn't mean—"

"What a clannish way to look at it. Not everyone thinks that being born in the same city is enough of a tie to make them favor each other over all others. I see a woman who needs medical treatment I am particularly well-suited to provide. Why can't we make this about medicine?"

160

The tense silence ended when I asked Isidro, "Is Lucas okay?"

"The medical status of another individual is none of your business," he snapped. "The only thing you need to concern yourself with is reporting where and when you're told to."

Anger tightened my mouth, and my cheeks heated. Even when Lucas and I bickered, he didn't use that kind of tone, so I'd almost forgotten what it felt like to be treated with such disrespect.

After Isidro left, a light hand on my shoulder made me jump.

"Don't worry," the new doctor told me. "I have some compelling arguments up my sleeve. You'll get the repairs you need, I promise you."

"Are we really from the same city?"

"Sorry to get your hopes up. I just meant to express my irritation at the assumption that one commonality in our files makes them think I can't be impartial. If you'll excuse me, I need to get to the administration before he does."

As soon as I was alone, Lucas sneaked into my room. "Hey, how're you feeling?"

"Thank God you're all right," I said, brightening. "I thought he'd killed you."

"Domino got me topped off with a bunch of the synthetic blood and paid my PIT fine. Even got them to clean this up so I won't have a scar," he said with a gesture at the skin Mauss had split with the rifle butt. The bruising was spectacular. "Why didn't you tell me you were so critical?"

"I was scared for your daughter and wanted to keep going, same as you."

"I never should've told you about her. But thanks," he said. He glanced to the corridor and ducked out of sight as Isidro passed by. Crouching down next to me, he said, "Before you ask, yes, Mauss was gone by the time Domino got to us. No photo this time, but he did leave that book on folk heroes. He didn't leave any notes or pictures in it, though."

I swallowed hard, but my voice still came out strangled. "He took my clothes off."

Realizing what I was waltzing around, he said, "No sign of rape. He wrote on you. Said you should be left to die."

I made a face. Why did Mauss pass on every opportunity to kill me? Was I supposed to just get more and more afraid? Hell, Isidro scared me a lot more than Mauss did. Isidro didn't hesitate to use his knife.

"Mauss put another chastity belt on you," Lucas said, half-amused and half-dismayed. "They had to saw it off."

"I hate this man so much."

He smothered his laugh in his elbow. "I'm just glad I didn't have to be the one to get it off you this time."

"They told me I'm off the case," I said. "Are you?"

He wouldn't reply. I liked that about him. He didn't lie to me, change the subject, challenge my right to ask, or pretend I didn't ask. He just looked me in the eye and refused to provide an answer.

"I want to nail this guy," I told him. "If you come across anything weird, you let me know. I'll take a stab at figuring it out."

At the sound of familiar, booted footsteps, he got to his feet. Domino's wide shoulders blocked the doorway as he told Lucas his call had come through. Lucas gave me a smile goodbye, though his smile tactfully disappeared as his gaze flicked to Domino's pumpkin-colored hair. The dye-job made the gold Aldebaran speck in Domino's eye appear to shine with an unprecedented brilliance, but that was the only advantage of his current color choice.

162

Domino's impenetrable gaze gave me no idea of his reaction to the contraband in my topside belongings. Had he expected it? At least the bag lacked weapons or signs I was working with someone on the outside. Granted, the unauthorized items indicated I meant to run, but I hadn't. He must've known I'd had countless opportunities to. Lucas said Domino understood extenuating circumstances, so this might fall under that category.

"Mauss said he wasn't done with me."

His brows knitted. "Lucas didn't mention that."

"Because he'd already taken a rifle butt to the head by then. Mauss said I wasn't functional like he thought, so he was going to come back for me."

"He told you this when you were dizzy and blacking out?"

"Don't make it sound like I'm an untrustworthy witness."

"I think you hear what you want to and ignore the rest, so yeah, your testimony doesn't mean much."

"Screw you. Why would I want to hear I'm still a target? Because I feel like I don't get enough attention?"

"There's no way for him to come through that door unless we open it and welcome him back in. I've made changes he can't get around. Or did you think we were so dumb we wouldn't change the locks?"

"No."

"Don't initiate contact with Lucas," Domino said. "I know you didn't this time, so I'll be reminding him about it, too. You know by now who they'll let you talk to down here."

"Seriously? We spent all that time together, but now we're supposed to ignore each other?"

"Do I sound like I'm joking? Your involvement in the Mauss case is done."

"Is there a problem?" Finley Goddard asked from behind Domino.

"I was reminding her she's not topside anymore," Domino said, pinning me with a hard look before leaving.

They were fools to think I would let the Mauss issue go just because I was down here. This was where it had started. This was likely where it was going to end.

At least I had a new lead doctor for a while. This Finley guy seemed interested in my quality of life, so maybe I could get more gym time to get stronger. I might even be permitted a dessert every once in a while. With Isidro, if I even looked at a brownie that bastard waved a feeding tube at me.

Wait a minute.

That second photo from Mauss. The timing was all wrong. He'd said I should've learned to stay away from cookies after Isidro had forced a feeding tube on me, but that happened days *after* Mauss had left the lab. How could he have known that?

I felt the tension tighten my neck around the surgical site.

Mauss either had a way in the lab Domino didn't know about or he had an accomplice. It didn't matter which. Locked in the lab, I was still prevented from getting out of the killing field. No access to allies. I contemplated sharing my revelation with Domino, but he considered me an unreliable witness. What were the chances he'd believe me?

How much worse was this going to get?

CHAPTER 21

WIDE VIEW

As soon as I was ambulatory a week later, I petitioned my counselor for an audience with the Director of Operations, and to my surprise, it was granted the next day.

Tuncay met me in the same conference room where my previous meetings had been held, robbing me of the hope they were going to let my world expand beyond the few corridors and offices I knew.

As I sat in the plastic chair opposite him, I said, "May I speak freely?"

"You can be free with your opinions but not free with certain subjects."

How did anything get said in a place with so much surveillance? "I'm aware I didn't capture Mauss, but I don't remember our agreement being contingent on that."

"It wasn't. He did initiate contact. Several times. It's not your fault your health failed and you needed to return when you did."

"May I be permitted to see for myself your end of our deal has been fulfilled?"

"You don't trust me?" he said, his eyes narrowing.

"Since I've lost almost everyone I ever cared about, I've got some irrational fears about losing the rest of them. I'm simply making an effort to meet my fears head on to take the force out of them. This is no different from my fear of drowning prompting me to ask for more pool time until I got over it."

"I'm very busy," he said testily. "I can't serve as your tour guide every time you get afraid of something."

"Understood. Thank you for your time."

Yet two days later, he did take me down into the basement again. We went directly to the icer with my name plate on it, and he showed me it was indeed empty. The cobwebs indicated it had been vacated months ago if not longer.

Too bad it wasn't in the correct place in the catacombs, and too bad the person who had swapped out the nameplates had slipped with the screwdriver, scratching the metal.

"Satisfied?" Tuncay asked.

I gave him a bright smile. "Absolutely."

As we walked back to the elevator, I asked, "Did Jason leave me a message?"

"He wasn't told you were involved at all. We told him he was deteriorating too fast. Like we talked about, not everyone is a good candidate for cryo. We kept him for a few days to make sure he was stable, and then he was released topside."

"To a jail cell?"

"I don't know. That's for the lawyers to figure out."

"Well, did he at least thank you for either accommodating his request to be here or for releasing him at the first sign his health was failing?"

His mouth pressed into a thin line, warning me his patience was at an end. "Yes, he did."

It was possible he didn't show me Jason's icer for a legitimate reason. It might be a smoking shell due to some accident during the thawing. That definitely would've pushed me into a big emotional response. But all his response did was prove he lied. Jason wouldn't have said thank you. Instead, he would've given some snarky comment about the quality of service or demanded to know who had butchered the dry cleaning of his suit.

"Anything else?" Tuncay asked.

I shook my head. "I won't ask about him again."

On the way back to my room, I realized I was biting my lip and made myself stop. It didn't matter how many reasons I had why it didn't make sense Jason would be here. Worst case scenario, he was here anyway, still having nightmares, still deteriorating one cell at a time, and for now I could do nothing but work on the Mauss issue to develop a bargaining chip.

Topside, I'd tried to predict Mauss's movements, but I should've been focused on his motivation. The man had a vision for me. I just had to figure out what it was.

To tie up any loose ends from the surface expedition, I went to retrieve the book about folk heroes to check it for anything Domino might've missed. When I saw the padre alone, I delayed that task and approached him.

"Father Brannigan, did Mauss have a Bible passage he particularly liked?"

His eyes widened and then narrowed. He'd measured then, learned I'd expanded my library centimeters at a time until I'd well and truly encroached on his side.

I prompted, "He repeatedly pushed a Bible at me like I was supposed to learn a specific lesson."

"There are a lot of lessons to be learned from the Bible."

Unsurprised by the lack of help, I turned to leave, but he stopped me, looking like he was at war with himself. He motioned for me to sit in the nearest pew. I wanted him to be permeated with the scent of incense and myrrh, but he smelled like cheap soap.

He leaned with his elbows on his knobby knees. "With Mauss, it wasn't a lesson to be learned so much as an explanation to you for what he believes."

"Why would I care what one man believes?" I asked, softening my tone so it didn't sound sarcastic or dismissive.

"Believe it or not, he does have some sympathy for what you've been through, but that sympathy conflicts with his beliefs, beliefs a great many share. Knowing those verses might help you understand and forgive people of a certain mindset." He went to the far side of the chapel and took a fresh black-faced Bible from a box and a sheaf of paper off a nearby stack. "When you're ready to go over these verses, please let me know. I would like to help you through this, Miranda. Of everyone in the lab, your burden may be the most difficult to bear."

He looked so unhappy for me that tears stung my eyes. "I don't understand."

"I know," he said. "But someday you will." He got to his feet and, with shaking hands, presented me the Bible and flyer. "If you don't mind my asking, do you pray?"

I frowned. "I do pray for the people I killed at Greyson, Padre. I haven't forgotten about them."

"I meant for yourself."

"I only pray for dead people. Everyone else can still choose to improve the condition of their soul."

He was about to comment, but he seemed to sense I'd about run out of patience, so he simply reminded me he was there for me if I needed him. Then he left the room to give me some privacy.

Seated in the pew, I looked up the ten verses on the list. They all related to God creating life and giving out souls.

Was Mauss pissed they kept bringing me back from the dead? But wasn't letting me die when they could do something about it sort of like murder? And if I gave up and died on my own, wasn't that like suicide? No, plenty of people were resuscitated and the masses didn't think twice about it. The padre said the verses justified a position.

Was it the cryopreservation? That definitely made me different, but again, it wasn't all that different from being in a coma. I hadn't ripped a hole in the universe through time travel or something.

I read the specific verses from Genesis, Psalms, Deuteronomy, and John again.

Wombs and children showed up a few times. I sat back, a sick feeling in my belly. Was finding out I was pregnant after my husband's death the thing I couldn't remember from those last weeks before I was shot and kidnapped? Had I gone into cryo pregnant and lost the baby? If Mauss thought I'd volunteered for a dangerous experiment while pregnant, he might've considered it something beyond endangerment. Was this about abortion? He certainly wielded the chastity belts with eagerness.

I asked the one person I thought would reply, the devil himself.

It wasn't often I startled Isidro with one of my questions. "No, you've never been pregnant, and yes, I'm sure. Why?" His voice sharpened. "Who said what to you that made you think otherwise?"

When I told him, he snorted, calming down. "The Bible thing again. Have you noticed how selective people are about believing what's in there? I mean, isn't there some kind of covenant about not killing people? Where was Mauss's faith then?"

I left his office, even more puzzled. The Bible thing *again*? What did Isidro mean? And why did the padre give me a pre-printed list taken from a short stack, like it was a matter he was used to counseling people on? Given the close quarters of the lab, I would've thought he'd be pushing verses about the power of getting along and people getting a grip on their tempers.

Ten verses about God creating man and giving them souls. Why did those words have people forming up on either side of some line? It couldn't be the creationist versus evolutionist show down. That had been going on for hundreds of years. And even if it was about that, why would Mauss put me in the center of it? As long as their beliefs weren't shoved in my face, I didn't care what people believed. As for my own views on the subject, I couldn't remember it ever coming up.

And why was the padre so grief-stricken about it?

"Miranda? Are you all right?"

I jumped at the sound of Finley's voice, hoping Isidro didn't think I was lurking outside his office. When Isidro was done with me, he expected me to immediately leave the medical suites.

Knot in my throat, I hurried away.

Finley clung to my side. In a low voice, he said, "I saw you by the elevators earlier. Did Tuncay take you downstairs? Why?"

I shook my head, my silence now a choice, too.

He put his arms around me like he was afraid my knees were about to buckle.

He murmured, "Don't be afraid. God's watching out for you." I snorted and pulled back, but his grip tightened. "Stick to the routine they want for you. Don't deviate again."

He released me and continued down the hallway. I returned to my room, bemused by the exchange. I'd been told on multiple occasions to settle down and play by the rules, but this was the first time someone made it sound like it would be part of a conspiracy to do so.

My heart fluttered in my chest. Someone had helped Puck escape the lab, and I would bet anything Finley was a part of that. But did I want to escape? They'd hunt me. They'd captured and killed Puck in another clan, so it wasn't like a border on a map would stop them. And what about Jason? What if the only way to get away was to leave him behind?

I paced the length of my cell, my circuit eventually slowing to match the rhythm of the cresting waves of the wall environmentals. Nothing had to be decided today. Perhaps I'd completely misread what Finley meant and—

No, something was going on there. I definitely needed to get to know this man better.

CHAPTER 22

FLOWERS AND SCALPELS

Conveniently, Finley still had the last ten percent of my recovery to work on, so we saw each other daily. However, he was maddeningly coy about elaborating on his hint something more could happen if I only fell off the radar by strictly doing what I was told to do. Despite the surveillance, he'd apparently managed to coordinate with Puck and smuggle him out, so why wouldn't Finley talk to me? The warm greetings and seemingly sincere interest in what I thought and felt were signs he liked me, but was he still deciding how far he could trust me?

Hell, vice versa. Every once in a while, he felt oddly familiar to me. One time, his voice held an odd echo of an accent I hadn't heard in more than a century. It brought to mind watching a professional baseball game with the taste of hot dog in my mouth, sweaty hair stuck to the back of my neck on a humid day, and the smell of Lake Michigan in my nostrils. But I'd heard him talk like he was from Chicago just that once.

Another time, he'd burst out laughing at something I also found unexpectedly funny, but everyone else looked at us like we were crazy. Was it an unintentional reference to an old movie? I thought so but couldn't place it. I still had plenty of holes in my memories of the late twentieth and early twenty-first century.

When I woke with flowers in my hair six months after my return to the lab, my first thought was that I was going to reevaluate my opinion of him. He'd never come into my room, saying everyone should have a private place, but if this creepy intrusion was supposed to be a sign of romantic intention, he was about to catch an earful.

The two sprigs of flowers were crushed from being slept on. One was from a mock orange, the white flowers releasing the familiar intoxicating scent, but it wasn't the correct shape for it to be from the shrub in the atrium. The other bloom was less familiar: unscented, pink, with five delicate petals cupped around ten stamens. An azalea? The atrium planters didn't contain those either.

I wrapped the flowers in a shirt and went to the security station. Domino looked up in surprise when I spilled the flowers on his desk and told him what had happened.

"Why are you telling me?" he asked.

"I want to know who broke into my room."

"People enter your room all the time, all of them with legitimate reasons. Someone was nice to you and you're going to freak out about it?"

"The only people in this lab who like me enough to do something like this are Finley and Lucas. Finley was my first thought because he usually acts like a gentleman who might bring a lady flowers, but he says people should honor my boundaries by knocking and waiting for my permission to enter my room. Lucas, who thinks of me as too young for a grown man to consider, would've left me books in the library, not flowers in my room. Do you know where these came from? The plants themselves, I mean."

He pointed at the white one. "Atrium."

"It's ruffled, not plain, and the atrium one isn't blooming. If these didn't come from the lab, I need you to get on the internet and find out exactly what these flowers are and what they mean in the Victorian language of flowers."

"The what? No, forget it. Even if I worked for you, you know we don't get internet here."

I was about to blast Domino when I saw him brush his finger against his lips, hesitating for a moment in the universal signal for silence. He swept the flora into the trashcan and covered it with the shirt. No, not covered it. Hid it.

"Little One?" Tuncay said, stepping around the corner. "What are you doing here?"

"I want to file a report. One of my books is missing," I said without missing a beat.

He gave me an odd look. "Your books? That's not your personal library, and no one needs your permission to take one. I don't want to hear you're pestering the security personnel again."

Jaw clenched, I walked away.

Two days later, Domino appeared in the doorway to my room. I was ten minutes late for my counseling appointment.

"Are you kidding me?" I said. "If you put an anklet on me, prepare to be punched right in your man parts. My button fell off, and I'm looking for something to hold my pants up."

Giving me a look like I was insane, he reached past me and tossed onto my bed the shirt I'd wrapped the flowers in. It had been cleaned and folded.

"Sorry," I said grudgingly.

He snorted and went on his way.

Putting away the shirt, I felt a small slip of paper in the fold. I palmed it and put it in my pocket to read as soon as I thought I could get away with it.

Domino had written the security feed to my room for that time period was unrevealing, but he didn't tell me whether it had gone to static or the person had been masked or whatever. He got a partial fingerprint off one of the stems, but it came back as mine. Both flower sprigs were externally sourced, but a location couldn't be narrowed down. He was alarmed by the freshness of the stems, seeing as no one had arrived at the lab in months and no one had arrived with any botanical matter for at least ten years. Not through what was supposed to be the only door, anyway.

The pink flower was a rhododendron, representing caution or danger. I was correct about the mock orange identification but startled to learn the sweetly scented flower represented deceit. At the end of the note, he had written he wanted me to let him know when I got an idea who the warning was from or who the warning was about.

The very last line told me the note was non-toxic.

Non-toxic? What was that supposed to mean?

It didn't matter. He'd answered my questions, and I had to get rid of that note before anyone found it and realized he'd helped me. But what was I supposed to do, tear it up and flush it? What if they retrieved the bits of it at the waste management end and were able to piece it together? It wasn't like I had a lighter, not that alarms wouldn't go off at the first sign of smoke.

Why did he give me a damn note anyway? He could've pulled me into a dark corner for ten seconds to tell me. I needed to give it back to Domino. He had to be able to get rid of it even if I had to shove his non-toxic note down his—

Oh. Non-toxic. Wonderful. I tore off a corner of the note and hid it in my hand. I surreptitiously sniffed it, but it didn't reek of chemically treated paper or have that sharp scent of ink. I poked the piece into my mouth. It didn't taste like anything. I swallowed it. Only about a hundred more tiny pieces to go. I went to the cafeteria to have some lunch to masticate with the rest of that note.

Caution. Danger. Deceit. Was it too much to ask for some specifics? Not that I could do a lot when confronted with a threat. My only defense down here was hiding until the shooting stopped.

The frustration from the warning faded, but the unease rooted in Domino's note didn't. It was bad enough I thought Mauss had a partner down here, but now we'd learned about another way into the lab and around the security cameras. This time I had awakened with flowers touching my temple, but next time it could be a gun barrel.

A year after my return to the lab, I was about to abandon the whole plan concerning Finley Goddard when I walked into the cafeteria one day and saw him sitting with Sam, my counselor. They were deep in serious discussion, almost painful from the look on Finley's face, so I didn't sit with them. At one point they both fell silent, and as if feeling my gaze, Finley looked around and gave me a shy smile. Sam said something, and the doctor blushed, forcing his attention from me.

I gave my counselor a sardonic look that made him grin before I took my apple and retreated to the atrium. I sat on the bench facing the nocturnal tank. Because the atrium was the central hub of the lab, the remains of the anesthesiologist who'd been murdered there were among the first to be policed, but I couldn't pass by the spot without remembering the carnage.

Had they ever caught Mauss? No one mentioned him. As soon as someone died or disappeared, it was like they never existed to the people who remained. No wakes or funerals, no moments of silence. Just silence.

I worked in silence, too, watching the people interact around me as I sifted through endless connections and observations. I had reached one dead end after another as I unearthed clandestine affairs or discreet morphine addictions. Whomever Mauss had been working with was still unknown to me. For now.

Sam joined me as I nibbled on the apple core and debated whether or not to bury it in the nearest planter.

I asked, "He's like me, isn't he? An American, so a victim of the cryo experiment. Was telling me I was the sole survivor supposed to keep me from searching out any others?"

"Finley's entitled to his privacy," he reminded me, accepting my invitation to sit.

"I think he was in cryo for a long time. Before America fell. There's a familiarity about him I can't explain any other way. There's a sadness, too."

Sam nodded as if deciding some of Finley's secrets were mine, too. "It's no wonder you two found each other. To be honest, we've been expecting as much for a while."

"He has skill, doesn't he? You guys didn't want him practicing old-style medicine on people, but he's picked up all sorts of cutting-edge techniques down here. He's probably better than a lot of modern surgeons."

Sam nodded again. "He's got a real gift. I hate to say this given the ugliness of what happened to you, but the man who selected the first generation of test subjects knew quality when he saw it. Artists, doctors, mechanics, physicists, computer and math wizards, you name it."

"I was still in engineering school, not a full-fledged contributor to society."

"You weren't a mistake, if that's what you're wondering about. It wasn't the engineering specifically that captured his attention. Something in the way you process information made you stick out to him. I believe he chose you because you had the potential to learn anything that needed to be learned to fill in any unexpected gap in the collective."

"Collective?" I said, eyes widening.

He waved his hand, looking embarrassed. "Pet theory. Anyway, you found you had an instinctive gift for flying, didn't you?"

"I had good instructors," I said, uncomfortable with the reminder of Jason. Unless I figured out something new to bargain with or I was free and could go to his family, he was stuck in the icer like he requested. But the next time I bartered for his freedom, I would personally see he was safe before I did anything for them.

"Can you tell me about the Asian boy who was killed a few years ago?" I asked Sam. "I mean, you're telling me the ice cubes were a wonderful lot, but he was terminated. Does the icer drive some of us nuts? Is there something wrong with Finley?"

"Let's go down to my office. I can help you sort through some of these feelings without the risk of anyone overhearing something they shouldn't."

I buried my annoyance about people guarding Finley's privacy despite hearing the same people bandy my personal information about like I was a celebrity.

Motioning for him to retake his seat, I said, "I just brought up that Asian kid because I don't want to get mixed up with a crazy man. I suppose in my meandering way I was looking for your opinion on Finley."

Sam's voice was reassuring. "He's a good man."

Isidro and Finley didn't see eye to eye, but the older surgeon did relinquish some of my care to Finley. Sam just confirmed what I'd noticed about the way other people regarded the younger man. Finley was well-liked, even trusted. But why not? He knew to give them all of his best and none of his worst.

"Am I allowed to discuss the past with him?"

"Your American past? Yes, but don't get your hopes up. He's far more interested in the present world, like you should be. He hasn't been topside since he was awakened, so he has a lot of questions."

"I can answer them?"

He nodded. "I'm sure he would love that, especially since you've lived topside in three clans now, even if only for short periods."

I hesitated. "Are you sure? Will you run it by the administration? Because it's been a while since I got into trouble, and I don't want to break my streak."

Before long it became clear that like Polaris, Dr. Finley Goddard was a fixed point upon which everything in my world revolved. My library was forgotten under layers of dust, and dramas developed and blew over beyond my notice. He was easily the smartest, cleverest, and most sensitive person I'd ever met, and it took everything I had to get closer to him. One carelessly expressed opinion or overly pessimistic view of the future, and I was shut out for months. I'd seen glimpses beneath his surface, though, found the connections between a few discrete facts. This man was definitely at the center of everything.

When I finally had the distinction of a bioscan so perfect Big Blue requested it be serviced because it couldn't find anything wrong with me, I showed Finley the full force of my gratitude. Like Isidro had said, the last part of my recovery had not been the least bit easy for the medical staff to accomplish, and I'd heard more than one of them ask if it was even possible.

179

Finley's incandescence was even greater than mine. With a teary-eyed, profound kind of pleasure, he watched me twirl in the medical suite.

"Are you going to get bored with me now?" I teased.

"Never," he promised me. "You always exceed my expectations."

"Will you have dinner with me? I'd love to celebrate."

"I'm sorry, but I still have a lot of work I need to catch up on." He shot me an embarrassed grimace. "I've been neglecting my other duties to work on you."

My cheeks grew hot at the reminder I was special to him. "Well, let me know when you're available. I can wait."

"Don't delay your celebration, please. You've earned it."

After I left him, I sought out Maria, the replacement anesthesiologist and most quintessential female in the lab.

"Little One," she said, her immaculately kohl-lined eyes widening. "What can I do for you?"

"I want to smell like flowers instead of antiseptic, and I want to learn how to play up my eyes with cosmetics. Will you help me?"

She grinned. "You already got his attention."

"It's not for any man. It's a special occasion for me, and I want to pamper myself."

Two hours later, I fought and screamed in fury while the medtechs struggled to get the restraints in place. They scrubbed off the scented lotion while I thrashed. Isidro surveyed it all from a safe distance, snapping a reminder to me: I was to stick to the skin products issued to me because some chemicals pass through the skin barrier.

"You just earned yourself two months of supervised showers," he told me.

"Bring it on, motherfucker."

Isidro's smile for my defiance was strange, brittle. "I think I saw her left eye twitch. There must be some degradation. Cut out her left eye, visually inspect the nerve, and then reinsert it." He leaned over me. "Comment?"

My eye. Christ.

"My apologies," I said hoarsely. "It won't happen again."

"What do I have to do to make you understand I won't tolerate you being cavalier with this body? I'll take whatever steps are necessary to protect it."

"I understand. I'm sorry."

He regarded the trio of scratches and the swelling on his tech's face. "Dislocate three knuckles on her right hand. Your choice which ones."

I was breathing too hard, but I couldn't control that.

After Isidro left, the pair of techs looked down on me in shock and dismay.

One of them asked me, "Why?"

I laughed.

Chapter 23

Splitting Hairs

I didn't see Finley for days, and I felt guilty he had so much work to catch up on. I hadn't asked him to make me his only patient, but since I wanted to be healthy and whole, I hadn't refused the attention either. Had he learned what Isidro had done to my eye? I hoped not. Unsurprisingly, I was healing well, so his worry would've been wasted.

I was prepping my lunch tray with an Isidro-approved meal when I overheard some people saying the administration was going to throw a party for the lab to celebrate their victory in getting me to a hundred percent. I doubted I would be invited unless they could muzzle me so I wouldn't ruin the atmosphere by demanding my rights be reinstated. Would they drug me, lay me out on a slab, and put trays of appetizers and drinks around me like I was a centerpiece?

Domino strode into the cafeteria, saw me loading my plate, and came straight at me.

He shoved the tray out of my hands, and it clattered against the metal rails, sending vegetable soup over the side to splatter on the laminate. He spoke over my rude comment. "Can you eat that?" he said, pointing out a slice of apple pie on the counter.

"No, of course not. It's got sugar and flour in it."

"Good." He forced me to take the small plate to avoid wearing it, and we left the cafeteria, his big hand pressed into my back to force me into a trot.

"What's—"

"Shut your mouth and move your feet," he said.

We went through the double doors I had followed Lucas through a lifetime ago and down several more hallways until he stopped short at a white door with a tonal circuitry pattern design.

As soon as he got the door open, he pushed me in. "You don't leave. No one comes in except me. You don't eat anything you normally would. Not even water from the tap. If someone forces their way in, don't be shy about knocking them out with a chair or something. Don't worry about injuring them. Just stop them from getting to you."

"What's going on?" I asked.

He faltered for a minute, searching for words. "Surveillance is down and your biological reserves have been wiped out. All your source material samples have been destroyed, too."

"Except for what's inside me, you mean."

He nodded. "They don't know if it was deliberate or accidental. I'm not taking chances."

"Don't forget about me."

"I won't," he promised.

I sealed myself in. I checked the perimeter of the room to learn its dimensions in case we lost power and searched for anything I could use as a booby trap or early warning system.

The suite was almost double the size of mine, and the occupant had installed a floor-to-ceiling screen to block sight of the bed. The furnishings were sleek and sparse thanks to the inhabitant's modern aesthetic. When I saw the toiletries lined up in the bathroom, I knew I was in Lucas's quarters. One of the reasons we got along was because my compulsion to line items up meshed perfectly with his innate tidiness.

I caught my reflection in the mirror and did a double take at my new curves. I wasn't voluptuous by any stretch of the imagination, but the hormone therapy had finally triggered more pronounced breasts and hips. It was pretty twisted to see how excited Finley and Isidro had been when I'd had my first period. I was sure Lucas was grateful to have missed that milestone.

I lifted the edge of his mattress, but nothing revealed he'd ever hidden a weapon there. The left bedside table was more lucrative, full of snacks and sports drinks. Domino could tell me to eat pie all day long, but he wasn't the one who had to deal with Isidro if I ate wrong. I wouldn't touch the supplies unless I had to.

A notepad was lined up with the edge of the desk, a pencil centered above it. The top page was blank. I skimmed the top page with the side of the pencil lead and was able to make out the impression of the words from the last page to be removed.

Little One: Home. Go Home. Just Go Home. H.O.M.E.?

When Mauss had left us photos, he'd said we should just go home. And that last time when Lucas was already unconscious, Mauss said something to me about home, too. I'd considered Mauss was referring to a particular place and not simply a designation of where we happened to live, and apparently Lucas hadn't missed the emphasis on the word either. An acronym would've been clever but impossible to guess with such common letters.

I did know Mauss was a game-playing sphincter who would've loved to serve us his secrets on a platter but encoded in a way to fit easily into conversation. I suspected hubris brought down a lot of villains.

Little One: flwrs in hair. Fin Godd big pollen allergies, hates plants. gut tells me not him anyway. but who? no one fits. doesn't feel like a threat. find Vict plant meaning bk for her. clever of her.

Domino: topside surv pointed at entrance fully op, show zero activity for 1 mo prior to Little One's flwr timeframe. either flwrs came from dif part of lab not allowed access to or from unk entrance to lab, prob unk entr. clear Javier. this is bad.

Domino: Fin Godd also a target?

I tore off the pencil-skimmed sheet and stuffed it into my pocket. I rubbed the smooth edge of a picture frame over the pad of paper in an effort to fill in any remaining depressions his original pencil pressure had left so no one else could find out what he'd written.

Damn Domino for keeping me from comparing notes with Lucas. It wasn't like this was none of my business. Now maybe Finley's, too, if Lucas was right. Had Finley ever thrown a punch? No, it would've damaged the surgeon's hands. Was the man supposed to defend himself with the parry and thrust of a scalpel?

Finley and I had to get out of the lab and out of this clan.

I knew I should've tried to get some sleep, but the forceful pulsing in my skull and around my healing eye kept me as awake as the whirling, frightening scenarios I envisioned if Finley and I stayed down here too much longer.

Around five in the morning, the door to Lucas's habitat chimed with the security override tone. It slid open, but no one was there. My hands tightened around the lamp I held like a bat.

"Lucas?" I called out.

"Put it down," Domino said and risked peering around the doorway. "It's me."

"Step inside and shut the door."

He did so, switching on the lights but keeping them low. He had lost his sense of urgency, but he remained wary as he sat on the couch watching me replace the lamp on the desk.

I asked, "So we're good?"

He seemed to be deciding how much he was going to tell me. Or perhaps he was deciding whether or not he believed my calmness. After all, I no longer had any back-up tissues. If I sustained injuries, the lab might not have the means to repair me anymore. If I suffered enough critical trauma, I might actually die. Perhaps that was supposed to scare me.

"They didn't just destroy your tissues. A woman was murdered," he said, scrubbing his hand through his dark blue hair. "Stuffed in the incinerator and burned to ash."

I didn't know what to say. Obviously, that was terrible. I glanced at the nearest security camera. "Is surveillance back up?"

"Tech's still working on it."

"Since what happened to my tissues came with a body count, are you thinking it was sabotage?"

He nodded. "You need to trust me to handle it. You have other things to worry about."

"Was Finley's biomatter wiped out, too?"

"What makes you ask that?"

"Well, you know he's like me, don't you?"

He hesitated as if deciding whether I was fishing for forbidden info or if I actually knew the truth of Finley's origins. I wondered if he'd even been shown a roster of the original experiment victims. It always sounded like Domino knew things despite the administration's attempts to control the information flow, not because of it.

"You think this is a hit on the first generation members like you two?" he said.

"Answer my question, and I'll tell you what I think."

"He had no reserves to destroy. I'm guessing his genetic code is too ordinary to bother with."

"Unlike my legendary code?" I said with a grim smile.

"Blame your parents."

"The more I know about this place, the less sense it makes. Finley went through the same hell in those cryo-tubes I did, and he's a talented surgeon. Why isn't he worth saving?"

Domino's gaze was unwavering, but I had the sense the question made him uncomfortable.

"I don't know that I would wish their attention on him," he said. "They're debating whether or not to harvest more source material from you."

"I'm surprised I'm not already being prepped for surgery."

"Well, Dr. Goddard said he fixed everything wrong with you, so they can't justify growing more tissues."

The flicker of hope I might be released dwindled and died. "Since when have they needed a reasonable excuse for anything down here?"

Domino lifted his shoulder in that peculiar one-armed shrug of his, not meeting my eyes. I didn't think he meant to tell me as much as he did. He must've missed having someone to talk to.

He said, "Maybe Isidro was right about Finley's proclamation being premature."

I snorted. "The fresh damage to my eye and my hand, you mean? This was straight-up retribution. Nothing was wrong with those parts of me before I opened my mouth and said something someone didn't like hearing."

"Retribution?" he repeated, shocked.

My eyes widened, and I retreated, jerking my gaze away. Maybe we were both saying things we shouldn't have. Did that make us friends?

"They can't find me in this part of the lab," I told him. "I need to return before the cameras come on."

He followed me out of Lucas's room and sealed it behind him. "Whose retribution?"

We'd reached the cafeteria when the security camera's red light flickered, catching his eye as well as mine. The camera's light became steady, now recording us staring at each other, our faces emotionless masks.

"I don't suppose you know where Finley is," I said, thinking about Lucas's supposition I wasn't the only possible target down here. "I'd like to see for myself he's unharmed."

"He's gone."

I tripped, catching myself with a hand on the wall. My heart beat dully, like the blood moving through it was already half-frozen. "He's gone? Like dead?"

He pulled me aside, glancing over his shoulder to see who was near us. Dropping his voice, he said, "Let's say if one kind of bait doesn't work, you reach for another."

"Lucas and Finley are going out in the field together? You found sign of Mauss?"

He nodded. "They left almost a week ago."

I clutched at his sleeve. "You've got to get them back."

"Yeah, why?"

"Why do you think, you big, blue-haired ox? Mauss wants me. Send me back out there if you have to send someone."

188

He pulled me aside, away from the odd looks levied my way. "The clue was meant for Dr. Goddard, not you. Even if they trusted you, they wouldn't send you."

His radio squawked, ending our discussion.

Less than a month later, I heard the news. Finley and Lucas were missing.

"Are you sure?" I asked Domino, my voice hoarse from the strain of getting words past my tight throat.

"There's no doubt," he said.

Jesus, missing. Not dead, not maimed, not fine, just completely missing. No further information. Nothing was worse. I didn't feel loss, just a mind-numbing terror combined with the staggering pain of failure.

I told Domino, "I need to go up there and find them. Now."

"Losing Finley cemented their decision to keep you here indefinitely."

My jaw clenched. The only difference between *indefinitely* and *forever* was false hope.

Later, surrounded by the stillness that comes from the middle of the night, I curled in the fetal position, trying to shake off my last horror-filled dream about Finley.

I stared at the wall, making constellations out of the minor depressions caused by moving furniture or past tenants beating their fists, whatever. I saw the leggy triangle of Libra, and my mouth flattened. Of course I would find The Scales.

Finley was up there with Mauss and Lucas. God, the streets were going to run red with blood.

I sniffed hard, but then I let go and sobbed until Blue's transmission caused Sam to intervene. Despite my protests, he firmly held my head and forced pills down my throat. I knew the drugs would soon drag me under. Christ, how much of my existence did the lab make me spend unconscious? If this was my life, did I even want to be conscious?

It was a hell of a way to spend my nineteenth birthday.

CHAPTER 24

CROATOAN

In the library three months later, Domino nudged me roughly to get my attention away from Nietzsche. It wasn't my love for his theories that caught my interest so much as my determination not to think about the word I'd found carved into the underside of another library shelf.

The library had a dozen new books—more classics, damn it—and when I'd rearranged the shelves to accommodate them, I'd remembered the graffiti underneath the one and searched the undersides to see if anything else was there that I needed to scrub off. I'd found one more writing sample, written in AMF's hand, whoever the hell that was.

Croatoan.

The word made me so uneasy I hadn't been able to finish sorting the new books. I'd snatched the nearest book and forced myself to concentrate on it instead of the legendary colonial colony where all the inhabitants had disappeared without a trace.

Domino told me, "They want you in the conference room."

"Why? I've been a model prisoner."

"They're considering you for release."

I sat on that for a long time, afraid to believe it was true.

Domino said, "I thought you'd be jumping and screaming all over the place."

I closed my eyes and leaned back in my chair, torn up inside. "If Finley makes it back, can he stay down here as long as he wants?"

Domino jerked involuntarily at the mention of Finley.

I asked, "That's what you guys want anyway, right? All the hatchlings to volunteer to stay down here out of trouble, out of sight, fighting the good fight with all our might?"

In a low voice, he said, "If you left now, it would be the best possible thing for you. Trust your instincts. Not your heart, not your head, but your instincts."

I murmured, "You make it sound like it's a matter of life and death."

He gave me a direct gaze. "Maybe it is."

"Why the random compassion?" I asked him. "Half the time you're a bully and a dick, but the other half you're saving my ass."

"Well, sometimes the hair on the back of my neck stands up and sometimes it doesn't. Come on, let's go."

We were both silent as he escorted me to the conference room, and I thought about Domino's heebie jeebies and Finley. Mostly I thought about Finley.

In the end, only one right answer existed.

I walked into the conference room and told the committee without preamble, "I want to stay."

They all stared at me in disbelief, but it was Domino's hard gaze I felt the most.

Tuncay spoke first. "Little One, under the witness protection program, you *will* be safe from Mauss, but we won't leave you without a means to contact us for emergency medical treatment."

"I understand."

"So you've changed your mind and want to work with us?"

"I didn't say that at all."

Silence.

Domino reluctantly said from his corner, "She's got feelings for Dr. Goddard, and it's not like we produced the man's body or anything."

I flinched.

Alan Tuncay scowled at Domino.

"You wanted an explanation. I gave it to you," Domino said. "She's going to stay until he either shows up dead or she realizes it's never going to work with him."

"Who died and made you Cupid?" I snapped, shoving away from the table. "You don't know me or Finley, and you definitely don't know the extent of our feelings for each other. I'm not dealing with the stress of his disappearance well, and the least you people can do after all the crap you put me through is to let me stay somewhere safe where I have access to a counselor I trust for a little longer."

And that was that.

On shaking legs, I made it back to my room and under the shower where I could cry in peace.

Freedom.

Now.

Those goddamned bastards.

Seven months and eighteen days after Finley and Lucas disappeared, my time at the library was interrupted by Domino once again. Before he could open his mouth, I stuck a page marker in my book and asked him, "Know what the difference between a Northern fairy tale and a Southern one is? A Northern fairy tale begins with 'once upon a time'. A Southern one starts out with 'y'all ain't gonna believe this shit'."

"You heard," he said in surprise, his words carried on a breath of wintergreen.

"Isidro was giving me a checkup when all hell broke loose. It seems our lost souls were in the basement all along."

His restless mint went still, and he looked thoughtful.

"Down by the icers?" he asked, as if testing my knowledge.

"In the icers," I clarified. The men had been discovered when the alarm sounded in Finley's cryotube. "Damned if I know how the psycho got them into the most secure part of the lab without anyone knowing about it. It seems he's cleverer than I gave him credit for, and when is that ever a good thing?"

Again came the repeated clicks of his mint being flung against his teeth.

"I can only patrol the areas they give me access to," he told me without apology. "Anyway, I just wanted to let you know the men were back."

"And to remind me to stay away from both of them," I said.

"Do you have any idea what my job is down here?"

"You're the law."

"I keep the peace," he corrected. "That means I keep the residents here safe from one another and themselves as much as I can. Mostly, this means preventing the curious and the self-entitled personalities from getting out of hand. I may not know all the details about what goes on around here, but I've worked contained environments long enough to know you and Dr. Goddard are not a good combination for maintaining the calm in this lab. It's nothing personal."

"Feels personal. All you ever do is tell me to shut up and color like I'm a child."

"As opposed to treating you like you're part of some crime-fighting team? Stop pestering people with your questions about Mauss."

"Well, apparently he's still relevant. Didn't you just come in here to tell me he hasn't forgotten about us at all? I mean, have you ever considered how far I got with Mauss topside when the only piece of information the lab ever gave me was a list of cities to go to by train? You sent me up as bait, but I proved I could be so much more. Think what I could do if you actually give me some clues to work with."

"You're not a crime fighter," he snapped. "If you're bored, get some schooling or waste your time on video games like everyone else."

"Of course I'm bored. I live in a sterile white cage. I serve no purpose. Once I get an education, then what? Seriously. Let's say I get a degree in astrophysics. That was one of my options. What am I supposed to do with a degree in astrophysics down here? Nothing, right? Getting a degree is busywork, and since no job will come from it, I'll finish another degree from their list. How about nano-pharmaceuticals? Perfect. Now I can walk the same corridors, go to the same appointments, and eat the same damned food with two degrees instead of one."

"It wouldn't go to waste."

"Wouldn't it? Even if they give me some stupid little corner in some office and let me design and run a little experiment, it'll still be more busywork meant to keep me calm and shut me up. Isidro would never let me take on anything using real radiation, real chemicals, or real nanomites. My body is too precious to actually be used."

"They offered you a release," he reminded me. "You ignored it to be with some doctor you're only attracted to because he's from the same century as you. How long is it going to be before you get bored talking about the good old days?"

"What do you care as long as it doesn't disrupt Utopia for everyone else? Nothing is real about what goes on down here, Domino. The surveillance in every corner, every bathroom, every bedroom makes sure of it. That zombie-like calm out there? It's nothing more than the dystopiate effect of living every moment under surveillance."

"Are you finished?"

I threw back my head and yelled, "Long live the revolution." Predictably, no one rallied around the battle cry. I shrugged. "Now I'm done."

"For the moment."

"Can't help it. I wasn't born in a cage, and knowing what freedom feels like is not something you ever forget. What do you think, counseling or medication?"

"It was a sizeable snit, so they'll hit you with both barrels. Was it worth it?"

I laughed.

He left me to my reading, but I abandoned it to chase him down. I pretended to trip and knock into him, spilling the box in his hands. When we both bent down to retrieve it, I said in a low voice, "If Mauss comes back here and all hell does break loose again, what do you want me to do?"

His brows knitted, and I felt a burst of unease as I realized I could very well be conversing with the man Mauss was working with.

"Never mind," I said hastily.

196

He motioned for me to return to the library. He stepped on my heel twice in his haste.

As soon as we entered the room, he stopped me from taking another step. I could feel the strength of his hand as it clenched around my arm. "Do?" he asked in a low voice.

"What's going on?"

We both whirled at Tuncay's voice.

With a false smile, he said, "I saw you two rushing down the corridor like there was a problem, but I couldn't imagine why it would require both of you."

Domino opened his mouth, but nothing came out. God help me, I couldn't come up with a reason for our actions either.

Tuncay leveled his strange smile between us, looking like he knew we were hiding something. I wished I could look sweaty and sultry like it had been about sex, but neither of us appeared the least bit amorous.

"Domino, walk with me," Tuncay said.

"I'm on my lunch break."

"I don't give a damn if you are. You work when I need you to."

Domino's mouth tightened, but he stepped out of the room.

Tuncay pinned me with a long look before he, too, left.

Hours later, Domino met up with me again. "Make it quick."

"Last time you were able to warn me, but I'm not banking on that being possible or even being your priority if he comes back in here again with murder on his mind. I'm sure I'm expected to hide again, but is there a panic room or something I'm expected to get to?"

"Until you can outrun a bullet, I want you to hide wherever you need to. You found a good spot last time."

Good response. If he wanted to funnel me toward a killing field, he would've told me where to go.

Unless he'd figured out where I'd hidden and wanted me to go there again so it would make it easier to kill me.

I said, "Good enough for that one event, if nothing else. I don't suppose I can get a gun yet."

"A good enough hiding spot and you won't need a gun."

"True." I couldn't help adding, "You know who hates the idea of citizens having a right to arm themselves? Tyrants."

"You've got no way to secure it," he reminded me. "Is a gun something you'd trust everyone in this lab to have access to just by entering your room?"

"That's a crappy answer."

"It is," he agreed candidly. "But you know what? They never authorized me to have a gun either. At least I've got the means to hide the one I smuggled in."

With a reluctant smile, I watched him leave. I envied the people who could read a man and know whether or not to trust him. Sometimes I wanted to believe Domino could be relied on, but was that based in loneliness and desperation? Or was I actually picking up on some subconscious indicators he was worth my faith? Knowing whom to trust would be better than having a superpower down here.

CHAPTER 25

GOD'S PLAYGROUND

Sam arranged for me to be able to visit Finley in the medical suite. Finley's eyelids cracked and fell again like they were made of stone. His lips barely parted as he said, "Hi."

I took his hand in mine. It was clammy, and I forced myself not to fling it away from me. "Are you going to be all right?"

"Yes. Are you? I heard what Isidro did."

"Did?"

"Your eye. Your hand. I'll fix anything he got wrong."

Every word he spoke seemed to tire him more.

"I won't let him do it again," he said. "I swear to God."

He couldn't possibly think he could stop Isidro.

"Finley—"

"I did warn you," he rasped. "Not to deviate from expectations. Was it that hard?"

"Shh, you can chastise me later. You look exhausted. I'd better go."

He wouldn't release my hand. Instead of the familiar smooth softness of his surgeon's hands, I felt the rough strength of a bricklayer. What had he been doing with his hands?

His voice was as hard and coarse as his hand when he said, "Tell me about your relationship with Jason Chavez."

Eyes wide, I said, "I don't have a relationship with him."

"Spell it out for me. Why does your file say you do?"

"I had a one-night stand with my mentor. I was lonely. These things happen. We never even came close to repeating it. I respect the work he does, though. Why are you asking me about him?"

"While I was topside, I realized they might release you. You're repaired now. I was afraid you'd run. To him," he said, regarding me with narrowed eyes, fist curling at his side.

"That was years ago," I said, frowning at the show of jealousy. So much for the hope Finley would help me free Jason. "Bobby Hamin wounded me more by breaking my heart in the eighth grade, but I'm not going to cross the border to throw myself weeping on Bobby's grave either."

The tension left his body, and he looked as fragile as frost again. Trembling from the exertion, he took my hand and kissed it in apology. "Bobby Hamin was a fool."

I turned away. "Get some rest."

My heart lurched as I left him. Did he see it? Did he see the moment I realized his exhaustion was real but the weakness wasn't?

Caution. Deceit. Those were the messages in the flowers that had arrived after I'd spent more time than was strictly necessary with Finley.

In the first photo, Mauss had wondered when I was going to meet God. He'd also said it was God's will I stay alive. Puck had mentioned God, too, saying He'd told Puck to warn me about the lab. He hadn't spoken like God was one of his best friends the way Mauss did, though. Puck had said he suspected God was insane.

Finley Goddard wasn't just the man who'd helped Puck escape the lab, he was also Mauss's accomplice. No, it was more than that. Mauss was working for Finley, not with him. God doesn't take a partner. He sure as hell doesn't take a girlfriend, either. What did Finley truly want me for?

That night, I was slow to wake to the light, persistent tapping on my door. When I opened the door, the sight of my visitor made my eyes widen.

"Finley?" I said, grogginess giving way to a fear I could taste. "What are you doing here this time of night?"

"Shh," he whispered. "Nothing's wrong. Are you up for a midnight stroll?"

I nodded.

"Good. Get dressed and meet me at the south end of the atrium. Don't let anyone see you."

He slipped down the hall.

I snatched up a fresh set of clothes. My eyes lit on the intercom. Could I get a call to Domino before Finley caught me? And really, what was I going to say? That Finley was God? I had to see this through.

Ten minutes later I was fighting down claustrophobic anxiety as I inched down a long tear in the flexible insulation surrounding the lab's cells. Insulation? Perhaps cushion was a better word for it. I supposed the flexible material would provide a little give and take during earthquakes compared to a rock and dirt fill.

Finley had offered me a flashlight, but I'd declined, deciding I didn't want to see the inhabitants of the foam I was disturbing. Hearing them and feeling fleeting touches of them was bad enough. His light cast a faint, eerie glow through the cushion. As I went after him, I smiled grimly at the thought I'd finally gotten my wish: technically, I was outside the lab again.

At first I thought Finley was winging it, working through the fissures with the hope they ended up somewhere, but he didn't hesitate or backtrack. He knew exactly where he was going. I couldn't decide if that was reassuring or not.

I was less than a meter away from him when the light disappeared. I stilled, listening in vain for him. He might've been nabbed as soon as he emerged. I waited patiently, unwilling to announce my presence.

What if we were captured? What if Domino used that as a reason to separate me from Finley? That would ruin everything, absolutely everything. I needed proof. If not proof, then an idea of Finley's endgame.

And what if catching us made Domino wonder if I was hiding more than trailing after Finley through the foam to God-knew-where? What if Domino thought I'd conspired with Finley? What if he said he was following my lead and not the other way around? Everyone would believe him over me because he played well with others while I was the rebel. Worse yet, what if Domino thought I'd conspired with Mauss to murder the first seventeen and that woman when my reserves were being wiped out?

A pair of hands seized me, scaring a gasp out of me before I was yanked through a gap that wasn't quite big enough for a person to pass through.

"It's like being born, huh?" Finley chuckled, dusting me off as he pulled me to my feet.

202

"I don't remember," I said nastily, finger combing cobwebs from my hair. The glow of readouts in ancient housings confused me. "Where are we?"

The overhead lights flickered on. As my eyes adjusted to the brightness, I saw we were in the basement. Empty cryotubes surrounded us.

Jason. I could finally check on Jason.

"Are you sure they won't be looking for us?" I asked in a hushed voice, pressing into the shadows.

"I know what I'm doing."

"But why come here?"

"No surveillance," he said, holding his hands out expansively to indicate the lack of cameras. "There are lines feeding information from the icers to the computers upstairs, but that's the extent of their monitoring for this part of the lab."

"You sure? Maybe they started a video feed or patrols after you guys were found down here."

He grinned at me. "They just changed the locks on the door. They're good locks, though. I know I wouldn't be able to bypass them."

"You're awfully happy to be in a place that screwed up your life twice. Those icers are nightmares in a can. For most of us, they were a death sentence."

His smile faltered before fading completely. "I know. A lot of good people died." He walked over to the nearest icer and wiped off the name plate. "Laura Sommers. I think you would've liked her. Her file says she was in her last year of school for aerospace engineering. That was her gift: engineering. You two would've had a lot to talk about."

"Yeah?"

He glanced at me. "She died while they tried to resuscitate her. A lot of them died because of the impatience, ignorance, and arrogance of the doctors here."

"A lot of them died because of the man who put them in these tubes," I said, making sure blame was laid at the correct feet.

"I know," he snapped. His apologetic smile followed. "Forgive me. There are ghosts down here."

He wanted to talk, so I kept the man talking. I pointed at the next tube. "Who died there?"

"Logan Duperre Treson," he said without needing to look at the name plate. "Microbiologist-slash-biochemist with a knack for finding bacteria that turned hazardous waste into something a lot less lethal. All that talent and his mentor took credit for every lick of work Logan did."

"You speak about him like you knew him."

"I did."

"Because you read his file?"

"You think you're the only one mourning these people?" he said, showing signs I was testing his temper. "You don't even know who you're mourning. You haven't read their files once let alone as many times as I have. You don't even know any of their names. Not one person."

"Robin Goodfellow."

He flashed me an irritated look. "And who's that?"

"A beautiful man of Asian descent who sat next to me at an airport and asked me if I dreamed. That was about ten seconds before a pair of lab security people killed him. The young man called himself Robin Goodfellow. Shakespeare's famous elf. Puck."

"His name was Wallace Lang. He was an oceanographer and a poet." Before I could ask how he'd sneaked Puck out, Finley said, "Come with me. I want to show you something."

"No, I've already had the tour. Why on earth would you bring me here? There's more negative karma here than anywhere else I've ever been."

"I wanted to be alone with you for a change. I wanted to be in a place where we could talk freely."

"You want free speech? Here's some. I—"

"Be quiet," he said bluntly, and I did my best to hide my surprise at the way he spoke to me. It belatedly occurred to me I'd only seen his public persona until now. I regarded him silently, regrouping.

He grinned and claimed my hand with one that was sweaty despite the chill in the air. "I want to show you the living quarters."

"You don't mean these, do you?" I said warily, jerking my chin at the nearest icer. "I'm sure the tech is fascinating, but I'm not in the mood for a study session."

"Will you trust me?"

He navigated the corridors easily, and I wondered how many times he'd made the journey through the walls.

A short flight of grated metal steps at the end of the main hallway led to the living quarters, although I couldn't imagine who'd want to stay there. The cell was barely enough for one person, perhaps two if the big desk was moved out of the sleeping area. I touched the aging rivets on the doorway, realizing this whole basement area must have been the original lab and that it wasn't until decades later Texas had added the upper sections we lived in.

"What do you think?" he asked.

"I think we got lucky someone stumbled on this secret clubhouse before we all finished dying," I said. "Can you imagine it? You're out hiking one day and when a storm blows up unexpectedly you duck into a cave that ends up leading to an underground laboratory stocked with fifty dying people with magnificent dossiers."

I turned and looked back toward the inhabited icers.

"How long do you suppose we were supposed to be in there? Was there a timer set to flush the tanks and set

us free after a hundred years? Or maybe it was only supposed to be ten or twenty years, but the U.S. fell and the
Clan Wars killed off or prevented the appropriate people
from springing us."

"I don't know. I've been busy planning the future, not
dwelling on the past."

"You must have a hypothesis, though."

"The future," he repeated, unwilling to humor me.

"I want to see my icer."

"No, I think it's better you keep a distance from an
instrument you consider a personal means of torture. I
should warn you if you squeeze between the seams on
your own, you'll get caught. I'm taking advantage of irreg-
ular hiccups in certain security cameras, and I'm not
about to tell you when and where they will hiccup. I took
a risk even bringing you down here."

So that was why he'd recruited Mauss. The surveillance cameras. "You wouldn't have brought me here if
you weren't sure, and I wouldn't have come if I weren't."

"Miranda," he said as if he just wanted to say the
word aloud.

Feeling like crying all of the sudden, I rested my head
on his shoulder to reassure myself he was not a god, not
a monster, just a man. "This is so strange."

He held me like I was infinitely precious to him.
"Unprecedented," he acknowledged.

We held each other until it was time to wriggle our
way back up to the main part of the lab. It was as disturbing as the few tender moments I'd had with Jason, but I
was able to smile at Finley when we could've parted ways.
"I'm wide awake. Do you want to go to the cafeteria for a
midnight snack?"

He reluctantly shook his head. "I really shouldn't
have left my bed. Too much exertion too soon."

"Can I stop by your room in the morning then? I'll bring you breakfast."

"I would like that."

At the cafeteria, I leisurely drank a small glass of unsweetened green tea in case he changed his mind about joining me, and then I walked through the atrium like I was headed back to my room. As I approached the seam we'd gone through, I couldn't take my eyes off it.

To hell with the surveillance. The camera may be recording every moment of that hallway, but that didn't mean human eyes were on me at that moment.

It took only seconds for me to push through the seam again.

CHAPTER 26

TRUE LOVE

As fast as I could, I struggled through the fissure in the darkness. I was going to Jason's icer. If a good look at the system showed me how to initiate the thawing sequence, well, the lab was about to learn what it was like to deal with a man who refused to follow the rules and punished anyone who got in his way.

Even with my reliable sense of direction, I got turned around in the foam. I should've reached the fissure leading down by now. Had Finley marked it? Is that why he needed a flashlight? I returned to the seam in the corridor, but I didn't breach it. I'd already been out of bed a long time, but if I ended up under tighter restrictions because I got caught, I would regret not making one last attempt to find the path.

Having found my bearings again, I slowed to the pace Finley had taken and tried the route again. Yes, there it was, that downward fissure. When I reached the basement seam, I pushed out, hit the lights, and ran like hell to get my answers before Finley, Domino, or someone else could catch me.

I came to a shuddering stop in front of my icer. My name plate had been restored to its rightful place, and Jason was still in there. "Tuncay, you bastard."

Unease prickled me like frost forming on my spine. Compared to the other icers I saw when walking with Finley, this one didn't look right. If nothing else, the plentiful growths on Jason's skin were the wrong color.

But Tuncay had said everyone was different. Different levels, different bacteria in their systems, different temperatures they stabilized at, everything. Variation in cryo was assumed. His boards still read green all the way across.

My hand hovered near the surface of the tube encasing Jason, feeling none of the characteristic coolness. But that didn't mean anything. I'd had so much nerve degradation there were bound to be some things that didn't register correctly at times no matter how perfect they said my body was.

I looked up into Jason's eyes and stopped lying to myself. Flattening my hand on the surface, I confirmed he was suspended in room temperature fluid. I crouched to take a better look at his readouts and saw the thin film covering them. I lifted the edge with my thumbnail and peered underneath. The screen read that the icer had automatically been switched over to a *Needs Maintenance* setting years before after the loss of all biosignals from the inhabitant.

On autopilot, I replaced the film that showed a green board. The bottom panel sat crookedly, and I discovered it was a drawer that hadn't been pushed in all the way. The inner label contained a checklist for the necessary contents: hardcopy medical files, silver-based photos that wouldn't degrade as fast as modern printed ones, and personal effects of the occupant. The drawer was empty.

It was like no one ever meant for anyone to know who he was or why he was there.

I wiped my fingerprints off the icer and walked away, shutting the lights off behind me. Without haste, I crawled back up to the main floor and emerged from the seam into the corridor by the atrium and kept walking. I didn't cross anyone's path. In my room, I stripped and took a long, hot shower before crawling into bed.

I feel asleep immediately.

The increasing illumination in my bedroom signaled daybreak. I opened my eyes to the majestic wonder of a beach sunrise. The unique salty, sandy smell touched me, and the sound of a collapsing wave flowed over me. The ocean was vast. The planet Earth was larger still. The solar system was immense. The Milky Way Galaxy was so gigantic I could barely comprehend it, and it was an infinitely tiny speck in comparison to the rest of the universe. One man's demise was nothing on the cosmic scale of things. That Jason had already been dead when Tuncay had showed him to me was even more insignificant.

But in my universe, Jason had been the most significant person in my life. I loved my husband, but I'd hidden big chunks of myself because I didn't think he could love me if he truly knew me. Jason was the one who was far more interested in what he saw through the cracks in my facade. It was because of him I was fine with being strange and grumpy and imperfect. Fine? Hell, I embraced who I was.

He died down here, naked and alone, nightmares pulling apart his mind. No one down here had given a damn.

Nearly a week later, Finley was back to his medical duties and confirmed Isidro had done no permanent damage to my eye. My dislocated fingers had also healed well. That night, Finley and I went back to the basement. We walked the corridor in silence. I was glad he didn't feel like talking because my throat was dry and tight.

No way could we keep getting away with this. Every breach through the seams left a slightly bigger hole, and people walked the lab at odd hours. For all I knew, Domino was already suspicious and was giving us enough rope to hang ourselves with. He came across as a goon, but I'd never had the impression Domino was a fool. Jesus, this could go wrong in so many ways I couldn't even begin to calculate it.

Finley's arm brushed mine at one point, and he laced his fingers with mine. With his other hand, he reverently touched the surface of each cryotube we passed. As if I needed any more proof he was sympathetic enough to help Puck escape.

"What's going to happen to us?" I asked Finley, moving aside so I didn't block his light while he ran diagnostics on one of the icers.

"I'm surprised you have to ask," he said. "We should leave this place."

"The minute they find us gone, they'll send everything they've got after us. We'd never get to see each other again if they didn't want us to."

"I know a place we could go," he said absently, still focused on the cryotube. "Did I tell you I figured out how to fix these to produce a perfect stasis condition?"

"Stasis for what? There's no space program. Never was. You know the moon landing was faked," I teased. "We're stuck here on Terra Firma. Well, within."

The woman in the icer floating in the murky liquid looked awfully vulnerable, and my hand rose to touch her face in simple comfort, only to hit the transparent surface of the cryotube instead.

He was looking at me sympathetically. "I do that, too."

"Who is she?" I said, tucking my hand in my armpit to take the chill from it. That idiot Tuncay made it sound like the icers were cold enough to make clammy skin stick to them, but it wasn't quite that intense.

"Sasami Allendine, one of the medical technicians. They stuck her in here almost twenty years ago even knowing she has diabetes, the fools. I've been keeping a close eye on her, but I don't think she's going to make it. I could pop her, but for what? Needless experiments like they did to you, me, and the others? Maybe wrongful termination just because they don't want to bother having to create insulin?"

He leaned his forehead against the frosty surface of the cryotube, his lips moving slightly as if murmuring a prayer or apology.

What was the appropriate thing to do for her? I didn't know. It wasn't like he had the tools to treat them down here in secret, but condemning someone to Isidro's blade wasn't something to be taken lightly. She'd no doubt been listed as deceased in all official records, so she would be without rights like I was.

Touching the original nameplate bearing a name different than Sasami's, Finley sighed and looked over at me. "Didn't you think things would've improved in the past century? Or that at the very least, the people who thawed the first generation would've embraced us, seeing us as an extraordinary set of gifts from a time that couldn't appreciate the need for us? The fifty people in these cryotubes could've worked miracles if only given the opportunity."

Pushing useless tears off my face, I shook with emotion.

212

The death toll was staggering. Life after life snuffed out, everyone responsible thinking they were doing righteous work. Somehow that made it more terrible.

Seeing me tremble, he wrapped his arms around me, clinging to me even as he tried to give me his strength.

"But you and I survived," he said. "There's still a lot the two of us can do. You saw what it's like in the outlands."

"I did," I whispered. "Those poor people. You're right. We need to act."

Something like a sob escaped him, and his embrace tightened until I could barely breathe.

"I knew you were special. Despite everything you went through, despite all the reasons you have to turn cold and dark, your soul remains good, strong. God, I love you. You have no idea how much."

I studied his face and saw he meant it. He truly thought I was something shining and whole. Something Paul-like showed in his expression, and the unexpected reminder of my beloved husband made all the lingering doubts about my actions evaporate. "How do you want to start?"

"Love, you're joining the game during the bottom of the ninth inning," he said breathlessly, framing my face with his hands. "We can leave immediately. Your last sample didn't reveal even a single nanobot."

"You're saying I can pass for human if someone runs a Big Blue over me?" I teased.

Something flickered in his eyes, a momentary unease.

"Finley? Is something wrong? Am I not healthy after all? You can tell me."

"No, you're healthy," he assured me, his smile genuine. "As perfect as a person can be made."

213

As he took my hand to escort me down the hall toward the living quarters, I said, "My clothes are too light a color to be hiking around the darkness unnoticed."

"I've got some clothes stashed down here for emergencies. You can wear those until we get home."

"Home," I repeated, savoring the word.

"You won't believe your eyes," he promised me. "It's beautiful, not like this place."

I stopped, releasing his hand. "Hold on. How did you get the money to build a secure location? The government? If the government gave us to the wolves here, what makes you think they'll leave us alone there?"

"Give me some credit," he said. "The place we're going was built before this clan even existed. We'll be safe, trust me. No one knows about it."

I hesitated, thinking about the possibilities of this one-way trip. He touched my face, and I flinched, startled. He snatched his hand back.

I caught his hand. "I'm sorry. I was a million klicks away, and you startled me."

His gentle smile returned, and he kissed my hand to tell me all was forgiven.

We headed toward the living quarters again.

At the top of the short flight of stairs, I stopped him. I didn't want to, but it was like an itch turning into a painful prickle demanding to be scratched. "Are you sure? I understand our needs are nothing compared to the millions who don't have enough food, water, and other necessities, but neither of us will be doing anyone any good if we get caught escaping the lab."

He stood on the top step facing me, his expression confident. "I can understand your reservations, but you have to trust I know what I'm doing. It's time to go. You're finally healthy enough to leave, and those people need us."

214

His passion for his cause was limitless and unflagging. "You amaze me," I said. "I've never met anyone like you."

"I meant what I said, Miranda. I love you."

He held my gaze for a moment longer, his bright, steady eyes showing me all his hope, all his faith.

When he turned to descend the steps and lead me to my destiny, I reached out and wrapped my fingers around his neck.

CHAPTER 27

THE SUPERHERO MISTAKE

Finley stilled at the feel of my bony fingers closing around his throat.

"I can snap your neck so fast you won't even feel it," I said quietly. "I can feel you wondering about me, wondering why your girl has suddenly turned on you. God help me, I need to tell you why. Mauss told me it was God's will I live, but he wasn't referring to our Lord in Heaven, now, was he?"

He surged. "Mauss? No, I had nothing—"

I jerked him back, tightening my grip ever so slightly. I expected him to ram his elbow back or stomp on my foot, but he did no basic self-defense move at all. He took the threat of me seriously, though. I could feel the pulse in his throat rabbiting.

"What are you do afraid of, God?" I asked. "That's who Puck said he got his orders from, too. Finley Goddard. Goddard isn't even your real last name, is it? It's the one you chose. What's the matter? Wasn't Christ high enough on the food chain for you to take a name like Christian or Christopher? But Christ died for God's children, didn't he? You've got no intention of doing that."

"Miranda," he sighed, using a voice I suspected was supposed to make me feel stupid for making such an outrageous claim. "You chose another name, too. They made us. My born name is Adam Finley. I chose Goddard after the rocket scientist."

"You had Mauss set up the hiccups in the security feed before you had him kill those people and bail. You had him lead me around the worst areas of Texas to see how people were suffering while shoving American heroes down my throat to remind me about the ideals of liberty and equality for everybody. You were grooming me to join your cause, just like you groomed him."

"You've got it all wrong."

"I seriously doubt that because no matter which angle I start working it, I end up coming right back to you. *Everything* comes back to you."

"I don't know what you're referring to," he said in frustration.

"The icers, Finley," I snapped.

His pulse leapt under my fingers.

I said, "You're the one responsible for arranging my kidnapping in 2014. You're the one responsible for fifty people losing a century in those icers. Those damn icers. What were you thinking?"

"You never would've realized your potential," he said, his passionate defense making the tendons in his neck stand out. "Especially after your husband died. None of the first generation would've reached their potential without each other's support and encouragement. Like a family, you would've been bound by the past and worked toward the future."

"*They're all dead*," I roared, throttling him. "You killed them."

He clawed at the hands on his throat. "Miranda, please."

Finley's desperate sound fed the carnivore part of my soul.

"Stop interrupting the monologue," I told him, forcing myself to calm down. "You snatched fifty more people, didn't you? Well, forty-eight. You and I would be the last two to be sealed in those new icers, right?"

He tried to pull free, and my fingers curled sharply. As soon as he forced himself to go still, I loosened my grip but not enough to remove the threat.

"Finley, how could you be so cruel? Wasn't the magnitude of the first round of losses enough for you? Don't you know your science fiction? Your chaos theory? Perhaps part of the reason the world is this ruined is because you robbed the twenty-first century of the talents of fifty good people, including yourself."

"You've got it wrong."

"The hell I do. You're stealing people again. Why can't you see how much you're weakening the future by stealing even more people this world desperately needs now? What will you do when we wake in a hundred years to a place that's even worse? Exponentially worse? How long are we going to skip ahead looking for fertile ground to seed your utopia?"

"It will happen," he said hoarsely.

"It should've happened more than a hundred years ago," I snapped. I released him, and he collapsed, his body weight carrying him down the stairs. I hurried to kneel at his side. "Are you injured?"

"Is there any point when I get to respond to the charges you leveled against me?"

"How about now? Why didn't you fix Puck?" I demanded.

"He sustained brain degradation from a lack of oxygen during a sloppy resuscitation. He was unable to perform at the level I needed. I couldn't operate on him because I was working through the last of my own nerve damage. He wasn't expected to survive his next scheduled surgery, so I helped him escape, and I suggested he warn you about the lab. And it was a suggestion. I don't give orders. I just make suggestions."

"Persuasive ones, apparently. Why did you delay contacting me?"

"It would've revealed things I shouldn't have known seeing as I was recuperating as a fellow patient myself. How did you figure out who I was?"

"Wait your turn," I said, pushing him flat on his back. "Who put the flowers in my hair that night?"

His eyes widened. "Flowers?" His eyes narrowed with sudden malice. "Flowers. Of course. Looks like someone overstepped himself. I'll have a talk with him."

"So it was one of your people."

"Stop making it sound like I'm the leader of a gang of thugs. Everyone acts of their own free will."

"A convenient defense. Why did you suggest Mauss kill my team?"

"Your team?" he repeated viciously. "You think they were on your side? After they removed you from cryo and got you stable, they prepped you for transport to the Hernandez knowing you'd be destroyed after enough of your DNA was harvested for their gene manipulation programs. Your team turned a brilliant, beautiful person with all the potential in the world into nothing more than a commodity. Every single one of them got what they deserved."

"You destroyed my reserves," I said, wide-eyed. "You did it."

"I did. God intended that genetic code to serve you so you can serve Him. The lab had no right to store it, to play with it, to steal it, to use it like a commodity."

"Finley, a woman was killed. Burned to ash. Please tell me she was dead when you put her in there and not that the incinerator was your murder weapon."

His eyes were full of emotion, but he didn't deny anything.

"Who else have you killed down here?" I demanded, thinking about his jealousy over Jason. No wonder Jason had to die. I might've had someone to run to otherwise.

"You've killed, too," he said hoarsely.

"Two people," I said wearily, sitting on the floor next to him. "I told them the tranquilizer darts would kill me in my condition, but they didn't believe me. They fired, and I fired. The Hernandez military didn't teach me to wing someone, so those two people died even faster than I did."

The smart man stayed where he was, lying on the floor on his back with one knee drawn up, a smile toying on his lips. He wasn't pleased by the turn of events, but it was plain he was as reluctantly impressed with my cleverness as I was with his.

"You always were an apt pupil," he said.

I thought of the shots fired while the Hernandez rescue team was saving me from that plane crash. That wouldn't have been Finley. That would've been the result of Isidro driving the other faction of the lab to get me back after he found me gone.

"What are you going to do now?" Finley asked.

"I don't want to kill you, if that's what you're asking. But I can't let you kill anybody else. All life has value. All this cryo has to stop, too. We're going to go to your lab, the one you were working on after you stuck Lucas in the icer, and we're going to thaw those people."

His smile broadened, showing his amusement. "What's to say I won't slip a tranq in your food one day and freeze you anyway?"

I smoothed the dark hair off his forehead. "Finley, can't you see I'm offering everything you truly want? If we destroy your working icers, the government will never find them and abuse them. We can change the world, and we can do it together, but we will do it in this world, not the next. Humanity is going to continue to devolve as resources run out, so we need to act now, not pray the future will be more welcoming. Can't you see?"

Finley stared up at the ductwork in the ceiling, looking thoughtful.

"Look, I'm not unreasonable," I told him. "If you're honestly not happy a couple of years from now, I won't interfere if you want to freeze yourself for a future generation. Not me. No one but you. But I don't think you'll go that way. We can change the world, just like you wanted. Dedicated people doing the right thing often end up with like-minded people, so we're likely to inspire others. Not just fifty of them either. Plenty of people want to make this planet a better place. They just don't know how or don't believe they're capable of making a difference."

His eyes shined, and I felt hope. Maybe he wasn't going to make me kill him after all. Not at this point anyway.

"It's possible," I told him earnestly, getting to my feet and stretching my hand out to him. "We can do this."

He placed his hand in mine and stood up, facing me. "You know, I think I've been waiting for you my whole life."

"So are we good? I want to meet our goal in a non-violent way, and, Finley, it is a combined goal. I want the same thing you do, but I can't tolerate anyone using the icers as a tool for it. I don't want to risk you in those things any more than I want to risk me. Let's just leave now, okay? Please?"

Slowly, he nodded, but I could tell he was distracted. "I love you, Miranda."

Most of his head disappeared.

CHAPTER 28

DIRTY LAUNDRY

I stared dully at the remains of Finley's head. The right side of his brain had been ripped out, bone and hair framing the residual pudding of grey matter and blood.

Immediately, a second shot sounded, and I felt the wet warmth splash against me this time.

Finley's body fell back, his hand leaving mine. His corpse thumped on the floor, the vibration coming up through the bottoms of my feet.

I couldn't breathe, couldn't feel my heartbeat, couldn't react at all.

Lucas rushed up, his rifle in hand. "I'm sorry I had to do that while you were so close."

My ears rang from the shots, so I read his lips more than heard him.

He said, "We needed him to reveal where the secret exit is, but he kept bringing the syringe closer and closer to you so we had to act."

Syringe? Jesus Christ, an uncapped syringe *was* in Finley's hand. I hadn't even seen him pull it out.

But no one ever had, I realized as I thought of his four dozen original victims.

I struggled to get to my feet, and Lucas helped me up with a hand on my elbow. He looked frighteningly cadaverous with his sunken cheeks and neck tendons standing out. Cryo did that to him, I realized. But, no, he hadn't been in there that long. *Finley* did that to Lucas.

Oh, Jesus, a head shot. Two of them. Two headshots leaving nothing of Finley's head but a dangling jawbone. I expected to feel relief because no matter how much spare tissue they secretly had on reserve, it would be impossible to bring him back. Instead, I feared technology could still perform some ugly kind of miracle. I didn't know much about modern computers and artificial intelligence. For all I knew, another part of the lab worked on uploading copies of a person's consciousness to a computer. After all, multiple paths to immortality existed.

"They'll be here any minute. Ugh, what a mess," Domino said as he saw the fluid leaking from Finley's corpse. "You should've whacked him over the grate instead of on the tile."

Whacked. It was one of my words, and I almost laughed hysterically that Domino had taken to using it.

Domino straightened, scowling at me. "I told you to stay away from Finley Goddard, a man who made my skin crawl for no apparent reason. What the hell were you thinking, coming down here with him like this? If you'd screamed, who would've heard you?"

My laugh was high-pitched and squeaky, sounding like I was on the edge of losing my mind altogether.

Lucas tabbed the safety back on his high-powered rifle as he studied me, gauging my reaction to his killing Finley. "Ease off, Dom. At least for now."

224

Acknowledging Lucas knew me better, Domino stepped away to give me space. When he stepped around the body to avoid the spreading seep, the air stirred and brought the scent of blood to me. I could smell it on my clothes, on my skin, everywhere, and it was getting more intense with every moment that passed. I sucked air through my mouth.

Stomach roiling, I stumbled toward the bathroom in Finley's tiny quarters, but Domino hauled me up short before I got more than two meters from the corpse. "You can clean up in a minute. Hold tight until Tuncay gets here."

"I-I'm not d-doing so well," I managed, clenching my eyes shut. "The b-blood..."

"Sit on the steps and put your head between your legs."

"D-d-dom-mm..."

He pulled me to the steps and pushed down on my shoulders to make my knees give way. Crouching in front in me, he poked one of his mints in my mouth, and the sharp, bright taste of wintergreen penetrated me like a winter wind.

"Look at me," he coaxed. "C'mon, you can do better than that. Really look at me. See what color my eyes are."

I locked onto the lifeline with an intensity and abruptness that made his eyes widen.

"Hazel," I said bluntly. Christ, why did I have to breathe so much? That blood smell was so *strong.* "Light brown with green and blue streaks, gold spot in the right one. Your Aldebaran spot."

"My what?"

"It's the yellow star in the Taurus constellation."

"That's what I'm talking about," he said approvingly. "Your color's coming back."

But as soon as he left me, I caught a glimpse of Finley again. I clenched my eyes shut against the sight of the blood. Attempting to ease some of the awful tension turning my muscles into hard, knotted ropes, I exhaled forcefully. The puffing of my cheeks caused something fragile to strain against the skin of my face and then shatter. It was almost like smiling with a dried face pack on.

Little chunks of Finley were drying on my face.

"Oh, Jesus. Oh, Jesus. He's *on* me."

Domino grabbed my hands before they reached my face.

I yanked at his grip, desperation making my voice shrill. "He's on me. I can feel him *on* me. Jesus, I've got to get *clean*."

"You'll get clean, I promise," he said in his familiar blunt tone. "I need you to stay here for another minute or two, just until they get here."

"Screw them. I—"

"I authorized a termination," he reminded me. "They need to see the threat to you was close and immediate."

Alan Tuncay and a medic ran down the corridor.

"What happened?"

Domino barely glanced at them as he retrieved a camera from the rafters. "I told you on the security circuit. Finley Goddard was the viper in our nest all along. When she realized that, he tried to kill her and escape the lab, unless I'm wrong and that syringe by his hand is a B-12 shot. You always say she's the important one because of the cloning on top of the cryo so I authorized termination. It's all on here," he said, pressing the camera into Tuncay's hand.

"D-domin-nooo," I whispered, touching the pieces of Finley stuck to my face.

226

Tuncay paled at his first look at me. "Oh, Christ, is that stuff on her face what I think it is? Get her out of here."

I made a frantic sound, and the medic came forward, dousing a wad of gauze in sterile water.

"Domino, you do it. Don't let anyone see her. Get her to her room and under a shower," Tuncay said harshly, jerking his eyes away from me only to have them land on Finley. His eyes jerked away again, only to see the spray of blood and bone and brain matter. Tuncay closed his eyes. "She doesn't leave her room, and she doesn't leave your sight until this is resolved to my satisfaction."

I tried to get to my feet, but my legs wouldn't hold my weight.

"Yes, sir," Domino said, hauling me up to my feet and holding me upright.

"Take this with you, and get rid of that footage," Tuncay said, shoving the camera back in Domino's hands. "I don't need to see the man die."

Domino gave him a strange look but pocketed the security camera.

The medic handed me the wet clump of gauze, and I frantically scrubbed my face as Domino pulled me toward the living quarters.

"No, I said her room," Tuncay said.

"It's on her clothes, too. I want to get the worst of it off her before I take her upstairs. It's not like the people here don't know what brain matter looks like."

In the tiny cell, I yanked my shirt upward, but I was shaking so violently it got stuck around my elbows and head. Bodily remains on my shirt touched my mouth, and a scream rose up my throat.

Domino pulled off my shirt and thrust it under the tap. In a low voice, he said, "Is there anything here we need to remove before Tuncay sees it?"

227

"I have no idea," I said honestly, the words muffled through the wet gauze as I scrubbed my face. "Finley only showed me what he wanted me to see."

He shook out my shirt and examined it. Deciding it was good enough, he wrung it out, his forearms bulging. I pulled my T-shirt over my head, now feeling cold, wet, and dirty instead of just dirty.

"Better?" he asked.

"Not even, but at least the chunks are gone."

Avoiding the sight of Finley's body, I edged around the corpse while Tuncay and Lucas fought over who was going to clean up the mess.

Seizing the opportunity, I sprinted through the maze of corridors until I stood in front of my icer with Domino skidding to a stop behind me.

"Did you get lost?"

"As far as you know," I said. Gesturing to Jason's body, I said, "Someone needs to tell his family he's dead. I know you won't tell them the truth, but they at least need to know he's dead so they stop looking for him."

Domino's brow furrowed. "Who is this?"

"Jason Alexander Chavez," I said, surprised he didn't know. Then again, he wasn't given much more information than I was despite his job replacing Mauss as the chief of security. Mauss's defection might've been why Domino wasn't told anything. "He was the clan's premiere weapons control officer for the clan's premiere combat aircraft. His family is important to the MoD. As was he. If you're asking what that has to do with the lab, my answer is that he used to be my mentor. He was pretty much the only person on Earth I cared about."

"Something's not right about this," he said as he committed the man's face and condition to memory. "Don't tell anyone about what you see here. I need to check on something."

228

"Don't you remember? This is all for the greater good," I said sarcastically.

"Watch your mouth. Better yet, shut it and remember who's been watching your back."

He took steps toward the main corridor.

I didn't. "What did you mean when you told Tuncay you knew I was important because of the cloning?"

CHAPTER 29

TRAPPED

Eyes wide, Domino went still. My question hung in the air around us as we stood next to my icer.

I shivered in the wet T-shirt, but it was the expression on his face that made a chill settle on my spine.

"Sorry, I thought I had a right to know," I said lightly, stepping past him.

He seized my arm and propelled me toward the elevator. "For decades they took DNA samples from each original icer victim so they could grow enough tissues to attempt resuscitation and repairs. At first, they couldn't come close to creating a full clone. But there's something different about your DNA. It's..." He faltered. "Sturdy? Like if they had fifty dishes full of tissues and only one survived past a certain point, it was always yours. I don't really understand it, but I know it's connected to why your body recovers faster than anyone else's. It's why you lasted so long after you found out you were dying at Greyson."

I didn't believe a word of it.

He said, "I know for a fact one Miranda clone lived into her early teens and another made it into her twenties. They probably created more than those two. Do you remember me telling you a woman was murdered when all your biologics were destroyed? She was the older one, and the only clone the lab had left. Your clone."

I was shaking my head. "That's impossible. There are big fat bans about human cloning."

With a glance at the hall to make sure no one was coming up on us, he said, "When the lab asked for permission to do limited human cloning, they were very careful with their wording. The government believed they were authorizing the use of cloning technology to recreate organ tissues. It wasn't until after the discovery of the first full-blown clone that anyone realized the special order actually provided the legal means for the lab to clone a full, intact human being from the samples taken from any of the people in Finley's original experiment."

"Domino, those doppelgangers they made from me have nothing to do with me."

"They have everything to do with you. Your kidneys were failing while you were at Greyson, but you had to know the rest of you wasn't much better off. The effect of the tranquilizer overdose was catastrophic on your organs. They had a clone with organs ready to transplant but no way to resuscitate you long enough to survive even one surgery, let alone all of the vital transplants."

The wall was cold metal behind me, and I couldn't stop pressing myself against it, wishing it would absorb me.

"They had nothing to lose by working it from the other way around. Your brain and some of your spinal column were moved into the clone's body."

"That's not *possible*."

"You're younger and shorter than you remember being because your clone was fourteen and hadn't fully matured yet. The more mature clone was fighting off a serious infection, so they didn't risk using her. Mauss has enormous respect for you as Miranda Donovan, but your clone body is something he means to wipe off the face of the planet because he says the Bible is firm on the subject. I believe Father Brannigan showed you those passages."

Again, the matter-of-fact tone. Sometimes it made him seem like an ass, but sometimes, like now, it made him seem patient and nonjudgmental. However, the content of the conversation was pure insanity. He didn't look like he cared for it either.

"Due to the way the current biotech laws are written, because the percentage of original tissue is so low, the lab is able to legally classify you as biotech property they own like they own your clones. You can be bought, sold, and destroyed like a laboratory monkey if they want."

"Why are you doing this to me?" I whimpered.

"They told me you were informed about your insertion into a clone as soon as you woke from the operation," he said bluntly. "You weren't. Great. One more lie. But you're right. You're entitled to know what you are."

My head spun. "No. I'm sorry, but you're terribly mistaken. I know who I am. Don't you think I know who I am? What I am?"

"I've been lied to before," he said eventually, his tone neutral as he retreated from the subject. "Let's get going. There's still some brains stuck on your face."

I felt my eyes rolling back into my head, but Domino's brawny arm kept me upright, urging me forward.

In the elevator, he took the dirtied gauze from my hand and worked on the spots I'd missed. "I'm sorry about stopping you from showering for so long. Sometimes it's just easier to make a point with a picture than an hour's worth of words. I had to show him something in case the surveillance unit failed."

"I'm still not doing so good," I croaked, the elevator's motion working against my efforts to keep my stomach calm. "Stop touching me. I feel smothered."

He ran block for me down the hallways, shielding sight of me as best he could when we couldn't avoid passing someone, and I wondered what people thought of me being a soggy mess with a security escort.

I barely made it to my bathroom before I heaved my guts out. Tears ran down my face to mix with the vomit. I staggered to my feet and tore at my clothes.

"Settle," he said, discreetly moving my soiled clothing out of sight. "He can't hurt you."

My legs failed me again when I stepped into the shower, but he was there. "I've got you."

He washed me impersonally, getting shampoo in my eyes and ignoring my girlie regions. When he stepped back, satisfied I was clean enough for government work, I picked up the soapy cloth and scrubbed my face.

As my touch became more and more brutal, Domino took the cloth from my hand and pushed me under the rinse water. "It's gone. You're clean, I promise."

When he shut off the water, I shivered, the water running down my hair and skin in shaky rivulets. I'd stood in this stall less than eight hours ago. God, how much had changed between one shower and the next?

He toweled me off with broad, fast strokes.

I saw the seam where the shower unit met the wall, and I backed away in fear. "Mauss could fit through the seams. Maybe that one. Maybe all of them. Maybe—"

"Doubt it. He's claustrophobic. Besides, he had keys and access codes to everything while he was here, plus access to the security camera feeds. He didn't need to grub around in the walls like a roach."

"You never listen to me."

"Mauss left through the front door, and I honestly don't think he's been back." He stuck the corner of the towel in my ear, making a high, startled sound escape me. "Got it," he said. "Just some soap."

"Do you think they'll let me leave now?" I asked. "I needed to stay here in case Finley came back because I wouldn't have been able to find him topside. I had to get close to him to find out what he was going to do, to make sure I was correct about who he was. But Tuncay's not going to let that get out, is he? That Finley was the one? He can't have a failure this massive on his record and remain in charge. I need to leave this place. Like for good. In a totally sanctioned way. I pretended I didn't have it together, but I do. I'm a little upset, but you would be, too, if you were me."

He stepped out of the room, using the comlink to reach Maintenance. I put on my sleep shirt but felt defenseless, so I pulled on a pair of pants, too. I sat on my bed, waiting because it felt like Domino was waiting. Two guys from Maintenance arrived with long, narrow strips of metal, which they affixed over the seams in my room.

"Thank you," I told Domino.

"This is so you can't get out, not so no one can get in."

My stomach seized. "What is this?"

"I'm doing my job. Not only did you fail to notify us of a massive security breach, you used it to access a restricted area. Because of that, one of the most valuable people in this lab is dead. And as for your freedom, well, they offered you freedom once, and you turned it down. Legally, they don't ever have to offer it again. Even if they had been considering it, I'm sure this reminded them why you can't be trusted. You definitely proved it to me."

Javier, one of the other security guys, arrived with a large plastic box.

234

"Completely strip her room," Domino said as he shut off the wall animations. "Sheets, toiletries, everything that's not bolted down. Did you bring the cameras?"

Too shocked to speak, I could only watch as Javier packed up my books and clothes while Domino installed battery-powered cameras between the ones attached to the power grid. In effect, they turned my room into a prison cell.

After it was empty, Domino did a final check, testing that no screw could be worked loose, that no crevice hid anything.

"I did the right thing," I whispered. "You know I did."

"You did what you wanted," he corrected before sealing me in.

But I'd done the right thing. I found the villain. It had gone wrong, true, and I'd almost taken a syringe full of poison for my trouble, but I figured out who was holding Mauss's leash. Didn't that benefit them as much as me? I'd earned my damn freedom.

They were never going to let me go. I was going to die in this room. Worse yet, I was going to live in this room, healthy and bored, no way to kill myself, no way to stop them from resuscitating me if I did. Finley was dead, so there wouldn't be another Puck-like extraction. Now that they knew about the seams and security feed hiccups, whoever gave me those flowers was out of reach, too.

God, why hadn't I said, "Let's go," as soon as Finley mentioned leaving? Why had I needed to get my answers then and there? Even impaired, Puck knew not to question God. Why had I been so sure the possibility of getting caught would spur him to respond to my questions quickly to get things going again? I was so stupid.

And the clone thing was too awful to contemplate. Growing a human being to cut up for parts for another was as unforgivable as Mauss thought it was.

No, Mauss and Domino were wrong about what I was. So what if it explained things that had seemed odd for so long, like my smaller stature and why I was regularly mistaken for someone else by people from other parts of the lab?

It couldn't be true. It wasn't cloning if some liver cells were harvested from me and stimulated to reproduce at an increased rate until enough liver tissue was available for my repairs. This whole thing was a horrible misunderstanding resulting from sloppy terminology.

Like the way I'd been preserved from 2014. It had been called cryogenics and cryonics, but neither term was technically correct. They were just easier to say than using the far more accurate explanation that cold temperatures and proprietary secrets had been used with limited success to slow my body's processes to the point where I could be preserved longer than would be predicted given the lack of food, water, and air my body usually needed.

My body? The lab's body, if Domino was correct about the legality of my position. Imprisoned in their body, never allowed to die, never allowed to live free. Jesus, could this get any worse? How much had I crippled my chances by not complying unless forced to, by not showing I understood the complications around my existence? I should've been willing to work with them to find a middle ground between what I needed and what they did.

I cried myself to sleep, tears pooling on the metal bed slab now that the mattress pad was gone.

I couldn't recover from the first nightmare. Even after Domino woke me up, I couldn't stop screaming, couldn't stop seeing the walls drip with Finley's blood and my own, couldn't stop feeling Finley's hand squeeze mine as if he were transferring his soul into me as the first bullet tore through his head.

As soon as I saw the light glint off the syringe in Isidro's hand, I fought with all my strength, but I still

236

felt the brutal stick in my flesh. The familiar, enveloping blackness came slowly. The panic and fear weakened, dulled.

Domino stood over me. I saw the Aldebaran speck of gold in his eye and the grim line of his mouth, and a new, strange peace swelled within me. I wasn't alone. Despite the things he'd said for the cameras, I'd never been fighting this alone.

Chapter 30

One Last Try

Dreams, so many dreams...

Screams. Dozens and dozens of them. Men's. Women's. Children's. Finley's victims screaming at me to help them or screaming at me because my generation hadn't been able to detect and contain Finley's insanity before he started playing God. Lucas was among them, and he was screaming, too, blaming me for not warning him he was in danger from Finley.

I woke with Lucas's name on my lips. I got out of bed to go find him and promptly had to sit down until the dizziness faded.

The hair lifted on the back of my neck, and I froze. I wasn't in my room in the lab. In fact, I wasn't in the lab at all.

"Austin," Lucas said without looking up from cleaning his pistol. As if realizing I might not find his pastime reassuring, he dropped a cleaning cloth over the pieces. "October nineteenth. And I'm Lucas," he added with a flashing grin, repeating the info I'd demanded of him the first time I'd woken in a hotel room with him.

"Stand up," I told him.

"What? Why?" he asked warily.

"Just do it."

When he reluctantly complied, I crossed the room and hugged him hard. "When I heard you'd left with Finley, I was afraid he was going to kill you."

"I'm fine."

"Finley sabotaged your cryotube. I knew it as soon as I saw you in the basement looking all raggedy and skeletal. Why did he want you dead? What did you see that you weren't supposed to? Did you see him leaving a message for Mauss? What a bastard. He didn't even kill you to your face."

"Wow, look at you," he said at my demonstration.

"Ah, shut it." Emotion spent, I stole a slice of apple off his plate and withdrew. "So what's going on? Mauss leave us another taunt?"

"Not sure. Domino got your bag out of storage if you want to shower and change."

I searched my bag and found everything exactly as I'd left it, telling me Domino had stashed it topside somewhere. Sometimes I could hug the big ox.

Domino was sitting across from Lucas when I emerged from the bathroom in a cloud of steam.

"I need new clothes before we do anything," I told Lucas, plucking at where the fabric stretched too tightly against my breasts and hips.

"Agreed," he said with frank assessment and a paternal grimace. "Dom?"

Domino produced a cash card and tossed it onto the table. I wished my other needs were so easily met.

Directing his gaze between us, Domino said, "I want you to find the other lab."

Lucas and I exchanged a glance. Scratching his chin, Lucas said, "Yeah, Dom, that's like expecting us to build a house with one piece of wood and two nails."

Domino said, "She'll have more by the time you get back from seeing your kid. Be back in eight days."

Lucas snatched up his gear and waved at me as he went out the door.

Alone with me, Domino looked no more comfortable with me than I was with him. He offered no words to distract me from noticing the dark smudges under his bloodshot eyes and the deep brackets on either side of his mouth. Had he slept since Finley's murder? Did he feel remorse? I wasn't sure what I felt yet.

I crossed my arms over my chest and broke the silence. "You never listen to me."

"I always listen to you," Domino said. "I wasn't about to let our alien overlords know that, though."

"How did you get me out of there?"

"Given the collusion between Goddard and Mauss, they were forced to admit topside was probably safer than the lab until they can get all the seams covered and establish security protocols in the basement."

"And since I'm up here you thought I could take a stab at figuring out where the second lab is? I'm not sure I can help you. Perhaps you didn't watch the recordings yet, but Finley didn't tell me anything about his secret location other than it's older than the clan and it's beautiful. He didn't confirm anything about more icers, let alone people in them. As much as I hate to admit it, Mauss beat my ass from one end of Texas to the other, and Finley got the drop on me, too. I suck at this. Isn't there a math problem I can do for you instead?"

240

"Well, I'm not saying you get the job done clean or easy, but I still want you to try."

"I will."

His eyes narrowed. "Just like that? You're supposed to ask me what's in it for you."

"And you're supposed to show me an icer housing someone I know," I said. "Domino, I recognize the difficulty, but Jason's family has to be told something. I'm not saying his body has to be handed over or anything, but they need to know he's dead, even if it's unofficial."

He showed me the face of his palmer, revealing an evidence processing form. "The body in the cryotube was determined to be synthetic."

"Define synthetic. Because if we've graduated to androids who look like people, kill me now."

"A mannequin. Nothing special about it except for who it was made to look like. The lab had it created when your initial counseling sessions first showed you would be susceptible to that kind of leverage."

"Leverage for what?"

He shrugged. "I think it was a contingency, not a plan. It has been removed and destroyed."

I studied the image of the dummy's body parts being fed into an incinerator. Could it be true? I totally believed the lab was willing and capable of such a deception, but if it was a dummy, that left one big question unanswered.

"Where is Jason Chavez?"

"After Greyson, he returned to Texas but dropped out of sight for almost a year. It seems he then had an unofficial meeting with the Defense Minister before flying to Rome with some kind of secret cargo," Domino said. "Maybe he did a courier job for her or something. I don't know. He stayed in Rome and has lived such a low-key life he might as well have become invisible. His family couldn't find him because he's done nothing related to aviation. And I mean nothing. There's no sign he's even touched a computer in years."

"You honestly expect me to believe you're referring to my Jason Chavez? There's no way the real Jason would give up planes for that long. His tech either. I once saw him lose his mind when he couldn't find his palmer for five minutes. Jason's dead."

He showed me a surveillance photo on his palmer. "He crossed the border back into Texas yesterday."

"Yesterday? Well, isn't that convenient. How new do you think I am?"

"Maybe someone just brought it to his attention petitions were on the books for the seizure of his extensive assets under the pretense he's presumed dead," he said with a ghost of a smile.

"Thank you."

He leaned back in the chair, finger tapping against the table. "What was your relationship with Jason Chavez?"

"Attraction and some affection, but I wasn't over my husband. Jason wasn't my idea of boyfriend material anyway. The man who broke my nose so I couldn't fly with Jason? Jason planted enough evidence on the man's computer to make it look like he was a domestic terrorist. Because of Jason, Kairo will never see the light of day again."

"So you didn't love him, but did he love you?"

I shook my head. "What he valued about me was what I could do with my brain or a plane and how he could use it to get back in his DM's good graces. He wasn't interested in a relationship any more than I was. Why does the lab keep asking me about him?"

"No, this is me asking, not them. The truth wasn't what I expected, so I won't ask again."

I scrolled back to the surveillance photo. Jason hadn't changed. He was still dark, elegant, moneyed, and arrogant. Annoyed, too, if that crease between his groomed eyebrows was any indication.

Domino's gaze was direct. "They only used his likeness. Jason Chavez is alive. Safe. He was never willingly a part of the lab's agenda. He was never coerced to help them. He knows nothing about them."

My relief Jason was alive suddenly manifested in a torrent of tears.

"I don't have a lot of time," Domino said, shifting in his chair. "Can I keep talking while you cry?"

I nodded, mopping up my face.

"So after Mauss neutered Lucas and took you, he was going to take you somewhere. Finley's staging area, maybe. Without any more first gens to liberate from cryo, I suspect Finley was on the verge of sneaking out when you were returned to the lab needing so much work done. Now, if he was so determined to get his few remaining chosen ones like Puck out of lab hands, why would he risk not giving you the clues to find a safe haven if something happened to him? They would be clues only people from your generation might get, like you knowing an older Route 66 existed."

I grimaced, understanding his reasoning even though I didn't agree with it. "That was already obscure knowledge by then. Same thing for the American folk heroes."

"Doesn't matter. You recognized them. You're as American as all the other first gens, and I think that's the key. I'm asking you to go over everything again."

"For what? Is this about finding a second lab full of new cryo victims or Mauss? What about the guy who left me flowers? Finley knew who he was. Are you sure all his people who have been declared dead in that lab are actually dead?"

"I'm not making any more assumptions," he said flatly. "But my biggest concern at this point is a lab with dozens of kidnapped people dying in cryo."

"What do the people funding your little expedition hope we'll find? Because I want to feel confident I'm not opening up a second lab to another bunch of amoral bastards."

His lips were pressed tightly together, and I almost let him off the hook. Almost. Domino never fit in down there, and I'd suspected for a while he was working for someone else, something the lab didn't know. He didn't have to tell me who, but it was reasonable to worry over what would become of any cache of functional cryopreservation units.

He rubbed his hand through his hair. "Honestly, I think you're going to find a bunch of dead people. Anybody alive won't be the lab's to deal with, if that helps. I hate all this talking. Find the lab. Everything else will probably fall into place after that. When Lucas gets back, have him escort you wherever you need to go, but if you think you've found it, have Lucas call me. I don't want you two going in. Am I clear?"

"Crystal."

"Yeah? Because there's no need for you to endanger yourself for some closure."

I made a face. "I figured out the identity of my nemesis, and Lucas eliminated him. It's already over as far as I'm concerned."

"It isn't, but we're close. I need you to try one last time."

He got to his feet, finger-combing his thick blue hair back into place.

"I always meant to ask you why you dye your hair," I said. "I like the blue on you best. I'm glad you settled on that one."

244

He looked in the mirror. "You can't imagine what it's like explaining something like this to your Nana."

"Your dye job will grow out. My piss-colored eyes are forever."

His gaze sharpened on mine as he evaluated the color. I hadn't put my brown lenses in yet, so my gold eyes were out there for all to see.

"I forgot they used to be blue."

"Really, out of everything weird in my file, you remember the one unremarkable thing in there?"

"Hmm?"

"My born eye color. My baby blues. The ones that rotted away in the icers. When they hatched me, they replaced them with gold ones, but that was long before your time."

He looked like he was about to comment but thought better of it and closed his mouth with enough force that I heard his teeth click when they met.

I turned away, unsettled. In the pre-Finley days, the lab hadn't stopped with my eyes. I woke up with a new nose one day. I looked too much like Miranda Donovan, so they changed it. My cheekbones and jawline were different, too. I just woke up and it was done before I knew what they were going to do.

Odd actions for people who never meant to let me go. Was it to support their charade that freedom was possible, or did they simply want their long-term test subject to be easier on the eyes?

Domino used to yell at me for not being grateful. Any ugly woman would laugh at my being pissed they made me beautiful, but I didn't see my family in my face anymore. I used to look a lot like my dad, but I'd seen my mom there, too, especially around the eyes.

Hell, I didn't even see me in my face anymore. All I saw was Isidro's heterosexual vision of what a woman should look like. I'd never felt more like an orphan.

"I'm sorry you felt like you had to handle Finley on your own," Domino told me.

"You got there in time."

"It shouldn't have reached that point," he said. "Sometimes the law is wrong, dead wrong."

I realized it upset him he couldn't save me from the lab's worst. Not legally, anyway. I almost told him I doubted they exposed him to more than a fraction of the amoral things both legal and illegal that were done to me, but that wasn't going to make him feel any better.

He made it to the door before I stopped him. "What am I supposed to do if Mauss shows up before Lucas gets back?"

"He won't. It'll take him at least a few days to realize something went wrong on Finley's end."

CHAPTER 31

GRAVEYARD DUST AND SALT

Trying to beat back a smile, I pushed back from the computer several hours later and paced the hotel room. Wait, the lack of surveillance meant I didn't have to downplay my reaction. I laughed and danced around in circles.

Cris Chavez was going to be speaking at a conference at the Harbinger-Ellis compound near where we'd met.

My reaction wasn't just because his return to his normal life meant Jason was home safe. As soon as I'd opened the curtains and the first rays of sunlight had caressed my face, I'd thought of Cris. The ruggedness and strength of him. The deep timbre of his voice giving me a fluttering sensation in my panties. His mouth on mine. God, that hot mouth on mine.

So if Jason was two years older than the me I used to be, and Cris was two years older than his brother, then Cris was thirty-five to my thirty-one? I was supposed to be nineteen, though. Would that be too young for him?

The man was an engineer. A rugged, hot engineer.

I threw myself on the bed and hugged a pillow, kissing it passionately. But how many people had put their heads there? Or other body parts? I ran to the bathroom and brushed my teeth.

Shopping for clothes, I thought of him, too. I replaced the cute airplane bra and panty set on the rack and chose a silky aqua set. No, the bra had push up pads, and I didn't want to lie. I floated through the stores trying on clothes and choosing how I wanted to portray myself.

I knew I wasn't going to meet Cris Chavez again, but I couldn't resist the fantasy of having a conventional life. Traveling. Exploring. Making love. Eating chocolate cake at some artsy bistro. Flying. So many fantasies pushing my hands toward the good hiking boots and skimpy lingerie and crazy jackets with a million pockets.

But as the sun dropped over the horizon and fatigue set in, reality returned. No escape was possible for someone like me. I bought plain, drab, sensible clothes that would make me invisible. I ate the way Isidro would've wanted, and then I returned to the hotel to go to work.

When Lucas returned from seeing his offspring, he set his backpack on his bed. "You know, it never bodes well when I walk in and see you pacing. It means you think I'm not going to like what you're about to tell me."

"I'm always right about that, aren't I?"

His smile flexed. "What's on your mind, Little One?"

I forced myself to sit down on my bed, but my feet were still restless on the floor, tracing the lines of the patterned carpet. "Look, are we doing the right thing? Overall, I mean. Mauss saved that lady and her dog from a fiery car wreck, so he still has a sincere desire to help people. You and I are both aberrations to the normal world: a man who assassinates God's children and a woman who keeps resurrecting after God takes her life. But we're the good guys? I mean, I know he killed those people, but if we're doing the right thing, shouldn't it feel better?"

Lucas's pale eyes showed patience. "Don't make it so black and white."

"I know, but does this have to come down to his death? He doesn't have superpowers, so any jail will hold him. I understand if secrecy about the lab bars a traditional public trial, but I'm sure the clan has other facilities to detain top-secret transgressors. Do you even have handcuffs?"

"Do you want my opinion?" he asked.

I nodded.

"Mauss has crossed a line there's no coming back from. He was a good guy. Before he went to work at the lab, he did a lot of work to improve his community. Yeah, he was sometimes considered an opinionated dick, but he probably had to dig deeply to get to a point where he could murder those people. But no matter how much you think you're justified, once you've done something like that, you're never again going to be the person you were. I don't think he understands that. I think he thinks if he wins, he can just go back to his old self. Like this is nothing more than some crappy chore he's chosen to handle because no one else would."

"But—"

"I'm tasked with stopping him. I'm authorized to kill him, but I have the option of sneaking up on him, knocking him out, trussing him up, and handing him over to Domino. But he's never going to make it back to the man he was, so I'm hoping he makes me kill him. It seems more merciful somehow."

I didn't know what to say.

"So let me stop you from making the next logical argument," he said. "Someone once told me terminating people the way I do robs bad people of being convicted and jailed for the rest of their lives. He said there wasn't enough punishment for the crimes committed and no justice for the victims."

"But?"

"But dead guys can't slip through the cracks of an imperfect legal system," he said with a ghost of a smile. "They can't repeat their crimes or think up new ones. They can't be released due to prison overcrowding or an accidental mishandling of a piece of evidence. When I'm finished, the threat is neutralized forever."

"I'm not arguing with you. But I'm taking some of the responsibility for the outcome, so I want to feel like we explored the options."

"This isn't your decision. It falls on the people who authorize it and the people who execute it."

"So you say. I'm still going to the grave knowing I had a hand in it." Before he could say anything else, I said, "Do you need to get something to eat, or are you ready to get back to work?"

"Ready. Where are we headed?"

Lucas surveyed the broken skyline of Oklahoma City. "Now what?"

"I told you. We need to go through the cemeteries," I said.

"I thought you were kidding."

I overlaid a map from the city's intact days over the modern satellite image Domino provided so I could figure out where in the sea of debris the cemeteries had been. "I want to start with this one."

"Little One, we had this conversation in every town the first time around. I don't do cemeteries."

"I know what to look for this time, and it'll go a lot faster with both of us looking."

250

"No. I'll wait by the entrance."

"Superstitious bastard."

"Cemeteries are full of dead people," he said. "It's unsanitary."

"For the love of Christ, they've been dead for decades. They are dust and bones in sturdy coffins two meters down. I promise you they carry less disease than some of the women you screw."

Outside the rusted gates to the large cemetery I'd targeted, Lucas shut off his engine, but he wouldn't take his feet off the pegs.

"Oh, my God, really?" I said.

"One lost grave marker and I'm standing on a dead person. Less talking and more searching. We're running out of daylight."

"All the more reason for you to help me," I snapped, snatching the powerful flashlight he offered and stuffing it into my back pocket. "At least use your scope to check the gravestones facing you."

"Just hurry."

Truthfully, I wasn't entirely at ease in a cemetery either. Mandatory cremations had begun during the Clan Wars, so any cemetery we saw was guaranteed to have so many broken or shifted markers I wasn't entirely sure of my footing sometimes. I didn't want to walk across anyone's burial plot because it felt disrespectful at a minimum. At the other end of the spectrum, stepping on a grave seemed like the way to wake a spirit that had been resting in peace. It flew in the face of logic, but it was a lot easier being logical when I wasn't exploring an old cemetery as the sky darkened.

During my second pass with the flashlight, I found the gravestone. It was nearly hidden by the dead grasses, but I knew it was the correct one as soon as I saw the carving on it. I pushed aside the frost-killed vegetation and snapped a picture with my palmer.

A sound like someone stepping on a branch made me break and run toward Lucas and my motorcycle. I apologized profusely to the dead people I trod upon.

"Go, go, go," I yelled at Lucas.

When we got to the crossroads, I didn't hesitate to take the direction that would take us straight back to Dallas. There were closer places to crash for the night, but there was no way I was going to be able to sleep near the derelict towns of north Texas. I needed the comfort of a city packed with intact buildings and crowds of live people. If it was a big enough city, I could probably even find someone who could exorcise any poltergeist now targeting me.

My heart didn't settle down into its usual rhythms until we were locked in a hotel room with all the lights on.

"Jesus Christ," I muttered, my hand over my chest.

"I told you we shouldn't be messing around with those places."

"A cemetery makes sense. Large tracks of land. Most of it only dug to two meters. Typically, people hesitate to disturb the dead. Headstones are good places to leave permanent markings." I flopped into the easy chair. "I'm going to have a heart attack."

"I told you it was a crappy idea. It's two days before Halloween."

My eyes widened. "Why didn't you say as much in the first place? Give me your gun."

"Guns don't work on ghosts," he reminded me.

A hasty online search drove us out to the nearest grocery store to get salt.

"Kosher or normal?" he asked me, foundering at the unexpected range of options.

252

Shrilly, I said, "How would I know?"

"Well, it's not like it says anything on the label," he snapped at me.

"Kosher doesn't have iodine added, does it? Get the kosher."

"Well, what about sea salt? That's natural, isn't it?"

"Get some of each kind. We need some shells for your shotgun, too."

"I told you, shooting ghosts doesn't do anything."

"It will if we fill those shells with salt, won't it?"

He looked at me like I was a genius. "Rock salt shells," he said, grinning. "Perfect long range solution."

"I need to find a church, too," I said, chewing nervously on my hangnail.

"Holy water," he said in satisfaction. "Do you think plastic bottles would ruin it? I don't have any glass ones. Wait, we need a metal flask, right?"

"What? No, we're not hunting vampires, jackass. I need to pray."

He frowned at me. "I don't want you thinking you're going to die. It sets you up wrong. The whole point of this is that you don't even come face to face with him."

"No, I'm not worried about that. I was already in one boss fight, and one was more than enough, trust me. If you tell me to hide under the bed while you go deal with him, I'll happily do so. I need to pray for the people whose graves I ran across, not for us. I only pray for dead people. Live people still have the choice to change their path to a more God-approved one."

"I'm sure that makes sense in your head. You can pray for yourself."

"Because it's worked out so well for me so far?" I retorted. "I'm on my own."

"You are not. God loves you. He's just not going to do everything for you."

"Look, just buy me a ton of salt while I find the nearest church. And for God's sake, don't tell Domino. We'll never live it down."

"You know I have to file an expense report, right? What am I supposed to say about all this salt if I can't tell him the truth?"

"I don't know. Tell him we made a ton of French fries."

We both stopped and stared at each other. Even the thought of Isidro catching me wasn't enough to prevent my mouth from watering copiously, and I knew Lucas's did, too. His Adam's apple bobbed as he swallowed.

"Fine," I said. "After we buy the salt, we'll get burgers and enough fries to make us sweat saturated fat, but I really do need to find a church after that."

CHAPTER 32

ROLL OF THE DICE

I woke late, the fat coma leaving me bloated and uncomfortable. It had been worth it, though. The fries had been awesome.

My gaze shot to the door, and the thick line of white crystals was still intact.

"Window's good, too," Lucas told me from his place at the table without looking up from cleaning his shotgun. If I had learned one thing from him, it was to keep my equipment clean and well-oiled. "Checked it twice. I put some around the drains in the bathroom and taped some to the outlets, too. Nothing is getting in."

"Wow. If this had been a ghost hunt instead of a manhunt, something tells me we would've bagged him within days."

He shot me a dirty look. "I was stuck protecting a situationally naive teenager when I should've been free to do things the way I always do."

My eyes widened. "It's a good thing you're not bitter about it."

"That icer probably took three years off my life," he snapped. "All this should've been settled a long time ago."

"I'm in complete agreement. Leave me a gun and the salt, and go find him."

He scowled and shifted his attention back to his weapon.

When he was finished, I showed him the photos of the gravestone.

He said, "So what if the dead guy was a gambler?"

"It's a pair of dice. Paradise. Heaven," I explained. "And don't tell me I'm reaching because you haven't heard the best part. It's a pair of sixes."

He looked at me blankly.

"Boxcars," I said in satisfaction. "That's train lingo, my friend."

He rolled his eyes. "I'm not the one you have to convince."

"Everything points at it," I insisted even though I was glad I didn't have to take any of this to trial. None of it sounded clever.

"Even the little girls who were kidnapped?"

"That was intended to stick a knife in your side, not mine. He was trying to rattle my bodyguard."

"Let's say everything else connects to the gravestone," he said. "Now what? Is it pointing us somewhere? Do we start digging straight down until we find the lab?"

I didn't reply.

"That's what I thought," he said.

I shuffled my digital notecards and sorted them into stacks to evaluate them again.

The Religion stack started with Finley's real name being Adam Finley, Adam being a biblical name. Adam and Eve originated in a garden, the Garden of Eden. The cemetery where I found the headstone was a garden, too, at least by name: Eternal Gardens. He'd chosen Goddard—God—for his new surname. He called the lab limbo, a religious term for the place where souls get weighed. He might've considered his second lab paradise, another religious term, one easily twisted into a symbol he could have carved into a headstone with a pair of dice. I could see him using the term to describe the destination of the souls he considered worthy after the judgment in limbo.

The Family stack was much smaller. Finley spoke about the first gen icer people supporting each other like they were intended to be a family. The old American Route 66 was called the Mother Road.

The Home stack included a card reminding me Finley and Mauss referred to home like it was a specific place, not just where loved ones resided. A town on the Mother Road even had the word in the middle of it, if only phonetically: Okla-HOME-uh City.

None of the cards alone resonated with strength and truth, and combined they were frankly ridiculous. But it had to be more than coincidence that no matter which way I approached it, I ended up staring at a headstone with boxcars engraved on it in a cemetery in Oklahoma City.

"Search on the name on the headstone comes up with nothing," Lucas muttered, reluctantly drawn in. "Did I get the name wrong? Kalvin Osmet Ilovich?"

"No, that's it. Let me think on it."

It definitely wasn't a name that triggered anything in my memories of America. Reverting to pencil and paper, I played with the name backward and forward, checking initials, alternate spellings, the meaning of each name, alphanumeric substitution, numerology, and anything else I could think of until I had a crick in my neck and a cramp in my writing hand.

I paced, resisting the urge to step in each of the medallions in the carpet's pattern.

Was the name from a folk tale I didn't know? The folk heroes had been more than just Americana. To Lucas, they sounded like lessons about sacrifice and man's fight against the very technology he had created.

My stomach knotted. Domino said Mauss thought I was far more clone than real person.

"Kalo 'smi loka-ksaya-krt," I said abruptly.

"Was that English?" Lucas teased.

"Sanskrit."

"You speak Sanskrit?"

"It's the opening from the infamous Bhagavad Gita line Robert Oppenheimer used to speak of his work on the atomic bomb. It's the first three letters of each name on that gravestone. Kal-osm-ilo."

"What does it mean?"

"Well, with any translation there are subtle variations, but the popular one is 'I am become Death, the destroyer of worlds.'"

The words clung heavily in the air around me.

"Is that mentioned in one of the lab's books?" he asked.

I glanced at him, surprised. "Yeah, it must've been. I wouldn't have recognized the Sanskrit otherwise. I knew the quote from a long time ago, but in English."

"So it was meant for you."

"Why?" I said sharply. "Because I can build an atomic bomb or because I am the destroyer of worlds? Why does Mauss keep suggesting the world is better off by my being dead when he keeps passing on chances to

258

kill me? It doesn't make sense. Finley thought I could help him save the world, and we know Mauss was working for him."

"Yeah, but Finley spent almost all of his time in the lab either being repaired or repairing you while Mauss had the freedom to come and go as he pleased. Finley probably gave him the necessary part of the task and left the details up to Mauss. Like the gravestone. If the two dice with six spots each on an old-looking tombstone in the right cemetery were the important parts, maybe Finley didn't care what name was put on there as long as it wasn't I.P. Freely."

"That still doesn't explain how a man who wants to kill me ended up working for a man who wanted me to live."

"They both believed in the goal of heaven on earth," he argued. "Mauss must've been thrilled to find out Finley had the nerve and the knowledge to actually attempt it. Did Finley ever say anything strongly pro-clone or anti-clone? Because if he was undecided, Mauss probably thought as his right hand man he could persuade Finley to authorize your termination, too. Finley obviously didn't have a problem pointing out people he wanted dead."

"Yeah, all right," I said, finally calming down. "Maybe. At least we've seen no sign he knows where we are this time. Even if he is tracking us, it must be driving him crazy wondering what we're going to do with all that salt."

Lucas burst out laughing.

"Better call Domino," I suggested.

He nodded and reached for his palmer. The conversation didn't go as expected, though. Lucas's furrowed brow relaxed, and he looked cautiously pleased.

"Domino's on his way to us," he told me. "They found something. We're to stand down until we talk to him."

It was late when Domino rapped on our door. My eyelids were heavy and my bones aching and tired, but my mind wouldn't have shut down long enough for me to sleep anyway.

As he walked in, he said, "We found it. Mauss slipped up, and facial recognition caught him on a train station security camera. They were able to track him to the other lab."

I felt my frown form. Mauss was a patient, careful man who knew how to avoid being caught on video surveillance. The other deviation was explainable. He'd stepped in front of a camera without thought to provide emergency care at a car accident. For him to look up just long enough to let some train station security camera capture his face was awfully convenient.

"Where was it?" I asked.

Domino shook his head to indicate he wasn't going to reveal that to me, but I got the impression his silence wasn't his choice.

"You can't even tell me the train station he was flagged at, can you? Well, how many people were in the icers there?" I asked.

"Four. All dead. We're working to confirm the names on the icers, but first look suggests they're all modern victims. Mauss got away by assaulting one of the cops and putting on his uniform."

It was all so ordinary. From the moment I woke on Hernandez lands, my world had been turned inside out by revelations I had been kidnapped, put in cryo for more than a hundred years, and experimented on. My fundamental belief about humankind's inherent goodness had been ground down until it was all but worthless. I'd even found my bogeyman and had seen him destroyed before me.

And one day Domino was going to walk in looking like a cop no matter what he wore or what color his hair,

260

and he was going to tell me Mauss was dead. And it was going to feel this way. This dull, empty feeling seemed such an anticlimactic end to Finley's legacy.

I didn't want a shootout. I didn't want to stand triumphantly on Mauss's corpse and whoop to the heavens it was over. I didn't need to be involved at all. I just wanted it to be finished.

Well, I wanted to be alive at the end of it, too.

Was the numbness rooted in doubt? Maybe that tiniest of hope deep inside was afraid to come out and be squashed again. It would've sounded naive and banal if I said it aloud, but I wanted to fall in love again. To share my life. I hadn't conceived while married to Paul, but perhaps now I was so healthy, I might be able to have a child to adore and explore the world with. What better sign my soul wasn't fractured beyond repair than to live a life of hope and love?

It was nearly midnight, and the scant blue-white light from the hotel room's television screen washed out the men's features. Both seemed to expect a response from me.

"So that's it then," I said without inflection. "Good."

They still seemed to be waiting.

My head throbbed, and I rubbed my temple. "Anything else?"

"Yeah, what's with all the white stuff?"

"Don't know what you're talking about," Lucas said, trying to keep a straight face.

Domino gave me a long, penetrating look, and then he and Lucas left to wrap up the last details.

I sat on the edge of the bed with my elbows on my knees and my head in my hands. With everyone acting like my mission was over, I assumed that after I fell asleep, I would be gassed and wake down in the lab. No one left down there would confront Isidro if he said I was falling apart and needed more work done.

"Run away, damn you," I whispered. "Do it now. Escape."

I ran for the door.

CHAPTER 33

YUP

The next morning I woke in the hotel room with Lucas snoring softly in the next bed.

I curled into a ball and burst into tears. I should've run, but I hadn't. Perhaps that was the only reason I hadn't been caught, drugged, and woken up in that subterranean hell. It had felt like the both of them leaving together had been a final test as if Domino and Lucas wanted to trust me despite everything I'd hidden from them. And maybe I stayed because I had faith in them, too.

Over breakfast, I asked Lucas, "Domino say anything about me going back to the lab? Because if that's happening tonight, I'd like to go to the botanical gardens or the zoo today. Something outside."

"It's raining."

"Real rain would be a nice change from the monotony of that place."

"I'm not going with you. I like being outside as much as you do, but I'm not standing in the cold rain when I'm not at peak health yet."

"A few hours. Three. I'll buy you a manly umbrella."

"I'm not going," he repeated, smiling to take the sting out his words. "Be back by dinner, though. I hate eating alone."

Since I was alone, I didn't visit the local sights. I went back up north, needing to see the vista open up in front of me. I was tired of being ringed in by buildings. The rain gave way to my hope, revealing glimpses of blue sky between the charcoal thunderheads. West of Oklahoma City, my stash by the decorative boulders was still there, but water had seeped in, so I drained the container before tucking it in my pocket.

I stopped the bike at the turn south to civilization. I still had plenty of time before I was expected back, and when I did, it would be to sit in a hotel room until the lab was ready for me. It was possible I would master deadening my emotions down there. I might learn to give up hoping and go mercifully numb to what was happening to me.

Why the hell wasn't I running? It couldn't be fear. What could anybody do to me topside that was worse than what I'd already lived through?

Who was I kidding? Even that stupid cemetery had scared the crap out of me.

I burst out laughing at what I must've looked like, all white-faced and hysterical as I sprinted away from some bird or stray cat stepping on a stick.

I checked my fuel supply, then turned my motorcycle east, and goosed the throttle.

Less than half an hour later, my palmer signaled an incoming call. I reluctantly opened the connection, expecting to be recalled.

"Where are you?" Lucas demanded.

My heart skipped a beat. His ignorance meant the data transmitter had been removed from my motorcycle. Was that how Mauss had been able to track us so easily? Had they disabled the kill switch, too? I didn't relish the idea of being scraped off the pavement from my enemy activating it now that Finley wasn't there to stop him.

"You're overdue," he told me.

"You said I had until dinner."

"I said lunch, and it's already past one."

"Sorry, I heard dinner. I'm back at the boneyard," I said.

"Why would you go back there? Why do you have to solve everything?"

"Actually, I came back because this place scared me, and I'm not leaving until it can't affect me like that anymore."

"I'm on my way to you. Be ready to come back to the city as soon as I get there. It's okay to be scared of cemeteries just like it's okay to be afraid of spiders. It's totally normal."

"Whatever. Why don't I meet you halfway?"

"I'll tell you when I get there. You in a safe place?"

"If there had been any sign of people, I never would've stopped. If I see any, I'm bailing your way."

"Good."

Trying to get out of the biting wind, I sat down against the broken wall of an old outbuilding to evaluate the remains of my cache and figure out how I could do it better next time. The tape came off too easily, proving it wasn't as waterproof as the label had promised, but the contents were dry in their separate baggies. What a pitiful stash, yet I'd been so proud of it: a small folding knife, needle and thread, matches and tinder, water purification and high calorie food tablets, utility tape, a cash card with twenty bucks, and a hand drawn map. Oh, and a pair of socks. My God, what had I been thinking?

I chucked the container and rolled everything in the socks before shoving the wad in my armpit where the tear in my jacket was. I'd grown enough that the additional lump was uncomfortable, but I didn't want to just discard the items.

I checked the palmer. Time dragged. Being outside the controlled climate of the lab was nice and all, but reality's nasty weather was losing its appeal. I should've met Lucas halfway, but it sounded like we would just be coming back up here if I did. I didn't relish the idea of shooting down the freeway with the bitter wind rushing over my thighs until they got so chilled they itched.

I pulled my sleeves down over my hands and called up the maps in my palmer so I could practice reading the rubble across the street. I had a great sense of direction, but I hadn't yet learned Lucas's dystopian navigation art of seeing a pile of debris for the building it used to be.

When I heard Lucas's bike, I trotted to the cemetery entrance to meet him.

"Hi," I said, pushing the hair out of my face. "Did you bring food? I'm hungry."

He surveyed the graveyard from the corroded fence to the crooked headstones to the dead leaves swirling in the ominous-sounding wind.

"I hate you so much right now," he told me, passing me a deli sandwich and a bottle of water.

"I know."

He flipped down his kickstand and eased his weight in the opposite direction of the lean of his bike until the kickstand rested on the concrete while his feet remained on the pegs. His finessed stubbornness still impressed me to no end.

"You do realize it's Halloween today, right? Did you even bring salt?" he asked.

"Yes, I know what day it is, and no, I didn't come armed. That would defeat the purpose. My brain knows there's nothing to be afraid of in this cemetery, ergo there's no need for salt."

He snorted and poured a line of salt in a circle around his bike, cursing the wind.

"I thought we were leaving," I said.

He pulled out a small, thick pad of tech from his pack. "I don't want to have to come back, and Domino wants to know if there's a body in the ground by that headstone."

"Are we missing one?" I asked, taking an involuntary step back.

He handed me the tech pad. "The instructions are on the screen."

When I returned from sweeping the scanner over the gravesite, he connected a line from the scanner to his palmer and studied the image. I peered over his shoulder at it, but the image was blotches of color and intensity. Nothing resembled a body to me, but I didn't know what the scanner read, so for all I knew it was the epitome of a decomposing corpse.

"Damn," he muttered, zooming out and zooming in again.

"I'm not digging it up," I warned.

"There's no body there," he assured me. He tilted the screen toward me, his blunt fingertip pointing out various areas. "But the ground's been disturbed in the last year or so."

"Within the time frame Finley could've been running around loose after icing you, you mean. So what if he used this place to stash something? We don't have to be the ones to dig it up."

"Little One, you're looking at a ventilation shaft. This color here is decomposing roots of the bushes that hid the grate and diffused the warm air rising to a winter surface. The shaft's been closed off and planted over with grass so it looks like any other grave." He showed me my photo of the headstone. "See the grass heads? See the way the seeds line up instead of alternate? It's not the right grass for this area. He probably sodded it."

I snapped off a mature grass head and saw what he meant. "Ah."

He snorted at my understatement. His lips tightened, and he stepped off his bike and left his circle of salt. "I need to see the site."

I led him to the gravestone, but he barely glanced at it or the misplaced grass covering the ventilation shaft. Instead, he slipped on his sunglasses and did a slow pirouette. He repeated it with his naked eye and then did it one last time with a different set of sunglasses.

"They found his other lab," I reminded him.

"Yup."

"So what are you looking for?"

"Anything else that doesn't fit." He called Domino. "She's on her period."

After he hung up, I said, "What was that? A whole four words? And did he even need to know that?"

He tipped his head at me. "Certain things said in certain ways make it possible to communicate over unsecured lines. He now knows we've found unexpected signs of a structure fitting the parameters, and I'm sure it's got to do with Finley or Mauss. Sheesh. You think we're idiots? Or that we care when you're on the rag?"

"Isidro does. I would prefer you caring about it, too, instead of what this is turning into. They found Finley's private lab. They found Mauss there. Whatever this is, it's been sealed, likely abandoned."

"Yup."

"Stop yupping me."

"What do you want me to say? Things happen."

I trailed after him as he picked his way back to his motorcycle. Balanced with both feet safely on the pegs inside his salt circle again, he built his rifle while I used his binoculars to survey the area around us like he'd taught me.

"Stop being so angry about it," he murmured.

"I'm tired of being right. Mauss let himself be seen. Finley must've told him at some point I was ready and willing to be extracted, and when we didn't arrive on schedule or when Mauss didn't get any further communiques from Finley, he knew Finley was dead. He had to reveal a second lab because he had to assume I'd already been told one existed. Once we were all up here together, he had to suspect that was why. Finley provided Mauss with a false one for this very reason. Only four corpses? Huh."

"Little One—"

"I had this fantasy all I had to do was stick my head up and have Mauss try to shoot it off, but we're standing on another lab. This is bullshit."

"Hey, you found it."

"You reported it."

"Doesn't matter. We're not going in it even if we find a big neon arrow pointing out the entrance."

"Why not? No, stop and listen to me. Mauss probably set traps for us a bunch of times, but we only stumbled across three. We emerged reasonably unscathed solely because Finley told him not to harm us a whole lot. I don't think we'll survive the next surprise round, Lucas. Finley's not around to stop him."

"I know, but—"

269

"I know traveling with me hindered your game, so don't take offense to this, but we sucked at tracking him down. All we could ever guess about his movements was what road he traveled. No one we spoke to saw him. We didn't even know what he drove. He was the one on our heels the whole time, and we never even saw him."

His jaw tightened. "Your point?"

"Maybe that airshaft was only for one section of the lab that was sealed off, and maybe he's down there. Maybe he doesn't know we're here. This could be our chance to finally get the better of him long enough to end this. You and I, we find the opening, and we breach it. Just a smidgen. Just enough to draw him out. We draw him out, and we take the bastard down. That's it. The threat's eliminated, and we go back to town for pizza while Domino and his people explore that place."

He shook his head. "We have no idea what's down there. It could be a fully militarized bunker."

"Or maybe it never got off the ground in the first place. What if it only serves as a partially finished living space or a way station for the handful of people he was able to smuggle out of the lab? Finley and all his icers were found in our home lab, not this one. If you had a big, beautiful lab at your disposal, wouldn't you want to wake up there instead of that industrial basement where our icers are? If Finley dragged out leaving our home lab because of me, it's because the medical facilities aren't up to his standards here, right?"

He seemed to be considering that, just like I thought over his scenario.

"Lucas, just because I can argue why I don't think this is a fully staffed lab, that doesn't mean I'm correct. You're correct that we have no information about what's down there. Even Mauss being down there is a supposition. I'm not a criminal profiler. I don't read people well enough to play poker for matchsticks. It could be argued

270

the best thing we can do is leave and spend the night at a different hotel. If this is a lab, Domino will handle it."

"Well, there's a site I want to check before we do anything else because if it's the entrance and it does look like the lab's been abandoned, Domino needs to know so he doesn't bring a full security team when they've got better things to do. Leave the bikes. We'll have to go over some rubble."

"We? You made me wander around the graveyard at night by myself. Go check it yourself."

"Fine."

Nevertheless, I helped him get our bikes out of sight and well-hidden before I followed him footstep for footstep. "I hate you," I told him as I slipped and banged my knee.

He laughed.

CHAPTER 34

HOME

"It couldn't be this simple, could it?" Lucas asked as we approached the abandoned baseball field near the cemetery.

"Well, most of Finley's people did end up with some brain damage. It's possible it was meant to be this simple," I said, standing on the spot where home plate should've been. Baseball was the American pastime, so that fit with Domino's hypothesis, too.

Lucas indicated the first base dugout where faded and peeling paint announced this was the Home of the Fighting Angels. "Another biblical reference."

I wrinkled my nose. "Awfully public location."

"Maybe this exit was created well after the city fell. With no one around, they could've made an easy entrance that just had to stand up to a casual glance."

"All right, I can see that."

He tilted his head and said, "Is it me, or does that paint on the word *Angels* look different than on the others? Like they were originally the Fighting Something Elses and it got painted over. The color's close, but the sun's fading it differently."

"Sometimes people run out of one kind of paint and use another. Look, I did some checking and this city did have an underground passenger tunnel system downtown once. Maybe we should check that out."

"Why the resistance?"

"No resistance, just no pragmatic reason for this location to be the lab other than proximity, provided this lab is of similar size to ours. These dugouts aren't sunk even a meter. There's no close place to hide a car and this scrabbly dirt holds prints too easily," I said, pointing out a fresh set of bird tracks.

"You're getting a lot better at site analysis. I'll make a guerilla out of you yet. Let's finish looking over this site anyway. We're already here."

"There you go, forcing that logic shit on me again."

He grinned and jumped down into the dugout.

As I got closer, I saw what he meant about the paint. It did look like someone had painted over the words and put their own. The paint was chalky and peeling with apparent age, but a plastic sheen showed underneath where the chalky decorative finish was lifting off.

Lucas stood in front of an old wooden door painted the same color as the wall.

"Does that go to a locker room?" I said. "I don't think I've ever been in a dugout before."

"A local field like this wouldn't have locker rooms. Probably a maintenance closet."

I opened it before he could stop me. It was either a large closet or a small room, and it was empty except for a pile of dead leaves, scat, and some garbage.

I asked, "Raccoon nest?"

He jumped at the sound of my voice and exhaled noisily. "Sure. Why not?"

"I doubt the entrance to a secret lab is a crooked wooden door," I teased.

"What's the matter with you, opening it up like that? It could've been booby trapped."

"You know, the perfect time to tell me things like that would be before I was within arm's reach of it," I snapped, my heart hammering against my ribs.

"Well, Christ, it's not like this isn't our first time dealing with him. We shouldn't trust any of it."

"We shouldn't even be here. Let's go back."

"Fine, we'll go back."

Neither of us moved.

I said, "I don't suppose I get a gun yet."

"You're not supposed to be in a position where you might need one. You're supposed to be in your room doing your crossword puzzles while Mauss goes underground again because we left the playing field."

"Ah. How reassuring." I swallowed hard.

"You ready?" he asked.

I nodded, saying sarcastically, "How wrong could it go?"

He laughed.

We entered the closet, our flashlights cutting through the musty air.

But nothing about the walls or the floor suggested it was anything more than what it appeared.

"I was so sure this was it," he said, unwilling to leave even though we'd checked it thoroughly.

"Might still be. Ground radar was inconclusive."

As Lucas stood on home plate and updated Domino, I noticed Lucas's gaze coming to rest on a point in the distance, his expression a little puzzled. He ended the conversation by telling Domino we were going to check on a church.

I peered where Lucas pointed and saw the slanting light bouncing off stained glass shards clinging to a gothic arch in a small stone chapel. "Why there?"

"I don't know," he said. "Just considering it from the religious angle. It looks like an old building, too. It might have a graveyard, too."

On our way there, I found myself balancing on a narrow beam of high carbon steel alloy.

"Or railroad tracks," Lucas said in satisfaction, walking on the other rail with his arms out for balance. "Look, they go right behind the church. Guess we had to go to the ballpark. Wouldn't have seen the building otherwise. This is it. I know it is."

CHAPTER 35

THE WAITING GAME

Seeing the broken stained glass was part of an image instead of an abstract, I thought of Father Brannigan and his big canvas of St. George fighting the dragon. He'd said he served all faiths, and I'd asked if he also served the dragon's. Once again, I wondered if Lucas and I were on the right side.

Lucas looked toward the setting sun, holding his fingers up to guesstimate how much daylight we had left. Not much. Maybe half an hour before sundown, almost an hour until full dark.

"We should come back tomorrow," I said, my voice a lot higher pitched than I would've liked.

He pointed to a sharp footprint under an overhang where the rain couldn't get to it. "Right size and right kind of boot."

"So this is it. He's here."

"Probably."

Probably. Huh. Even I felt the portent and finality in the air. "One favor. Don't leave me covered in body fluids this time."

"Don't worry about it. I'll find you a place out here, and then I'm going to look for an entrance."

"Or we could both hide out here and wait for him to come out. Domino's on his way, isn't he?"

"I'm going to try to identify an entrance before it gets dark, not storm it. If the psycho comes out, I'll deal with it. You stay hidden."

"How will I know if you need help?"

"I won't, and even if I do, you need to stay hidden. No need for both of us to go down."

"What if he throws a little girl at you? He knows it'll knock you sideways. What if he's got a recording of a girl in distress and—"

"My baby is safe. I know this beyond doubt. Anyone else's little girl will be safer once he's taken care of, even if I have to step over her to get to him. I've thought through all of this, trust me. And there's no what-if-he-tries-it? He will try it, and I can handle it."

"All it would take would be a recording of your daughter crying or her doll or—"

"I can handle it," he assured me with a smile. "Desensitizing to that kind of stimulus isn't rocket science. My daughter is disappointed she can't melt me with her eyes or devastate me with her tears anymore, though."

"Poor thing."

"Well, my ex isn't too happy about it. I stopped giving the kid cookies and ponies and instead taught her how to poke a man in the eyes, punch him in the throat, and knee him in the balls. That might've been okay as far as the self-defense thing, but my bloodthirsty daughter's got a powerful, accurate strike. My ex is already imagining playground lawsuits," he said with a grimace, making me grin. I don't think he even noticed his hand covering his crotch protectively as he spoke.

"Hey, Lucas. Thank you," I said sincerely.

"You can thank me by staying safe where I put you."

Lucas found me a snug cranny well away from any of the predictable hiding spots, and he backtracked carefully. When he got to the entrance of the church, he looked back and scanned the street. He nodded slowly to confirm I was invisible from his angle.

His rifle slung on his back, he took his pistol in hand and stepped through the open door, disappearing from sight.

I realized I was holding my breath and my fingers were digging into the brick with enough force to bend back my fingernails. The torturous wait had begun.

Full dark. It was full dark, and Lucas hadn't reappeared. So much for just identifying an entrance and then leaving. The temperature dropped quickly, increasing the discomfort of my statue posture. At least the wind wasn't in my face.

Trust him and wait.

I shifted my weight from side to side to ease the muscle strain.

This was taking forever.

What was I going to tell his kid if something happened to him? That I stood there doing nothing well after events hadn't gone as planned?

I counted to a hundred. Then two fifty. Then five hundred.

Nothing happened.

That might be a good sign. No gunshots might mean a lack of something to shoot at, not that he'd been ambushed.

Maybe he found Mauss and was trying to talk him down. It'd be awesome if Mauss gave himself up once he realized we weren't going to stop looking for him. The shooting was three years ago.

Christ, three years.

It felt like I'd been standing in that cranny for three years.

Man, how cold was it going to get? It must've been fifty degrees. I automatically corrected myself, switching from the old-fashioned Fahrenheit to the modern Celsius. It was ten degrees. Stupid metric system.

No, fifty. That sounded warmer. Ten definitely sounded like a temperature where I would freeze.

With careful movements that wouldn't give away my position, I tucked my hair down my collar and slid my hands into my pockets. Nope, still cold.

What a dick. Lucas was probably messing around because I was as much a pain in his ass as he was in mine. This was payback for the cemetery.

It worked, too. I was definitely sorry we'd ever set foot there.

The sounds of an approaching helicopter made me frown. Was it Domino?

The helo reduced speed as it reached the city, and I watched it pass overhead, its spotlight sweeping the area.

It had to be Domino. Who else would it be?

But why was he using a searchlight? My motorcycle had a beacon on—

No, it didn't anymore. Damn.

Lucas had missed his last check-in, and all Domino had for topside signposts were a cemetery, a baseball field, and a church within walking distance of each other in Oklahoma City. That probably wasn't a unique combination.

The helo descended at least seven klicks away. Since the airport was adjacent to the old Route 66 and the Bethany Cemetery, it must've made sense to start there.

I swore, leaving my post, and envisioned a long trot in the dark to intercept him.

If it was him.

I would be careful, not exposing myself until I could confirm his identity. If it wasn't him, so be it. I would retreat to my crack in the wall and wait it out. If no one appeared by sunrise, I'd get on my motorcycle and return to our hotel.

"Hang on, Lucas," I murmured, stepping lightly and quickly on the railroad ties toward Domino's position. "I'm getting help."

A kilometer away from the church, the rotted timbers gave way, and I fell into the darkness below.

CHAPTER 36

THE BEST LAID PLANS

At first I felt like I was falling through air, but then I hit something that groaned metallically and gave way with the force of my body. The sound of breaking glass was accompanied by bright, hot sparks. The sudden stop whoofed the air out of me, but as I struggled to a standing position in the debris, I realized I wasn't injured. Cuts and scrapes, a few lumps, but nothing serious.

"Well, all right," I said, delighted, stepping out of the slow rain of dirt from above. "Yay, me."

The hair stood up on the back of my neck.

The lights had come on at the sound of my voice.

I was in the lab.

The room wasn't large, but it was richly appointed with lush upholstery, oriental carpets, and crystal light fixtures on the gleaming wood tables glowing softly even through the layers of dust. It could've been mistaken for someone's basement, but the dual layers of sliding doors were something straight out of my home lab.

I shined my flashlight through the broken overhead lightning and rusted metal ceiling to a gaping space where the flow of underground water had carried away much of the dirt above this lab cell. The top of the sinkhole was edged by the jagged teeth of dry-rotted railroad ties.

I lifted one of the fancy tables on top of the debris pile, but pulling myself through the hole in the ceiling triggered an avalanche of dirt that knocked me back into the room. I scrambled to get aside as earth poured through the hole. Shaken and coughing, I hit the door release and darted out of the room, sealing it shut behind me.

Christ, no wonder Finley hadn't rushed to make this his number one lab after he woke. The last century hadn't been kind to it at all.

Not trusting the metal ceiling to hold, I hurried down the corridor, anxious to find a perpendicular hall that would take me in the direction of the church.

I glanced nervously at the security camera and pressed on, moving as lightly as I could in my boots to muffle the sound.

A deep rumble made me jump and whirl around. A thick, clear partition quickly slid across to block the corridor by the sunken kiva I'd escaped from.

Did I trigger that? Or did some sensor trigger them when the integrity of that room was lost?

I jumped again as another transparent wall dropped down to block the entrance to the corridor that opened to the east next to me.

I broke into a run, glancing down corridors to see if any of them led toward an exit or an atrium. Being trapped like a specimen on a microscope slide? Not going to happen. Suffocating or starving to death in some hallway sealed off at both ends in some abandoned lab? Like hell.

I saw Lucas come skidding around a corner, barely getting through before the branching corridor he came from was sealed off. As it was, it looked like it had clipped his shoulder. Another partition was coming down between us, and I picked up speed.

"Get down," he yelled at me, raising his pistol and firing as I dropped to the floor. The bullets didn't penetrate the barrier.

I rolled onto my back and saw Mauss.

"Get out of there," Lucas yelled from the prone position he'd taken, firing under the transparent wall before it settled firmly into place. I saw a spray of red as a bullet pierced Mauss's thigh, making him jerk.

I tried to get to my feet, but Mauss shoved me, sending me sprawling. I had nowhere to go. The barrier had reached the floor, the corridor walls were on either side, and the man with the gun was in front of me, another clear partition five or six meters behind him.

"Your days are over, gem," Mauss said as I scrambled backward.

Lucas's weapon discharged in vain on the other side of the barrier. He'd switched to his high-powered rifle, but it did nothing more than make tiny stars in the glassy surface.

"Out of respect for who you used to be, I gave you every opportunity to do the right thing and kill yourself. A handful of pills and you could've gone to sleep and never woken up," Mauss said, snatching my foot and dragging me down the tiled floor away from Lucas. "But no. You arrogant clone, you seriously think there's a place for you here."

"I'm not a clone, you crazy bastard," I said. "There's no such thing."

He pushed me back and raised his gun as I scrambled to my feet.

"*No*," Lucas screamed, the sound muffled by the barrier. "Mauss, don't do it."

Mauss caught my lunge and spun me against the partition, making me taste blood.

"How did you think you could survive, Miranda?" Mauss demanded as I whirled around for another go. "They put your brain in a fucking *clone*. You're now classified as a godless, soulless *clone*. That cloned tissue can't be allowed to live, to breed, to poison the rest of humanity. For what it's worth, I'm sorry."

Bang.

It was deafening.

What a sick joke, I thought in disbelief as I stood there. Mauss had aimed squarely at my chest and pulled the trigger. I'd been knocked back and I peed myself, but I was still standing.

I gave him a cool smile. Apparently he hadn't heard it took a hell of a lot more than a bullet to kill me.

I turned to tell Lucas it was going to be fine, that Mauss was messing with me again, but I felt a strange tension in my chest. I looked down and saw a starburst of a hole in my motorcycle jacket.

Bang.

Another jerk and another hole in my jacket. Was that a trickle of blood?

My jaw set, I tried to launch myself at the gunman to make him stop shooting at me, but my knees gave way, one then the other.

"No," I managed to say. I coughed, and my mouth became coated in blood. I used the corner of the wall and the partition to start hauling myself upright again. "Mauss, stop. I'm a real person. You know Finley thought so."

Bang.

284

The world tilted.

I barely felt the pressure on my ankles as the limping Mauss dragged me down the corridor, keying in the release code for the transparent walls to retreat as we went. I barely heard Lucas's voice screaming after us. I wanted to tell him it wasn't his fault. I barely felt the pain in my chest as my arms trailed behind the rest of my body or the coolness of the tile as my jacket and shirt rode up enough to expose the skin of my lower back.

What I did notice instead were the finely stamped tin tiles in the Victorian style.

Finley was right. This place was beautiful.

Chapter 37

Burning in Hell

Consciousness returned with a burst of pain in my skull. Another burst speared the same spot as my head bounced off another riser. Mauss was dragging me down a flight of stairs.

I kicked him as hard as I could, and he lost his balance and fell, hands shooting out to slow his descent. Done with running and hiding like the Texans wanted, I did my best to keep up with him, thrusting my heels viciously into the tumbling mass of him like a Hernandez native would have.

At the bottom of the stairs, he moved sluggishly, and one of his hands went to his head as he got his feet underneath him. I rammed into him with my shoulder to knock him down again.

When I hurried to get off him, I felt his hands pushing frantically at my leg, and I saw my shin was across his throat. I shifted my full weight onto it.

Beneath me, he twisted, both hands pushing at me, but I rode it out until he went limp.

Panting, I climbed off him and glanced around for a weapon in case he regained consciousness before I found something to tie him up with.

A low-pitched mechanical hum caught my attention, and I realized where in the lab we were. The incinerator was fired up. The bastard had meant to throw me in there, and I doubt he would've made sure I was dead before he did.

Gun.

Bits of my body armor were embedded in my chest, and the sharp pain when I turned toward Mauss suggested some of them were driven in deep.

Get the gun.

It wasn't in his holster. I found it halfway down the stairs and checked the magazine. Eight shots left.

Coming down the stairs, I saw Mauss looking at me, but for once he showed me no hatred. He was just sort of blank.

"You stay down," I warned, pointing the gun at him. It felt hard and uncomfortable in my hand. "The safety's off."

He didn't react.

At all.

Puzzled, I edged around him and sat on the edge of the steel table, gun pointed at him. I thought unconsciousness would've come with his eyes automatically closing. It would've kept the eyes moist and protected from dust and debris. The way he'd been moving slowly, clumsily, and the weakness of his defense made me wonder if he'd been stunned from falling down the stairs. But it wasn't even a full flight.

The longer I stayed still, watching him, the more my thoughts gave way to my own condition instead of his. My head rang like a bell, and my fingers found a lump forming on the back of my skull.

The flesh over my heart was all torn up and my T-shirt was soaked with blood. I needed medical attention fast.

Gun at the ready, I nudged Mauss with my foot. "Simons Says get up, motherfucker. I want to know why— Ha! Not this time. No monologuing with the villain. See? I can be taught. Get to your feet, Mauss."

He ignored me in that irritating way unconscious people do.

I didn't like the look of him. His breathing was awfully shallow. In fact, I couldn't see his chest rise at all.

Heart lurching in my chest, I pointed the gun at his face and sank down. I gingerly touched the bullet wound in his thigh. He hadn't lost too much blood, and I was relieved he hadn't been hit in his femoral artery. He would've bled out before he could be questioned by Domino.

I grasped Mauss's wrist and felt for a pulse. I checked the pulse in his neck next, willing that big carotid to throb with the movement of his blood.

I backed away, shaking.

The thrum of the incinerator seeped into me, and my strained swallowing couldn't stop my throat from burning with acid.

On wobbling legs, I let the source of the fire draw me in, but unlike a moth I turned aside at the last moment and put the incinerator on standby. I saw a bed of ashes inside. Were they the remains of the person who'd given me those flowers to warn me?

I dragged Mauss's body to the table. I pulled his arms over my shoulders like I meant to wear him like a backpack and strained to get to a standing position. Once his corpse was laid out on the table, I checked his pockets. They were empty.

I paused, waiting for a part of me to object to what I was about to do.

My inner voice was silent.

I put my palmer in his pocket and rolled the table to the incinerator before hitting the lever to tilt the surface toward the gaping maw. With a few pushes, the body made it all the way in, and I lit the candle on it.

God knew I didn't intend to kill him, but I was going to sleep a lot better now that he was dead.

I wasn't going back to the lab. Lucas didn't know I had any body armor, and he saw me take three shots to the heart and go down. He saw Mauss drag me away, no doubt with a grin on his face since he thought I was dead.

Plenty of bloody smears in the incinerator room, most of it from me. It'd be easy to wipe the table with my blood like my body had been the one to slide into the inferno. The ashes of at least one other person were already in the incinerator, so they couldn't weigh ashes and realize a woman of my size wouldn't have created so many.

It was like the whole scenario was perfectly set up for me to fake my death and run while they kept searching for him. I was more than happy to oblige the fates. Trust was one thing, but Domino had already admitted he adhered to the law even when it didn't favor human rights. Anyway, the second lab had been found. Mauss was dead. It was over, whether they knew it or not.

I shoved the gun in the back waistband of my jeans and looked for a way out.

CHAPTER 38

The Special One

Between any security cameras, clear walls blocking corridor access, and Lucas, going back up through the lab wasn't an option.

I zipped my jacket so no bloody smudge would reveal I'd squeezed through the seam behind the incinerator. The foam buffer was still intact, and it took everything I had not to scream and claw my way out of the smothering blackness.

I went down. Perhaps something had gone wrong. If they found the incinerator before the cycle was done and saw a man-sized corpse, they'd know I was alive. If the seam didn't reseal properly or I left blood there despite my efforts, they would expect me to bolt straight toward the surface. I went down instead, almost sobbing in joy and relief when I found a fissure to wriggle through.

When the buffer dead-ended against the earth, I turned, traversing fissures in the insulation and testing the walls until I found a seam that yielded enough to push through. I peeled it back and listened hard. The air coming in was cool, dank, and musty. No light. No sound.

I forced my way through the seam as quietly as I could, but my boots echoed on the metal flooring. I used my foot to confirm the surface was free of obstruction and took a few cautious steps forward.

The overhead lights came on when I reached the main walkway, revealing the occupied icers around me.

As I walked down the bay, more motion-sensing lights came on to reveal the length of the icer bay. Fifty icers in all, all occupied. I briefly considered staying around long enough to make sure Domino found these people so they could be released, but the tell-tale chill of functioning icers was absent. I was surrounded by rotting corpses.

With typical Finley thoroughness, each icer had a name plate as well as a list of charges I supposed he meant as justification for the termination.

I knew the loss of Finley's treasured ones upset him a great deal. The shock of the abuse of his gift to the future was something else he said he never got over, so the carnage around me made sense. After all, a society isn't only enhanced by the addition of great people but the removal of rotten ones. I wondered if he smiled that angelic smile of his when he shut off the icers and let these people die.

I imagined he at least savored the death of the man in front on me. The label said he was T-ADM Harry Fischer, and he was charged with the decision to send me to the Hernandez for their genetic manipulation research, the same event that cost those lab personnel their lives when Finley found out about their participation in it.

When Puck had intercepted me on my way to Greyson, he'd told me he didn't know why my plane went down, but he did know Tadman was responsible for my being on it in the first place. Like someone with the surname Jones being called Jonesy or a MacAvoy becoming Mac, Tadman seemed to me to be a casual reference a

Tad or Ted or Theodore, so I'd kept an ear out for some-one with that name ever since. At the time, I hadn't been living in the clans long enough to remember that in a conversation with references to the same position across multiple clans, the clan initial was used. The Assistant Defense Minister from Texas was called the T-ADM. Tad-man, indeed.

With more than a little wonder, I recognized the decomposing corpse in front of me as belonging to the second most important person in the Ministry of Defense. Bagging him couldn't have been easy, but Finley had done it. I was unwillingly impressed with his reach.

Looking around, I wanted to feel some compassion for the people who'd been kidnapped and killed in here, and I wanted to muster up some moral outrage they'd been condemned without a proper trial.

What I felt was relief, though. These fifty people here meant he'd left fifty good people to make a difference in this time and place. It gave me hope.

At the end of the bay was a locked metal door. Per-haps portal was a better word. The circular door was ornately engraved with a nude man and woman sitting beneath an apple tree in a world rife with life and inno-cence. I might've thought it Eden if there'd been a snake.

I couldn't pick the lock on that door, so I found a seam and pushed through the insulation until I found a seam into the locked room.

The room was small and luxurious with a truly lovely oriental rug underfoot and a pair of antique chairs flank-ing a small table with a crystal decanter and two glasses. The chairs faced a lavishly detailed icer raised on a cir-cular dais, its technical workings hidden beneath brass covers engraved with flowers. In fact, the way the base was shaped reminded me of a lotus, a flower rising out of the mud and opening to reveal pristine white petals. Two bands of frosted glass wrapped around the icer's tube, intended to discreetly shield the inhabitant's groin and breasts.

This icer was empty, and the name plate read Miranda Elena Donovan.

I didn't see an icer for Finley anywhere, and again I felt the regret of not asking him the right questions while I still had the chance. Even if Mauss had survived long enough to be questioned, I doubted he knew what Finley's intention for me truly was.

This icer also had that clever drawer in the base for personal effects, and I found my wedding ring along with the missing hardcopy files Mauss had stolen. I took it all, careful to wipe my fingerprints off the gleaming metal of the icer after I shut the drawer. The ring didn't fit my ring finger anymore, so I slid it onto my index finger for safekeeping.

So this is what it felt like.

Closure.

It was sort of pokey and uncomfortable in places from the few questions that would never have answers, but knowing most of the puzzle had been solved and the primary villains had been neutralized felt like coming out of a cold wind to sit down with a cup of hot cocoa and a thick blanket. I sent waves of gratitude toward the heavens.

I discovered the envelope containing the hardcopies wasn't sealed when I shifted it and some photos spilled out.

I saw the image of my pale, broken body as it had looked when they'd transported me from Greyson. My chest looked sunken beneath the flightsuit. My brittle ribs must've collapsed from the force of the medic's attempts at chest compressions to restart my heart. In the photo, one of my eyes was partway open, and the sliver of the gold iris was a startling contrast to the paper-white face.

Another photo showed the fourteen-year-old clone of me sitting on a gurney, her soft blue eyes trusting as she regarded the smiling Chase through her eyeglasses. The next image showed my old body and the clone's side by side and face down with dozens of tubes and feeds keeping her body going while my brain was being transferred to the empty hole where hers had been. The robot arms had been moving so fast they were blurry in the photo.

I slowly pushed the photos back in the stack.

I'd been able to pretend I didn't know what I was for a long time. To be fair, they'd told me upon my awakening what they'd done to get me back, but I'd recoiled from the idea, telling myself it was scientifically impossible.

Accepting it as the truth just complicated my predicament. I wasn't sure what a clone's rights should be because I wasn't sure they were born with souls and that innate gift of knowing right from wrong. Would I still fight for the reinstatement of my rights if it meant granting them theirs? Would it be any better if the law did separate us? Free me but keep them enslaved? Could I live with abandoning any offspring of my genetic code to the whims of the lab from their unnatural births until the reaping?

God, how could the lab do this?

Well, they did it because they could. And how much of a hypocrite was I to reject cloning on every single level but still be alive because of it?

I thought of the man who'd shot me in that Illinois parking lot, the man who'd kidnapped me for Finley. The man had told me we were going to change the world. With the Bhagavad Gita line, it had been said again, but as a warning, not as a sign of hope.

But even if I supported the full termination of cloning to the point where I agreed to die for it, that didn't help me out with the post-death destination of my soul. Killing myself was a massive sin. Even if I didn't pull the trigger myself, letting it happen was the same thing.

And on a purely emotional level, I hated the idea of someone making more of me. I had plenty of flaws, and child-rearing theory, nutrition, and medicine must've improved until any modern clone was better than me in virtually every way.

My grimace at the thought made me taste salt and metal. Mauss must've split my lip.

Poor Mauss. Since his issue had been with my body, not me, sentimentality and pity for my circumstances hadn't let him shoot me in the head. I was grateful for his weakness and said a quick prayer for him.

I never would've admitted it to him, but I had read the Bible cover to cover. I still didn't understand a lot of it, but I drew comfort from certain passages, and that might've been part of his plan, too. It's what I chose to believe, anyway.

I turned away from the icer, and sharp pain flared anew in my chest, reminding me of my injuries. Streams of blood stained my jeans.

Christ, I'd be joining Mauss soon if I didn't get myself together fast.

I hit the room's door release and the circular portal swung open. A drop of my blood from the edge of my jacket hit the gleaming brass.

I hurried to the narrow door in the back of Finley's room, figuring I could take a towel from his bathroom to wipe up the droplets and press against my chest until I could snatch a first aid kit from somewhere.

The door opened with a squeak, and I saw my reflection. I froze. Something inside my mind broke free from its moorings and tilted dangerously. My vision went out of focus.

When the feeling wore off, I released my grip from the doorknob and wiped off the fingerprints.

It couldn't have been my reflection. I didn't look like that anymore.

I risked looking again.

Gold eyes. Early twenties. Ordinary face verging on pretty, perhaps even beautiful in certain light. Thick, light brown hair cut shoulder length. Tall for a woman. Broad shoulders and hips and a nicely indented waist. Not voluptuous exactly, but a sturdily built, inarguably female example of the species.

And what a species. We liked it so much we found new ways to create more of us.

It was funny. I'd looked like that for a lot of years, but I hadn't seen the beauty until that moment. Perhaps it was because I now resided in a slightly dwarfed and overly sculpted version of myself. Perhaps I just missed being who I was when I resembled the woman in front of me.

Gem. Mauss had called me that often, and now that I saw my twin I understood. It was short for Gemini. Domino had said a full-blown clone had been killed and her ashes found in the incinerator. How clever Finley was. They hadn't even noticed he'd stolen her instead, planting in the hot incinerator ashes saved from the burning of my past surgical waste. Had he meant to save her parts for me?

She was actually in full suspended animation. Finley had told me the icers could work as intended, but I hadn't believed it. Was she his last test before he froze me in the lovely one, froze me until he figured out how to reconcile the mind he wanted being dependent on the body he never intended?

The realization she was in perfect stasis didn't matter. I couldn't just leave her there. I followed the instructions inside the housing, and before I knew it, I was face to face with a naked, wet, shivering Miranda.

CHAPTER 39

MIRROR, MIRROR

The Miranda clone used her arms to cover herself, and her teeth chattered. "H-hi."

So that's what I sounded like to others. Intelligence raced through her wide eyes like chain lightning as she glanced over my face—so similar to hers. At the sight of my blood-soaked clothes, her face became an emotionless mask, but she spent no more and no less time eyeing the carnage as she did viewing the cryo system she'd hatched from and the elegantly furnished room housing the other icer. In mere moments, it looked like she'd evaluated the situation and made her conclusions.

She opened her mouth, and my heart leapt in my chest, hands tightening in fear of what she might say.

"I don't suppose you've got a towel or a robe or something? I'm feeling a little... exposed."

The corner of her mouth twitched with humor at the dryly spoken word.

Oh my God.

I would've said that. I would've said that like that. That was my mouth she spoke from, my body she clutched in an attempt to warm, my mind she thought from. No, not my mind. My mind was nothing but hard, gray scar tissue resulting from years of torment, guilt, and betrayal. This woman in front of me looked like she still had an innocence to her. Hope. The capacity to love and trust. She was who I had been. No, she was who I *should've* been.

Elemental terror filled me as I stared at the woman who was more me than I was.

Seconds later, I raced past the icers, visions of death flickering in the corners of my eyes. I fled to the seam I'd emerged from. Wriggling through the insulation and shedding the photos and files in my wake to decay in secret, I refused to think about her. I had no obligation to her. None. She wasn't my mother, my sister, my child, or my friend.

I started to say a prayer for her but faltered. Since she was a creation of man instead of God, did she even have a soul to pray over?

It didn't matter. I was going to do my best to pretend I'd never gone into that room.

I practiced the memory. I saw the engraved door, and I created a snake amongst the branches tempting Eve with knowledge. I saw myself reach for the door handle even if the snake made me feel uneasy. The door was locked. The chill on my spine got colder. I turned away.

No, that wasn't me. I certainly wasn't tapped into the universe enough to get a heebie or a jeebie. I needed to use logic.

I envisioned standing in front of the locked portal. I knew I could likely find a way around it, but it was neither necessary nor to my advantage to do so. This was the land of the dead and wouldn't have the first aid kit, food, and change of clothes I needed.

Yeah, but—

No, for once in your damn life, don't ask the question. How many chances to get free of the lab are you going to get? The time is now and you know it. Turn your back on that door and run away.

Okay.

Are you sure? Be sure. I can't have you change your mind.

No, I'm sure. I'm getting worried about blood loss. I need to close these wounds, get some water in me, and rest if nothing else.

In my mind's eye, I saw myself turn away from the door and return to the seam, bringing me to where I was at that moment.

"I turned away," I muttered over and over again. "I turned away. Eight pounds, eight ounces. Born vaginally after twelve hours of labor. I was born in this body, born in this body, and I turned away from that damned door."

Three or four days had passed by the time I found my way to the surface. I used the driving rain to mask my tracks as I darted down the city streets. I had no destination. I took a street until the surface changed to something that wouldn't hold footprints or show other signs of my passage, and then I changed direction. I was in a residential neighborhood when the rain let up, and I ducked into a house with an eastern exposure. When the sun rose, I'd need the light to take a good look at my chest. The stabbing pains were still there, but I'd lived with them long enough to realize the damage hadn't reached my heart or lungs.

After plenty of debate, I stepped outside to hide the gun on a cinder block under the back porch. If someone on Domino's team did catch me, I wasn't going to get killed because they saw Mauss's gun and thought I would shoot first.

Inside, I curled up behind a musty, overturned easy chair in the living room and ate the last food tablet from my stash before curling up to get some rest.

I woke to the sound of a gun being cocked.

"Come out. Slowly."

"I don't want any trouble," I said. "I thought the place was empty."

"You from the city? You sound like you're from the city."

Arms away from me, I got to my feet. The stranger was as young as me, and her eyes showed she'd seen more than her fair share of human cruelty, too.

I said, "I was carjacked."

"Is that blood?" she asked, gesturing at my torso with her antique twelve-gauge.

"A little. They shot me."

"Take off your jacket, and toss it over here."

Grimacing, I did as she asked. She fingered one of the holes in the jacket and swore when the sharp edge drew blood.

"Body armor," I explained, teeth chattering. "Look, I truly mean no harm. I was just hoping to rest then check my wounds before moving on, but I'll leave now. I need my jacket, though."

A man peered around the corner. "Lady, did you say you're hurt?"

"Show us," the woman said, her shotgun never wavering.

I pulled the rain-soaked, blood-stained T-shirt over my head.

"What is that?" the man said, coming closer. "Duct tape?"

300

She laughed.

"I had to stop the bleeding," I muttered.

The man shrugged out of his coat and gave me his cardigan. It was too big and stank, but it was warm from his body heat, and I thanked him profusely.

They escorted me to another house, and the woman settled her shotgun into the scabbard attached to a kitchen chair while the man motioned for me to take a seat. He looked at the holes through my jacket and then indicated the first piece of tape on my chest. "Bullet still in there?"

I nodded and handed over my folding knife. "Shrapnel from my armor, too, I think."

The woman plunked down a small leather bundle tied with a thong. He opened it to reveal a pair of forceps, a probe, and other basic surgical tools. He sterilized them with alcohol and went to work.

"Carjackings are uncommon here," he told me as he removed a bit of alloy and dropped it into the dish she provided.

"I didn't think you'd believe me if I told you my husband shot me and left me out here to die," I said through clenched teeth, hands gripping the edge of the scarred table as he dug around in the first hole.

The woman snorted. "Happens more often than you'd think. Do you have somewhere to go?"

"One step at a time," I said. It hadn't escaped my notice my wounds were swollen and oozing pus. Hopefully it was my imagination that produced the sight of the angry red lines radiating from two of them. "What do you guys use for antibiotics out here?"

"Antibiotics," the man said while the woman glared at me for assuming they were so backward.

"No offense," I said. "I've just had better luck with homeopathic methods. Raw honey and garlic are pretty good antibiotics for flesh wounds. I've only got my emergency cash card so it's not like I can afford some designer antibiotic."

"What have you got?"

I showed them the twenty dollar card and my wedding ring, knowing my husband Paul would've preferred I be alive without the ring than dead wearing it. "The two remaining panels of body armor in my jacket, too." They snorted, and I grinned at them. "Kept me alive, didn't it?"

"Sort of," the man said. He flushed the bullet hole with something that burned like battery acid before sewing it up and moving on to the next one before I could catch my breath. "Iga, will you heat some tea or broth? Her skin's awfully cold. Maybe find her some clothes?"

"Thank you," I said.

He shrugged it off. "We have to take care of each other. Otherwise, what's the point?"

"I wish I had more to offer you."

"Someone helped us when we were down, and we're helping you. You just keep the chain going."

"I will."

When I left them three hours later, I was warm and well fed, and my blood carried a bolus dose of an only slightly expired broad-spectrum antibiotic. I had four days of medicine, plenty to get me to another town where I could wrangle more. The man insisted I keep the cash card, but he eventually accepted the ring. The woman cried when he slipped it onto her finger, and I cried, too, awed by the fierce currents of love that flowed between them.

With great hesitation, I retrieved Mauss's gun before I left. I didn't want that horrible death-dealer in my possession to remind me of how wrong things could go sometimes, but I needed to be able to protect myself, plain and simple.

As I hiked, the gun's weight became familiar, and it was relegated to being just another tool in my inventory. Days turned into weeks, and that couple stayed in my thoughts. Despite the dwindling resources and poisoned earth, people still had hope. Their lives were short and painful, but they still loved, still risked, and still trusted. I wished I had recognized that when I was in the outlands the first time. I might've been able to make Finley understand this world, with its balance of light and dark, was so much more perfect than any utopia he could envision.

CHAPTER 40

JASON

Domino might've figured out I was alive, so I had to assume he'd flagged certain places where I might show up. I stayed away from Jason's house and the military flight academy in his hometown of Austin, but it was unlikely Domino would think of the man's tailor. I staked out Dmitri's for nearly two months before I saw my mentor.

I wasn't there to get confirmation of Domino's story. I trusted him to tell me the truths he could. In the seven months since I'd escaped, the pain of betraying Domino and Lucas hadn't eased. Nevertheless, having a clone's body meant the only way I was going to have freedom was if I stole it. It meant going without the lab's assistance when my body failed, but I preferred to live and die as a free person up here on the surface of the planet even if my life lasted only a hundredth as long.

Still, if Domino or Lucas ever found me and needed a favor, I would grant it if I could.

———— ✳ ————

I didn't recognize the sun-faded black Mustang as Jason's when it was parallel parked with ease in the spot that just happened to open up, but no other man walked with that combination of arrogance, strength, and grace. He was immaculately groomed with his dark hair short and fashionably styled, but he wore a casual white shirt, open at the throat, tucked into black trousers instead of any of the suits he favored.

He was fat. Well, fat for him. Plenty of men would've killed for his swimmer's build, but he was more than a little vain, so the scant softness around his middle was more shocking than if he'd shown up in a bra. I didn't like it. I wanted him muscle and sinew wrapped in an Italian suit, a god among men.

He retrieved a garment bag from the trunk, and when he walked through the doors of the tailor's, even from across the street I could hear the exuberant exclamations.

Amused, I watched as the senior tailor reverently hung the precious cargo on a hook before he and the son orbited around Jason like satellites helplessly caught in the pull of money and exquisite taste.

Like a deity, Jason accepted the adoration as his due. I grinned even as I rolled my eyes.

Yeah, Jason's home.

I'd come to thank him for teaching me the things I needed to know to dig deeply and fight the battles on my own terms, but none of the practiced words came to mind. I didn't even have clumsy ones. That was all right. He was safely home now, and I could try again another time.

After I finished my cappuccino at the bistro, I took the path down to the river to feed my sandwich crusts to the ducks in defiance of the sign prohibiting it.

"I don't appreciate this."

305

Jason's cold tone faded into husky surprise as he got a good look at me.

I was just as surprised to be confronted by him. "What?"

Absently, he said, "My tailors just refused to measure me because they felt it was more important I woo the 'prekrasnaya devochka' who stared at me through the window while she ate her lunch."

He thoroughly eyeballed me as he spoke.

"I know I'm beautiful, but people usually stop staring at some point," I said dryly. "At least long enough to blink."

"You remind me of someone," he said bluntly.

"Is that good or bad?"

He ignored that. "You know who I am."

"That's pretty arrogant. I just got a sandwich and looked over when the tailors yodeled like it was Christ's second coming."

"I wasn't asking if you knew who I was. I can tell you do. Why are you following me?"

Jason's perceptiveness was something I wished he'd been able to teach me.

"Yes, I recognized you," I said grudgingly. "You're famous. Well, infamous. You haven't published anything in years, though, so I thought you were dead or something."

"I took advantage of the opportunity of a lifetime."

"Something more important to you than flying?" I said doubtfully.

"Obviously."

An odd emotional depth resonated in his voice. What on earth had he been up to?

"Ended badly?" I guessed.

"Obviously," he snarled, but there was a catch in his voice. It almost sounded like a vital part of him had been torn away.

I was disappointed by the lack of information about his absence, but the look in his dark eyes signaled he wouldn't tolerate another question or comment about it.

He kept searching my face as he spoke, and I kept waiting for the point when he knew it was me. Even if I wanted to, I couldn't have changed every single mannerism, speech pattern, or any of the million details that made me Miranda.

The moment of recognition never happened. His eyes returned to the features Isidro hadn't changed, but he saw them only as isolated similarities, just like when I'd looked for my husband in the faces of other men after he'd been killed.

With a strange burst of grief, I realized if Jason couldn't see any of the Miranda he knew beneath my surface, that meant she was gone. Even if I told him exactly who I was and how I came to be there, he wouldn't have believed it.

"Enough with the expectant look," he said impatiently. "I don't write recommendations, give out money, or come up with training programs for random stalkers. I definitely don't have sex with them."

I struggled to find my voice. "Perhaps I'm just looking for the feeling we're alike in any way. I've been told my genes indicate I'd be a talented Axe pilot."

Bite, damn you. I used to be your damn partner, for Christ's sake. See me.

He said, "What's in your mind is a lot more important than anything in your genetic code."

"Genetics is the bedrock. Fighting your genetics is like swimming upstream."

"Human potential can't be quantified," he said, amused at my argument.

"Because of the soul?"

"Because of our capacity to think beyond what our senses—and tests—show us."

"There are still quantifiable limits. A person can't bend a spoon just because they think they can."

"But they can convince themselves and everyone else the spoon is bent. Perception is completely malleable. Everything your senses show is an interpretation of the truth, not the truth itself. You vary your interpretation as your beliefs evolve. Why are you letting some test tell you what you should be? Do you have so little faith in your interpretation of the world you must let others choose another for you?"

"Yes."

He burst out laughing.

"My judgment hasn't always been the best."

"But you've never made a correct call?" Before I could respond, he said with an unapologetic smile, "This is boring, and I'm going back to the shop. If I see you looking through that window or crossing my path again, I'll have the police pick you up, and when they run your file, I'll make sure there's a record of prostitution or heroin dealing so they'll detain you."

He would, too.

"It's not my fault looking at me gave you an erection," I said in irritation.

"It's not for you," he assured me. "It's for the woman you vaguely resemble."

"It's a lot more than vague, though, isn't it? Nobody looks at me like you do."

"Don't flatter yourself. She saw possibilities where everyone else saw certainties, and she never would've let some blood test define her or fear stop her," he retorted. "Leave me alone. This is your only warning."

"And an unnecessary one, you arrogant prick," I snapped. "You stay away from me. How's that? You stay away from me."

I was speaking to myself. He'd turned his back to me and strode away. Brakes squealed as the traffic gave way to his will.

Uncertain, I retreated. At the river, I peered at my wavering reflection, seeing yet another twisted version of myself. I'd never considered the possibility of Jason not knowing me. I didn't mean for him to see me, but I'd been prepared for his accusations if he had.

Miranda was gone. Entirely.

What was I supposed to do now?

Relief bubbled up. With no Jason, the pressure to get back in the cockpit was gone. I'd loved flying, but it came with too steep a price tag. After my time in the lab, it would be intolerable to live under military rules and restraints. At this point, I couldn't tolerate making an appointment or reservation for anything, let alone keeping to an ordinary work schedule. Hell, it was so bad, I'd walked to Dmitri's instead of taking the train because I resented being told when I would have to get on and then off the train.

No, Jason's response had truly freed me. My world was my own to shape at last.

CHAPTER 41

FREEDOM AND THE PURSUIT OF HAPPINESS

The penetration was slow, exquisite. As the sun crested the hill and incrementally illuminated my face, I savored the pleasure of its heat sinking into my skin like the benediction after a long night of prayer.

I was mortal again, and a hybrid mortal at that. I'd relaxed my rigid stance about what I could pray for without feeling greedy, so on long, perfect nights under an endless sky, I asked for help to accept what I was after I prayed for the souls of the clones who'd been killed through the years to sustain me. Jason would've argued the clones' outcomes weren't my decision, so I shouldn't take responsibility for it, but it felt right to me. I also prayed for the people I'd killed, finally admitting to the Holy Father those two people I killed at Greyson need not have died. Mauss either.

God, the sun felt good. No wonder people had worshipped the sun gods Apollo and Ra. After the sun rose above the peak, I sent my appreciation of the sight heavenward, and with more than a little regret, I reached for my sunscreen.

I'd retrieved the last of my Route 66 caches and had hiked west across north central Texas toward Harbinger-Ellis. The plane manufacturer intrigued me, but not as much as the hope of seeing a certain engineer out there.

Free of the lab and free of Jason, I let forbidden hope out of its box and dreamed of his brother now seeing me as an adult. I knew my husband would approve. He would've hated me ruling out having another mate after being widowed at twenty-four, and the smart, contrary, hard-working Cris Chavez would've met with Paul's approval. An affair with Cris wouldn't last, couldn't last, but I wanted it anyway.

Hesitating at a blind curve, I retreated and found a better approach the way Lucas had taught me. The two-lane road I'd been loosely following for the past day came into view along with a trail of oil leading to a vehicle with its hood up. His head already out of sight, a man wriggled under the engine, booted heels driving into the dusty earth. The black T-shirt disappeared under the vehicle, leaving long legs clad in denim exposed.

Vulnerable. Too vulnerable.

I approached slowly, silently, and I felt better about his safety when I saw the sawed-off shotgun within range of his other tools.

He drove a battered four-wheel-drive vehicle, and I suppressed the excitement. Other men had a deep voice, too, as they chastised their misbehaving trucks.

The sensible course of action would be to hide until I was sure. I didn't need any more reminders of what could happen to a lone woman in a lawless part of the clan.

"Would you like a hand?" I asked, willing to risk everything.

Cris Chavez pulled himself out from under his vehicle and squinted up at me.

I wondered if it was too soon to tell him I was in love with him.

"Tycho Walker, bounty hunter," he said in wonder. "Are you eighteen yet?"

I nodded. "And then some."

He got to his feet and rammed the hat back on his head. "Damn, did you turn into a beautiful woman."

"Thank you. Would it be creepy if I said I was headed to H-E in the hopes I'd see you again?"

"Since I found out Jason was home safe, I've been back and forth on this road looking for you."

"Why?"

"I recently read an article about ley lines drawing certain people together. I was curious to test the hypothesis."

"You can't be serious. Montgomery's a quack."

He laughed. "I thought so, too, yet here we are."

I grinned. It wasn't smart to want the brother of a man the lab thought I still had a sensitivity to. I didn't stupidly assume I'd gotten away clean in the first place. Someday soon the inevitable collision between the lab and me would come. I felt a strange hunger for the confrontation, suspecting it was going to be Hell's own battle.

I felt the sun's heat on the back of my neck and saw the rugged man in front of me, and my smile widened. The war was coming, but it wouldn't happen today.

His smile grew in response. "What?"

I laughed and jumped into his arms to kiss him soundly. "Nothing. Let's fix your wheels. There's a whole world to explore and not a lot of time to do it."

"You've got what, only another eighty years?"

My smile faltered, but only for a moment. "One can only hope."

Visit author Jordana Wells at:

JordanaWells.com

Be on the lookout for

Anaphase: DNA Strand 3

Having escaped the biotech laboratory that rebuilt her, test subject Miranda Donovan celebrates her freedom by starting a life below the radar with Cris, a passionate engineer. Everything changes when a medical emergency proves that the effects of her being a clone-human hybrid may be far-reaching, not only for her but for everyone else. Torn between love and duty, she must choose between living the life she fought so desperately to have or risking everything to bring down a biomedical lab no one else realizes is a threat.

Coming soon!

www.ingramcontent.com/pod-product-compliance
Lightning Source LLC
Chambersburg PA
CBHW020909200626
46814CB00001BA/253